D1366516

The Umbrella Maker's Son

KATRINA LENO

ILLUSTRATED BY DAVIDE ORTU

Little, Brown and Company

New York Boston

Copyright © 2023 by Katrina Leno
Illustrations copyright © 2023 by Davide Ortu

Raindrop art © MG Drachal/Shutterstock.com
Umbrella art © Sloth Astronaut/Shutterstock.com

Cover art copyright © 2023 by Davide Ortu. Cover design by Gabrielle Chang.
Cover copyright © 2023 by Hachette Book Group, Inc.
Interior design by Gabrielle Chang.

Little, Brown and Company
Hachette Book Group
1290 Avenue of the Americas, New York, NY 10104
Visit us at LBYR.com

First Edition: June 2023

Little, Brown and Company is a division of Hachette Book Group, Inc. The Little, Brown name and logo are trademarks of Hachette Book Group, Inc.

The publisher is not responsible for websites (or their content) that are not owned by the publisher.

Little, Brown and Company books may be purchased in bulk for business, educational, or promotional use. For information, please contact your local bookseller or the Hachette Book Group Special Markets Department at special.markets@hbgusa.com.

Library of Congress Cataloging-in-Publication Data
Names: Leno, Katrina, author. | Ortu, Davide, illustrator.
Title: The umbrella maker's son / Katrina Leno ; illustrated by Davide Ortu.
Description: First edition. | New York : Little, Brown and Company, 2023. |
    Audience: Ages 8 to 12. | Summary: Twelve-year-old Oscar Buckle is determined
    to discover the real reason behind why his town is so rainy.
Identifiers: LCCN 2022031750 | ISBN 9780316470872 (hardcover) |
    ISBN 9780316471145 (ebook)
Subjects: CYAC: Rain and rainfall—Fiction. | Weather—Fiction. | Magic—Fiction. |
    Schools—Fiction. | Fantasy. | LCGFT: Fantasy fiction. | Novels.
Classification: LCC PZ7.L5399 Um 2023 | DDC [Fic]—dc23
LC record available at https://lccn.loc.gov/2022031750

ISBNs: 978-0-316-47087-2 (hardcover), 978-0-316-47114-5 (ebook)

Printed in the United States of America

LSC-C

Printing 1, 2023

For Alma & Harper

Blanderwheel (Part 1)

OSCAR BUCKLE WAS RUNNING like his life depended on it.

Because his life *did* depend on it.

Because what had only a moment ago been a tremendous but manageable amount of rain was now *anything* but manageable.

It was now *life-threatening*.

It was now the worst of the worst of the worst of rains.

It was a blanderwheel.[1]

And everybody knew—

You didn't go outside in a blanderwheel.

So Oscar ran.

And ran.

---

[1] A rain of epic, monsoon-like proportions. Dangerous. Avoid at all costs.

He ran as the skies darkened.

He ran as great bolts of lightning shot across the sky.

He ran as the clouds split open and dumped buckets of rain down over the earth.

He ran as the ground beneath him began to shake and tremble with—

Rain

WAIT, WAIT, WAIT.

Let's back up a little.

I'm getting ahead of myself.

There's some backstory we need to cover before the blanderwheel. Just a thing or two to go over. Like—

Oscar Buckle lived in a city called Roan, in a country called Terra, on a planet called Erde, in a solar system called Virginia.

In Roan, it was always raining.

And when it wasn't raining, it was *about* to rain.

There were forty-seven different types of rain. Any two-year-old in Roan could name all of them, for it was one of the first things children were taught.

"You don't go outside in a blanderwheel."

"What a lovely wib[2] we're having today."

"It's a full spillen[3] outside, but I don't mind it at all!"

"It was shlinking[4] this morning, but it's a proper bliggot[5] now!"

Oscar Buckle's favorite type of rain was a gentle wib, the way it fell soundlessly from the sky, kissing against your skin as you stood in the street, gazing up.

But he also loved the more impressive displays, a cater-whail,[6] for example, when the sky lit up with lightning and the thunder was so loud the windows rattled in their panes.

And he *also* loved a warm and sunny gennal.[7]

Honestly, he loved most kinds of rain.

You learned to love rain if you lived in Roan, mostly because *hating* rain was sort of pointless.

It would be like hating air, or hating trees, or hating mountains or lakes or the ground beneath your feet. It was just easier to embrace it. It was a constant presence in the city, and that was just how it was.

Well...

That was just how it was *now*.

---

[2] A gentle sprinkle. The nicest kind of rain. Warm and welcome.
[3] A steady shower.
[4] Just shy of a spillen. A modest but persistent rain.
[5] Quite a lot of rain, and particularly unexpected.
[6] A summer thunderstorm.
[7] A rain that occurs on a bright-blue day with not a cloud in the sky from which it might have fallen.

It hadn't *always* been like this.

Although the weather in Roan had usually tended toward the wet side, things had gotten particularly stormy in the past ten years or so.

For a while, meteorologists tried to explain it.

But they couldn't.

"An underground tectonic shift!" some of them claimed.

"A gravitational anomaly!" others insisted.

"Honestly we haven't the faintest idea," the more honest among them admitted.

Eventually they recommended that everybody just get used to it.

And everybody did.

For the most part.

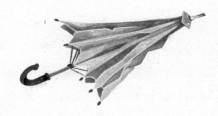

Buckle Umbrellas

BECAUSE OF ALL THE rain, the most popular accessory in Roan was, of course, an umbrella. Similarly the most common footwear was a good, strong, sturdy pair of rubber-soled rain boots and the most common coat was a rain jacket. Some people wore plastic hats over their hair or wrapped their heads in a sort of thin rubber scarf called a flouse.

Because you could get used to rain all you wanted, but most people agreed that it was still rather unpleasant to be wet.

This was where Oscar Buckle differed from *most people*.

Oscar never carried an umbrella.

In a sea of black pointed domes all jostling and fighting for airspace, he was a nimble, darting body among them.

His favorite shoes were a beat-up pair of sneakers with a hole in each big toe.

His favorite jacket was *no* jacket.

And he certainly didn't wear a plastic hat or a flouse to protect his reddish-brown hair and white, freckled face. He thought those were ridiculous.

It was more than a bit ironic, then, that Oscar's father was...

An umbrella maker.

Buckle umbrellas were known citywide for being strong, reliable, and long-lasting. They were made of the highest-quality materials, assembled by hand by Bilius Buckle (Oscar's father), and sold for anywhere from forty to one hundred skiffs[8] apiece.

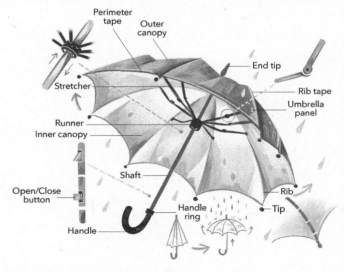

Perimeter
tape
Outer
canopy

End tip

Stretcher

Rib tape

Umbrella
panel

Runner
Inner canopy

Shaft

Open/Close
button

Rib

Handle
ring

Tip

Handle

---

[8] The exchange rate of one skiff to one dollar is confusing and varies greatly depending on what you're trying to buy. But for our purposes, let's say it's more or less one-to-one.

So *reliable*, yes, but also...quite expensive.

"Quality work takes time, and time costs money," Bilius Buckle liked to say.[9]

"But if you made them just a *little* bit worse, and sold them for just a *little* bit less, wouldn't we sell *more*?" Oscar had once asked his father over dinner.

Bilius had choked on a bite of soup, turned red in the face, and proceeded to lecture his son for the next hour about *integrity* and *value* and *my very reputation as a craftsperson*!

Oscar hadn't brought it up again after that.

---

[9] He usually said this when someone stopped by the Buckle Umbrellas shop, took one look at a price tag, and left without buying anything.

Brawn Umbrellas

But what could a person do if they weren't able to spend a sizeable chunk of their paycheck on a Buckle umbrella?

Well, in Roan, on every single street corner, at the intersection of every road, outside of every important building, whether north or south of the Wall,[10] you could find a person manning a little wheeled cart, and you could go up to this person and buy an umbrella for two skiffs.

These umbrellas were made by machines in one of the factories in the Toe.

They were made with cheap materials and assembled haphazardly and quickly. They would last, if you were lucky,

---

[10] The city of Roan is shaped a little bit like a stocking, and this stocking is divided into two parts by the Wall, which is twenty feet high and slices the city in half from east to west, just underneath the heel. Everything south of the Wall is called "the Toe."

for exactly one afternoon before a strong gust of wind turned them inside out or tore a hole in the fabric or blew them out of your hand and into the murky depths of the Gray Sea.

If you were *not* lucky, they would last you far less than that. They would get you a couple of city blocks, from your office in Commerce City[11] to a restaurant where you were meeting an important client for lunch.

The wastebaskets of Roan were absolutely filled with these cheap umbrellas. *Stuffed* with them.

Because, for a lot of people, it was just easier to spend two skiffs every few days than it was to spend sixty skiffs all at once. This was especially true in the Alley, where folks often lived paycheck to paycheck and found it harder to save up for an expensive purchase.

These cheap umbrellas were made by a company called Brawn Industries. They owned the biggest and foulest factory among all the factories in Roan. It vomited thick, toxic smoke that made the back of your throat itch and caused everything to smell like a burning chemical soup.

Brawn Industries had been making umbrellas for the past decade. In that time, they had caused almost every other umbrella maker in the entire city of Roan to go out of business.

Almost.

---

[11] Which is north of the Wall.

Buckle Umbrellas still hung in there, although what had once been a booming business for Bilius Buckle was now a scramble to pay rent at the beginning of every month.

Sometimes Oscar thought the struggle of keeping a small business afloat wasn't worth the headache at the end of the month when Bilius sat down to (narrowly) pay the bills.

Sometimes Oscar thought Bilius should just admit defeat and take a job at Brawn Industries.

And sometimes[12] Oscar wanted to collect every single umbrella in the entire city—Brawn *and* Buckle—and throw them all into the Gray Sea.

---

[12] A lot of the time.

Blanderwheel (Part 2)

HE RAN AS THE ground beneath him began to shake and tremble with violent quakes and jolts!!!

The lighthouse must be close now, and he knew he had to reach it or else he'd be swept into the Gray Sea, carried away by the rising waves that were crashing viciously across the small island. Could an entire island flood? Would the lighthouse and Oscar and this tiny outcrop of land end up at the bottom of the sea?

As he continued to run, he thought he heard a voice screaming on the wind....

But then he realized it was *him*.

It was *his* voice.

He was screaming.

And even as he realized that, a wild wail of wind stole his voice away.

Suddenly he could hear nothing except the white noise of the storm.

And then everything went black....

East Market

I'M RUSHING THE STORY.

I keep doing that.

Let's rewind just a bit, just a few short weeks, to a nice, calm Tuesday afternoon around three o'clock.

We'll get to the blanderwheel in due time.

For now, here is Oscar, heading to East Market, one of his favorite places in the entire world.

Oscar loved navigating the long, skinny aisles and cramped, packed stalls of the outdoor market, searching for a barrel of glamps[13] or a bushel of ollins[14] or the rarer svin,[15]

---

[13] A root vegetable similar to a potato.
[14] A root vegetable similar to an onion.
[15] A root vegetable similar to honestly nothing we have in our world. I can only say that it is versatile and yummy, and a little bit goes a long way.

which was Oscar and Bilius's favorite treat (but sadly not often available and rather pricey when it was).

He loved the sea of overlarge, black umbrellas[16] that hung over the entirety of the market, keeping the rain out (and, a long time ago, keeping the sun out as well).

And he loved Tuesdays at the market most of all, because Tuesdays were when Neko—one of Oscar's closest friends and the owner of the best stall at the market—received fresh shipments of fruit from all over Terra.

Oscar beelined toward Neko's stall now, weaving his way in between shoppers and merchants and ducking under ropes of garlic and jumping over crates of glamps.

To Oscar's right was the Wall.

Oscar waved at a pair of guards who were currently stationed at the East Door.[17]

They did not wave back.

Through the East Door, Oscar glimpsed Central Market. Like most things north of the Wall, Central Market was bigger, cleaner, and nicer. But Neko was from the Toe, so he always made sure to save some of his rarer treats for East

---

[16] These umbrellas were made by none other than Bilius himself and had hung over East Market for almost twenty years now. Which is a testament to the durability of the Buckle umbrella!

[17] The Wall has three doors total, and these are manned by guards at all hours of the day and night. While *theoretically*, a resident of the Toe could pass freely through them at any time, these guards are known to turn people away for any number of reasons.

Market. He set the prices in East Market lower, too, so the people of the Alley could eat the same sweet, juicy fruit as the people from Roan Piers.[18]

Oscar heard Neko's booming laugh before he saw him. Neko was a big man, at least seven feet tall, with tan skin, a barrel-shaped body and hands the size of encyclopedias. He was always happy, always laughing, and always overjoyed to see Oscar.

Today was no exception.

As soon as Oscar popped into view, Neko beamed and tossed him a small, bright-yellow object.

Oscar caught it and yelped in surprise—it was burning hot!

"Shooting star fruit!"[19] Neko said, cackling with laughter. "Super fresh!"

Oscar tossed the fruit back and forth between his hands, trying to cool it down a bit. "Is this...edible?"

"Of course it is," Neko responded, still laughing. "Make a wish and blow!"

So Oscar thought for a moment, made a wish,[20] then blew on the fruit.

It cooled instantly.

He took a cautious bite.

"Tastes a little burnt," he said.

---

[18] A very fancy, rich neighborhood north of the Wall.

[19] A wonderfully rare, sweet fruit that is a bit like a lemon mixed with a mango, with a smoky aftertaste.

[20] He wished he'd find a svin to bring home for dinner.

Neko made a face, then whisked the rest of the fruit out of Oscar's hand.

"No appreciation for the finer things in life," Neko mumbled. He popped the fruit into his mouth and made a loud sound of contentment.

"Do you have any apples?" Oscar asked hopefully. "I like apples."

"Yes, yes, I have your boring apples." Although Neko pretended to be grumpy, he was smiling as he dropped two apples into Oscar's canvas tote. He looked around his stall, grabbed two midnight oranges,[21] and dropped them in, too. "For your father," he said with a wink.

"Thanks, Neko."

"And do you have anything for *me*?" Neko asked. "You're overdue, you know."

Oscar never paid at Neko's fruit stand.

He traded.

You see, Oscar was a wood-carver.

He had been carving animals and other objects[22] out of wood for as long as he could remember.

He smiled sheepishly now as he slid a hand into his pocket. He rummaged around and then withdrew something small.

---

[21] These taste like a cross between an orange and a blueberry and are the color of the sky at—you guessed it—midnight.

[22] Like mugs and plates and paperweights and candleholders and flock pieces (more on flock later!).

It was a delicate wood carving of a bird, no more than four inches long, its wings outstretched, captured in midflight, its beak sharp and pointed, its eyes watchful and piercing.

Oscar held the carving out to Neko, who turned it over in his hands, studying it.

Oscar practically wiggled with anxiety. He rarely showed his carvings to anyone—just Neko, Bilius, and his best friend, Saige Cleverer.

Neko let out a long, low whistle.

"Oscar," he said. "This is incredible."

"Oh, I dunno," Oscar said. Compliments made him feel a little squirmy, and he shifted his weight from foot to foot as Neko continued examining the bird.

"Your talent is growing, my small friend," Neko said. "The detail here, in the feathers? In the face? The eyes are so expressive. Remember the last one you gave me, the tiger a few months ago? I can see improvements even from that."

"Thanks, Neko," Oscar mumbled.

"This certainly deserves a few more of these," Neko said, and tossed two more apples into Oscar's bag. "Now get going. Your dad'll be wondering where you are."

Oscar smiled and waved goodbye and then, his bag laden with apples and midnight oranges, he continued down the skinny aisles of East Market.

And sure enough, he found two svins for dinner.

Château Buckle

Oscar and his father lovingly referred to their Alley apartment as Château Buckle,[23] and as far as apartments went, it was warm and cozy and safe and clean and cluttered and, according to the two of them, absolutely perfect in every way.

It had two floors: On the first floor was the kitchen and living room, a small bathroom, and a curtained-off space where Bilius slept. The second floor was much smaller and consisted only of Oscar's bedroom and another bathroom with a big bathtub and shower.

Château Buckle was located in Building 4 of the thirteen apartment buildings that made up the Alley, and colloquially,

---

[23] *Château* is French for "castle." There are indeed people in Oscar's world who speak French, in a tiny country to the northeast of Roan called not France but Frunce (long story). They do have an Eiffel Tower there, and it's pretty similar to *our* world's Eiffel Tower, except it's three feet shorter and bright blue.

among its tenants, it was called Dove. All the buildings were named after birds. Saige, who lived just across the way with her mother, father, and baby brother, lived in Woodpecker.[24]

Oscar and his father usually arrived home around the same time. Bilius spent most of his days in the Buckle Umbrellas storefront and workshop, which was located in the middle of the thirteen apartment buildings, in a small arrangement of shops where the people of the Alley bought their clothes and their books and their shoes and, yes, their umbrellas.

If it was a good day, Bilius had managed to sell one umbrella.

If it was a very good day, he'd sold two.

If it was an *extraordinary* day, he'd sold three, to rich people who came down from Roan Piers to buy something fancy and expensive to impress their neighbors.

But if it was a bad day, he'd sold none at all.

Today was a bad day.

When Oscar got home, he found Bilius sitting on the floor in the living room, his shoes still on, his coat still on, his umbrella still open by the door. Bilius had his face in his hands, but when he heard the door open, he looked up quickly, trying to shake the darkness from his eyes, smiling for his son.

---

[24] Everyone just thought it was nicer to call the buildings names like Dove and Woodpecker, as opposed to Building 4 and Building 5.

"Oscar," he said. "I was just resting."

"On the floor?"

"Long day."

"Any sales?" Oscar asked, even though he already knew the answer. There hadn't been a sale for nine days now.

"It's a lull," Bilius said. "It's been wibbing for days. People only buy umbrellas when it's really coming down."

"Look what I got," Oscar said, trying to improve the mood. He took the svins from his tote. "I'll cook a svin casserole tonight, okay, Dad?"

"Oh, Oscar. That sounds lovely," Bilius said. "That sounds like exactly what I need."

"Why don't you head upstairs and get showered and I'll start cooking," Oscar suggested. He held out his hand and helped Bilius to his feet.

"You're too good to me," Bilius said, ruffling Oscar's hair. He kicked off his shoes and headed upstairs.

Oscar went to the kitchen, dropping his tote on the round table and washing his hands in the sink. The kitchen window looked out to the east, and he could see Woodpecker and Saige's kitchen window and, above that, Saige's bedroom. It was dark now; Saige took piano lessons after school and her parents both worked late.

It was one of the things they'd bonded over, when they'd first become friends. Their bedroom windows faced each other. They did Morse code with flashlights and had once attempted a string-and-can telephone. It had worked for a few weeks, until a particularly bad tranklumpet[25] had knocked the whole thing down.

Oscar washed the svins, then he got a cutting board and sliced them into thin, perfect ovals. He found a can of crushed tomatoes and lined a casserole dish with them, then added a layer of svins and a layer of cheese. He popped the casserole into the oven and set a timer for one hour. And then, because they had enough flour for it, he made two individually sized loaves of quickbread[26] and slid them in next to the casserole.

Oscar looked out the window again. The Cleverers' apartment was still dark, and the rain had increased from a wib to a plinker,[27] falling just slightly more heavily now. Oscar was glad he was inside. If he had a *least* favorite type of rain, it was the creeping, tickly, skin-crawly drops of a plinker.

If he craned his neck and looked upward, Oscar could just about see a sliver of sky between the two apartment buildings. As usual, it was gray, smoky, cloudy, and generally miserable. Oscar couldn't remember the last time he had seen the sun. Which feels like a good time to discuss—

---

[25] A rain characterized by its sudden bursts of downpour lasting a few seconds at a time, creating a distinctive pulsating effect.
[26] It is what it sounds like: quick bread.
[27] A very ticklish kind of rain that slithers down the back of your collar and crawls into the cuffs of your socks.

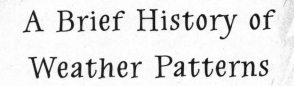

A Brief History of Weather Patterns

As I've mentioned, it wasn't always like this.

When Oscar was a baby, when his mother and father had been a young couple, they'd taken him to the beach, to the park, on long promenades around the city. There were pictures of the three of them, the sky blue and cloudless above, the sun a bright-yellow spot high above them.

But then, just about ten years ago, everything changed.

Of course it had always been rainy in Roan, but now there was nothing else. Now it was *only* rain.

And gone were the days of gennals and enmerals.[28]

Now the sun was a distant memory and the smoke from

---

[28] Summer showers that begin and end with a brilliant double rainbow.

the factories blotted out any scrap of blue sky that might have been left.

Now it was only rain, and only smog, and only ever an endless expanse of gray.

And now, where the Gray Sea met the gray sky, you could barely tell the difference.

A Decision

THE SVIN CASSEROLE TURNED out perfectly, golden brown on the top and cheese melted impeccably and svins soft and chewy and wonderfully filling. Oscar ripped bite-size chunks from his quickbread and used them to mop up the sauce from the bottom of his dish, and Bilius let out a long, contented sigh when he'd finished, stretching out his legs under the table and patting his belly with a smile.

After dinner, Oscar and Bilius usually played a game of flock,[29] so Oscar cleared the dishes now, set them in the sink to soak, and got the flockboard down from a shelf. He'd carved both the board and the pieces himself, and over the years, the

---

[29] A two-player strategy game, not unlike chess, where each player receives ten pieces, each with their own complicated move requirements. First to make it to the other side of the board wins.

wood had become well-worn and smoothed by their fingers. A good set of flockboard and flock pieces felt like an extension of one's own hand, and Oscar and Bilius always took the same ten pieces, setting them carefully into their starting squares.

Generally in flock, the youngest player goes first, but Oscar and Bilius took turns, and tonight it was Bilius's turn to make the first move. He stared at his pieces for a long time, his eyes half-closed, then he moved his spanner[30] to A2, and the game was afoot.

---

[30] The name of one of the pieces in flock.

The rules and regulations of flock were complicated and changed depending on what day of the week it was and whether you were playing in the morning or the afternoon or the evening, so I won't bore you with the details, but I will tell you that Oscar won by an enormous margin, and it wasn't a very exciting game overall.

It seemed like Bilius's mind was on something else entirely. He was distracted and slow, and he made quite a few moves that were absolutely terrible.

After the game was finished, when Oscar started to gather all the pieces and put them back into their velvet-lined wood carrying case (which he had also made), his father reached out and put a hand on his wrist.

"There's something I'd like to talk to you about, Oscar," Bilius said, and Oscar felt his stomach do a weird little flip-flop, because Bilius had a strange expression on his face, and he was suddenly looking everywhere but at his son's eyes.

Oscar put the flock case down and settled back in his chair, waiting.

Bilius cleared his throat.

Then he cracked his knuckles.

Then he scratched just under his left ear.

Then he—

"Dad?" Oscar said.

"Right, yes. Well. I've made a decision," Bilius said. "And

it wasn't an easy decision or a light decision. And it's also not up for debate. I'd just like to tell you what it is and be done with it."

This wasn't like Bilius Buckle at all.

Usually Oscar and Bilius decided everything *together*, whether it was as simple as what they should have for breakfast on a Saturday morning or something more important, like how they should celebrate Oscar's upcoming twelfth birthday.

Bilius wasn't one of those parents who didn't allow for discussion, so the fact that he had made a decision and hadn't consulted his son and proclaimed it "not up for debate" made Oscar feel...

Not good. He twisted in his seat.

"What do you mean?" Oscar asked. "What kind of decision?"

"Oscar, things are...tight," Bilius said. "I know I've been promising you a trip to Commerce City for your birthday, but it just won't be a possibility this year."

"Oh," Oscar said, disappointed, of course, but also understanding. "That's okay, Dad."

"And you won't be returning to school in the fall," Bilius continued quickly, in the manner of someone who had started to rip a bandage off and knew they must keep going or they would lose their nerve entirely. "You'll be taking an apprenticeship instead."

This made Oscar freeze. He felt suddenly chilly, like his blood had turned to ice water.

He had never particularly *loved* school, but that didn't mean he wanted to stop going. Plus, Bilius had always stressed the importance of education and Oscar knew his mother had wanted him to complete his Uppers.[31]

Oscar didn't remember much about his mother, since she had died when he was young.

But he thought of her now.

What would she have said about this?

He didn't think she would like it....

"An...apprenticeship?" Oscar asked, his voice quiet.

"With me," Bilius said. "You will start to learn the family trade."

"But I don't want to be an umbrella maker," Oscar replied.

To which Bilius stood up, brushed imaginary crumbs off the front of his shirt, and, still without looking at his son, said, "I believe I said this was not up for debate. If you'll excuse me, I have paperwork to do."

And he turned abruptly and disappeared behind the curtain that separated his bedroom from the rest of the living room.

---

[31] School in Roan is divided into three parts: Lowers, Middles, and Uppers. Lowers and Middles are required by law; Uppers are voluntary. Oscar will finish his Middles in about just a couple weeks' time.

Fort Cleverbuckle

Oscar didn't move for what felt like an eternity, and when he finally stood up, he found his legs numb and tingly and his arms wooden and stiff, and he kept dropping the flock pieces as he tried to tuck them into their velvet home. Finally he just left everything at the table, abandoning the dishes in the sink and walking quietly through the apartment. He put on his sneakers, slipped into his jacket, and walked out the door.

To leave most apartment buildings, one walks *down* many flights of stairs.

But Dove wasn't most apartment buildings and Oscar wasn't most tenants, and so instead of going down, he went *up*.

The apartment he shared with his father was on the seventh floor of the thirteen-story building, and although it had a small, rickety elevator, it was usually broken. Oscar preferred the stairs, anyway, and he took them all the way past the thirteenth floor, to a door with a sign on it that said: NO ROOF ACCESS!

And then, using a small, straight pin he always kept in his pocket, he easily picked the lock and stepped outside into the plinkering rain.

Ugh. He hated when it plinkered.

This rain felt like it had a million tiny fingers, and it dripped down his arms and creeped down his legs and slithered down his neck.

He headed for the edge of the roof.

To the west he could see the factories.

Past those, surrounding the entirety of the Toe, was the Gray Sea. Wide, churning, and treacherous.

To the north, the Wall snaked across Roan, dividing the city with brick and mortar.

And to the east was the roof of Woodpecker, where Saige lived.

The roofs of Dove and Woodpecker were connected by a long, sturdy plank of wood. Oscar had put it there himself, of course, and it didn't give him any pause to walk across it now, the street looming thirteen stories below him, the darkness of the night surrounding him. He felt like a daring tightrope walker[32]

---

[32] For legal purposes, do not try this at home!

(although the wood was significantly wider than a tightrope and only about five feet long).

Oscar rounded a big exhaust fan and there it was: Fort Cleverbuckle. He and Saige had made the entire thing themselves, and it fit both of them comfortably, with plenty of room for them to stand, and for Saige's wheelchair (which she had named Dot). The sides of the fort were made from thick plywood, there was an actual working door, *and* it was completely waterproof.

Although the roofs of Dove and Woodpecker were mostly identical, they'd chosen Saige's roof for the fort, because even though she loved heights, she (understandably) wasn't thrilled

with the idea of taking Dot across a makeshift roof-spanning bridge.

The elevator in Woodpecker was far more reliable than the one in Dove, at least, so Saige never had trouble getting to the roof. That was probably because Janet, Woodpecker's handywoman, had a soft spot for Saige and her love of heights, and made sure to prioritize elevator maintenance.

Both normal maintenance...and then some. You see, Woodpecker's elevator went right up to the roof. Janet had set it up this way herself—if you pressed buttons 5, 6, and 8 at the same time, held them for three seconds exactly, and then let go, the elevator shot right up past the thirteenth floor.

Saige was the only one besides Janet who knew this secret code, and she made sure to only use it when she was alone.

Oscar and Saige met at Fort Cleverbuckle most nights after dinner. It was their preferred spot to do homework, talk about their days, or just read a book or comic and ignore each other in comfortable silence. Today, though, Oscar had forgotten both his homework *and* a book. He'd been so upset when he'd left his apartment that he hadn't thought to grab anything. Lucky for him, Saige left her entire comic collection in the fort, because her parents didn't like her reading them. They thought the only things worth reading were big, important books about boring people doing boring things.

The design of Fort Cleverbuckle had been Saige's. She

wanted to be an architect when she grew up, and she'd drawn up the plans for the fort entirely on her own. All Oscar had to do was grab the things on her list of materials. Together, over the course of a few months,[33] they'd completed construction. And now, aside from the two of them, the only person who knew about Fort Cleverbuckle was Janet (who sometimes invited herself over for tea or dropped off a plate of freshly baked cookies).

Oscar let himself into the fort now, happy to get out of the plinker. He plopped himself down in one of the two beanbags they'd procured for the space (his was lavender; Saige's was a pale moss green) and took a deep, heavy breath.

Since he'd left his apartment, Oscar had been trying his best not to think about anything at all. Moving made this easy. He could concentrate on climbing the stairs, picking the lock, not falling off the wooden plank, putting one leg in front of the other as he stomped toward his destination.

Now that he was sitting down, though, everything hit him like a wave.

You won't be returning to school in the fall.

You'll be taking an apprenticeship instead.

You will start to learn the family trade.

Oscar's father was an umbrella maker.

Oscar's grandfather was an umbrella maker.

---

[33] And with a lot of help from Janet, who was thrilled by the idea of a secret rooftop fort!

Oscar's great-grandfather was an umbrella maker.

Oscar's great-great-grandfather was an umbrella maker.

Oscar's great-great-*great*-grandfather was an umbrella maker.

And so on.

Umbrella making had always been the Buckle family trade.

So why had it never occurred to Oscar that he might someday be forced to make umbrellas, too?

Well, for one thing, his father had never directly said it: *You must be an umbrella maker, and you have no say in the matter.*

Of course Bilius had hinted that he'd *like* Oscar to be an umbrella maker, but as Oscar had grown up, Bilius had also mentioned dozens of other things Oscar might one day do.

"You'd be an excellent chef, Oscar!"

"You're a natural at torchball,[34] Oscar!"

"Look at how well you fly this kite, Oscar!"

So why now?

Why the sudden—incredibly abrupt—change of heart?

And it's also not up for debate.

Oscar felt his eyes prickling with tears.

It was just so *unlike* his father.

Why would he have said that?

Why would he be so...

Mean?

---

[34] Which is a lot like our soccer, except the ball is on fire and most of a player's time is spent running away from it, so as not to get burned.

Oscar felt the first tears spill over onto his cheeks, and he angrily wiped at his face as it continued to plinker on the roof above him.

And since being sad and angry made him tired, he quickly fell asleep.

He awoke with a start when the door to Fort Cleverbuckle opened, and Saige came inside.

"Oops! Were you asleep?" she asked.

"Just dozed off for a minute," Oscar replied. He sat up and wiped a dribble of drool from his chin. He could tell the rain had picked up to maybe a shlink or a bliggot; he couldn't tell without seeing it. Saige closed her umbrella and shut the door behind her. She raised the left arm of her wheelchair and lifted herself from the chair to the green beanbag.

"Are you okay?" she said just as Oscar asked her the same thing—because Saige's eyes were unmistakably red. Her curly brown hair was in two braids on either side of her head, her brown skin was wet, and her silver wire-rimmed glasses had a few spots of rain on them. The tips of her ears were wet—her left, slightly pointed one[35] and her right, round one.

They both laughed a little at saying the exact same thing at the exact same time, and then Oscar stopped laughing—

---

[35] When she was three, Saige had toddled after her mother into the bathroom. Not realizing her daughter was there, Mrs. Cleverer had slammed the door shut—catching just the tip of Saige's left ear. It had been slightly misshapen ever since but was usually hidden by Saige's thick, curly hair.

Because Saige had just burst into loud, chest-heaving sobs.

"Saige! Oh my gosh, are you okay? What's wrong!"

Oscar slid out of his beanbag, landing on his knees in front of his best friend. Saige had put her hands over her face, so Oscar touched her knee to let her know he was there.

"I...don't...want...," Saige said in between sobs.

"You don't want what?" Oscar asked, feeling a bit frantic. "Saige, you're scaring me. Can you tell me what's going on?"

"I...don't...want...to *go*," Saige managed, and then she dissolved into a fresh round of sobs. Not knowing what else to do, Oscar squeezed himself onto the beanbag next to her and threw his arms around her. She leaned into him, still sobbing, and he just held her and waited until she calmed down enough to talk.

It took a few minutes, but finally Saige wasn't crying so hard, and when Oscar pulled away from her, she wiped her face with her hands and took a big, shaky breath.

"Saige," Oscar whispered. "Go *where*?"

"We're moving," Saige said.

And if the conversation with his dad had made Oscar sad, *this* news made him want to throw up and scream and cry and throw up again, all at the same time.

"You mean, wait...," Oscar said, reeling. "You mean, like, you're moving to a new apartment building? Well, that's okay. I mean, we won't be across from each other anymore, but the Alley is pretty small, you know?"

"No, Oscar," Saige said, her sobs turning into little hic-cups, the tears still falling freely from her eyes. "We're not moving into another apartment building. We're moving out of the Alley."

Oscar didn't say anything right away. His brain was try-ing to make sense of it. There were a few apartment buildings on the west side of the Toe, above the factories—maybe Saige was moving there? But it was only a twenty-or-so-minute walk, so that wasn't the end of the world, either.

"The Goms Apartments?" Oscar asked hopefully.

Saige shook her head. She took a few breaths, closing her eyes and trying to calm herself. When she opened her eyes, she looked so, so sad. Almost too sad to look at.

"North," she said. "Above the Wall."

Oscar forgot how to breathe. For a few long seconds, he just stared at Saige, gaping, and then he took a shaky, faltering breath. He couldn't feel his fingers. He couldn't feel any part of his body, but then Saige took his hand and he could feel that.

"My parents just told me," she continued. "Just now. I came straight here. I wanted to tell you because—"

"*When*?" Oscar interrupted.

"Two weeks."

"Two *weeks*!"

"They want me to finish up my Middles. We're leaving the day after school ends."

"Saige, I..."

"My dad got a new job. I wasn't really listening," she admitted. "I had sort of tuned out by then. I didn't hear anything after they told me we were moving. My parents, they're so...*happy*."

"Commerce City?" Oscar asked. He knew there were apartment buildings there, high-rises that dwarfed the ones in the Alley, double and triple the size.

"Roan Piers," Saige answered, her voice soft and...almost ashamed.

"You're moving to Roan Piers?" Oscar repeated.

"I guess it's a *really* good new job or something," Saige said. "I don't know. Like I said, I just kinda tuned out." She let go of Oscar's hand and looked into his face, her eyes wide and wet. "But this is totally fine. We'll still be friends. You'll come and visit me, and I'll get my parents to bring me back here. We can see each other all the time," she insisted.

And although Oscar nodded enthusiastically, although he swore they would still be friends and nothing could ever, ever change that...

Inside he knew the truth.

He knew that once Saige moved, they'd never talk again.

The people who lived in Roan Piers weren't friends with the people who lived in the Alley.

It just didn't work like that.

How It *Did* Work

THE PEOPLE ON THE north side of the Wall barely *ever* talked to the people on the south side of the Wall.

That was just how it was.

I mean—there was a literal *wall* between them.

Oscar himself had only been north of the Wall a few times: when he was a toddler, when he was eight, and when he was nine. He loved everything about it—the bustle and excitement of Central Market, the skyline of Commerce City to the northeast, the fancy stone-paved roads that led to the west, to Roan Piers.

And because the guards rarely let the people of the Toe through the Wall, it was highly unlikely that Oscar would ever get to visit Saige.

And certainly not with any sort of regularity.

But of course he *said* he would, if only to stop her from crying.

If only to make the sick, aching feeling in the pit of his stomach ease up a bit.

He promised they would see each other all the time.

But his fingers were crossed behind his back.

Wib

OSCAR WALKED FROM WOODPECKER'S roof to Dove's roof that night through the shlinking rain, feeling sadder and more depressed than he could ever remember feeling before. When he got back to Château Buckle, the apartment was dark and quiet and the curtains to Bilius's bedroom nook were still pulled shut. Oscar stared at them for a moment before locking the front door and heading upstairs.

He went into the bathroom first and changed into his pajamas, which hung on a hook on the back of the door. He tossed his dirty clothes into the wicker hamper, then washed his hands and face, brushed his teeth, used the toilet, and trudged to his bedroom.

He fumbled along the wall for the light switch, found it, flicked it on, then shut the door just a little too quickly—the rattle caused something to fall off a nearby shelf. It was a wooden woolly mammoth.[36]

Oscar groaned as one of the animal's tiny tusks snapped off and rolled under the bed. With a sigh, he knelt down to fish it out.

The space underneath his bed was crowded with piles of driftwood and scraps of cheap pine and fallen boughs of local trees; he spent much of his free time collecting the wood he later carved into his animals, and he wasn't picky about what kind of wood that might be. He couldn't *afford* to be picky. Good-quality wood was expensive, and he much preferred the free stuff that washed up on Bleak Beach. It had more character. It had lived a fuller life, and it was often from exotic places. He sometimes couldn't even identify the tree it had come from, which felt exciting and strange to him.

He found the tusk underneath a pile of such wood, worn flat and smooth from the waves of the Gray Sea. He sat up carefully and fit the tusk back into its place.

"Sorry about that," Oscar whispered to the tiny beast, before setting the animal back on its shelf.

Oscar's bedroom was his sanctuary and his studio. Every inch of wall space was taken up by shelves he had made himself, and every inch of shelf space was filled with the animals

---

[36] Although there are none in Terra and haven't been for many years, woolly mammoths are not extinct on the planet of Erde and roam freely in the High North.

he carved. His room was overrun with them; they even took up the two small windowsills, stood sentry on the four flat posts of his bed, and cluttered his nightstand.

He considered the animals to be some of his closest friends. He told them his secrets. He confided in them.

His favorite of all (although he would never tell *them* he had a favorite) was a wooden dog named Wib. Wib held the place of honor on Oscar's nightstand, closest to the bed, and Oscar picked him up now, feeling better as soon as he felt the dog's familiar weight in his hand.

Oscar crawled underneath the covers of his bed, Wib still in his hands, and fell asleep with tears on his cheeks.

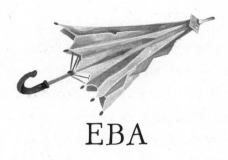

EBA

Oscar was late getting up for school the next morning, and when he walked downstairs, his father had already left to man the shop for the day. It felt like Bilius was avoiding him, and on one hand, that made Oscar uncomfortable, because his father had never avoided him before, but on the other hand, it made Oscar feel relieved, because his father was pretty much the last person in the world he wanted to see right now.

Oscar ate his breakfast standing up at the kitchen sink, got dressed in a haze of sadness, and decided to keep Wib in his pocket for the day—something he usually didn't do, but the thought of having the dog with him made him feel a little better.

Oscar's school was north of the Alley, and usually he and Saige made their way there together. But Oscar didn't really feel like seeing Saige, either, and plus, she'd probably already left without him. He was going to be at least ten minutes late for first session.[37]

He took a slightly circuitous[38] route, walking around the west of the Alley, then through East Market, where he stopped to treat himself to a hot chocolate.[39]

Oscar waved hello to the two guards currently manning the East Door.

One of them pretended not to see him.

The other nodded.

Oscar's school was just next to East Market, tucked against the Wall on one side and the Gray Sea on the adjacent side. The building held each grade level, and every child south of the Wall went here. Lowers were on the ground floor, Middles were on the second, and Uppers were on the third.

Oscar paused outside it, staring up at the drab, slightly lopsided building he had spent so much of his life in.

He had been prepared for another four years of school.

He'd turn twelve soon, and his Uppers would have lasted from twelve to sixteen.

---

[37] Middles consist of four sessions a day, with a break in the middle for lunch.

[38] He generally thought walking in a straight path was overrated, and on this particular morning he wasn't in any big hurry to get to school.

[39] Mrs. Flanders, who sells hundreds of different types of chocolate and candies in her market stall, is a good friend of Neko's and always eager to supply Oscar with a free cup (or two…or three).

He didn't know how to feel about the fact that he only had two more weeks left....

And then he'd be done.

And Saige would move to Roan Piers.

And he'd start an apprenticeship with his father that he apparently had no say over whatsoever.

He continued to stare at the school.

And the name of the building, spelled out in two-foot-high gray letters over the entranceway.

Elenore Buckle Academy.

EBA, as everybody called it.

Elenore Buckle.

His mom.

Sometimes he thought he might have remembered bits and pieces of her—her laugh or her smile or her eyes—but he thought all of that was probably wishful thinking.

She'd been the principal of this school for twelve years.

Seeing her name every day had always been comforting to him.

Like she was waving *hi*.

But he realized—with a pang of sadness—that pretty soon, he wouldn't see her name every day anymore.

With a small frown, he drained the last of his hot chocolate, tossed the cup into a nearby garbage bin, and pushed his way into the building.

Principal Gundersen

THE CAFETERIA OF EBA was in the basement, but if it wasn't raining too heavily on any given day, the students were allowed to eat on the back lawn of the school, on picnic tables that overlooked the Gray Sea. On Wednesday, the students were overjoyed to discover that it was barely misting,[40] so most everyone took their lunches and headed outside at noon, claiming picnic tables or spots of grass beneath the oak trees that dotted the property.

Oscar chose the farthest oak tree from the building, and he sat with his back against it, facing the Gray Sea, so that nobody would be able to see him from the direction of the school.

---

[40] A mist in Oscar's world is the same as a mist in our world (i.e., barely raining at all).

Usually he and Saige ate lunch together.

But he still wasn't ready to see her—not just yet.

He always packed himself the same lunch: tomato, cheese, and lettuce on two thick slices of bread. He'd grabbed one of Neko's apples today, too, and although he was feeling pretty miserable, the sweet-tartness of the fruit made him sigh contentedly.

That contentment was short-lived, however, as two of his least favorite people rounded the oak tree, one appearing on either side of him.

Gregory Fairmountain and Tim Klint were easily the meanest kids in school, and Oscar (and basically everyone else) tried to avoid them at all costs.

"Scram," Gregory said now, kicking Oscar's shoe. "This is our spot."

On any other day, Oscar would have wordlessly collected his lunch, gotten up, and avoided confrontation.

But this wasn't just any other day.

And Oscar didn't feel like moving.

So he retorted, "I didn't know you owned this oak tree."

Gregory was not used to people talking back to him. He stared at Oscar, his mouth open like a fish's, not knowing *what* to do.

And then he came to his senses.

He ripped the apple out of Oscar's hand and threw it as far as he could.

Which was quite far, since besides being a jerk, Gregory was the star of the school's torchball[41] team.

The apple landed with a quiet splash in the waters of the Gray Sea.

Oscar set his sandwich on the ground beside him.

He calmly rose to his feet.

He calmly brushed off the front of his shirt.

And he calmly punched Gregory Fairmountain square in the face.

Oscar had never punched anyone before, and right away he was surprised by just how much it hurt. His hand *throbbed* even as Gregory screamed out in pain, even as Tim launched himself at Oscar, knocking him to the ground and pummeling him with punches to his stomach and chest.

Adrenaline was coursing through Oscar's body and he hardly even *felt* these punches. But he *did* feel the sharp, burning sting of his hand. That was clear and loud and bright, a tether to reality that Oscar clung to as Tim kept punching him and, eventually, someone started screaming bloody murder.

It was Saige.

He'd know his best friend's voice anywhere. He felt one of the wheels of her chair bump up against his leg as she leaned over and attempted to pull Tim off him.

---

[41] Occasionally the rain would extinguish the flaming ball, and when that happened, you were allowed to pick it up and throw it.

And pretty soon there were more voices, and then a deep, booming shout that belonged, Oscar realized with a sinking dread, to Principal Gundersen.

As soon as Tim was successfully lifted off Oscar's body, Oscar became aware of a couple things:

His hand still hurt.

And now *every single part of him* hurt.

And he couldn't open his left eye.

And he tasted blood.

"What in the devil is going on here!" Principal Gundersen bellowed.

Principal Gundersen was, in general, a quiet, even-tempered man.

When he bellowed, you knew you'd done something really wrong.

"He started it!" Tim insisted, pointing a finger at Oscar, who still lay on the ground, one eye open and one eye swollen shut.

"You jumped on him!" Saige said. "I saw it!"

"Yeah, well, did you see Oscar punch Gregory in the face?" Tim said.

Oscar turned to his right, where Gregory still lay, writhing in pain in the dirt.

"What I *saw*," Saige said, "was Gregory kick Oscar first. This was self-defense, Principal Gundersen. Oscar didn't do anything wrong."

"This school has a zero-tolerance policy for fighting. I am calling all three of your parents. I want you all in my office, now. Ms. Cleverer, you can come along, too, and give me a full report on what happened here."

"This is ridiculous," Gregory said, finally pulling himself to his feet, holding his nose with one hand. "She's his *best friend*. Obviously she's going to side with him."

"By that same logic, you're my cousin," Saige pointed out.

"Yeah, but you hate me," Gregory mumbled.

"Gee, I wonder why." Saige rolled her eyes.

"Enough," Principal Gundersen said. "Office. Now. Move."

Principal Gundersen led the way, followed by Tim and Gregory and then Oscar and Saige. Oscar felt a bit wobbly on his feet, so he kept one hand on Dot to steady himself.

"You don't have to lie for me," he whispered to Saige as they went.

"Everything I said was one hundred percent accurate," she replied.

"I mean, he *barely* kicked me."

"But he *did* throw your apple into the sea. And you shouldn't touch other people's food. That's disrespectful *and* wasteful."

They reached the school building, and Oscar and Saige waited for the elevator while the others took the stairs.

Once they were inside and the door had shut behind them, Oscar turned to Saige.

"I'm sorry," he said.

"What do you have to be sorry for?"

"I was avoiding you."

"Actually, *I* was avoiding *you*."

Oscar made a face. "Right. So we were literally both just avoiding each other."

Saige smirked. "Sounds like it."

"Well, I *am* sorry."

"I'm sorry, too."

"But if you were avoiding me, how did you see what happened?"

"Well, I *had* been avoiding you. But then I was *looking* for you, because I wanted to talk to you. I just happened to find you at the same time *they* did."

"Talk to me about what?"

"The Night Market! Haven't you heard?"

"The Night Market? What about it?"

"Oscar!" Saige said, her eyes flashing with excitement. "It's *coming*!"

Suspension

THE ELEVATOR DOORS OPENED before Saige could say anything else.

Over the next forty minutes, Principal Gundersen spoke to Oscar, Saige, Gregory, and Tim separately. When that was done, he called everyone into his office together.

"It's interesting," he said, "because two of you say *one* thing, and the other two of you say something else entirely."

"Principal Gundersen, if I may—" Saige said, but Principal Gundersen held up a hand to stop her.

"I've already heard your account of events, Saige," he said, not unkindly. "The fact of the matter is I don't think I'm ever going to know *exactly* what happened, because you four are the sole witnesses. Saige, you weren't involved in the fighting, but as for the rest of you—there are only two weeks left of school, and it would be a shame to suspend you with so little time left. So I am prepared to send you home today, with your parents, for a one-day suspension. Well, technically I guess it's a half-day suspension. I will welcome you back tomorrow, *if* I have your word that nothing like this will ever happen again."

"I promise," Oscar agreed. "I'm sorry, Principal Gundersen."

"I'm sorry, too," Gregory said. "It won't happen again."

"It won't," Tim echoed. "We swear."

Mrs. and Mrs. Fairmountain arrived just as the four students filed out of the office. Julia Fairmountain yelped in shock when she saw her son's face (Gregory had a quickly blossoming black eye), and she enveloped him in her arms, sobbing quietly while Clara Fairmountain patted Saige on the shoulder and looked vaguely disapproving of the entire situation.

"You better watch yourself," Tim whispered into Oscar's ear as his own mother entered the small waiting room.

Oscar ignored him and sat down heavily in a chair next to Saige and Dot.

"What a bunch of jerks," she mumbled.

"I shouldn't have punched him," Oscar mumbled back, and he knew it was true, no matter what they had done to him first.

One by one everyone left, until finally it was just Saige

and Oscar in the small waiting area, and Oscar was able to ask the question that had been burning inside him for almost an hour.

"The *Night Market*? What do you mean it's coming?"

"Oh!" Saige said, her eyes lighting up at once. "Oh my gosh, it's all anyone can talk about! Somebody found a flyer on their way to school! Stapled to a telephone pole! Oscar, can you believe it!"

Oscar could *not* believe it, and he also couldn't allow himself to have even the slightest bit of hope that it might be real. It would be too much of a letdown if it turned out to be a false alarm. And there had been *plenty* of false alarms over the years.

Oscar had never actually been to any Night Markets, which were things of legend in Roan.[42] They were unpredictable, arriving randomly, with no set interval of time between them. The last one had been six years ago, occurring just seven months after the previous one. Before that, two years had passed, and before *that* it had been four years and seven months.

The Night Market was run by Farsouthians,[43] who arrived in massive ships and caravans and erected their tents at night. You woke up in the morning and everything was ready, and

---

[42] Actually, they were things of legend all across the entire country of Terra.
[43] A not entirely clever name for people from the Far South.

then *that* evening, the Night Market would begin. It lasted for three days each time, and when it was over, everything was disassembled and carted away and gone before the first light of morning. There wasn't much advance notice. About a week or so before the event, simple sheets of paper would start appearing all over the city.

But while the idea of a flyer found by a student on their way to school was promising...

It wasn't a sure fact.

Flyers had been faked before.

"Did you see it?" Oscar asked finally. "I mean, yourself?"

"No," Saige said, her shoulders falling slightly. "But Whitney did!"

"Keep your eyes peeled," Oscar said. "There are always a lot of flyers."

"Yeah," she agreed. "I will. Well, I better get to class."

"See you tonight," Oscar said.

Saige smiled. "Yeah. See you tonight, Oscar."

Oscar was the last one left in the office's small waiting room, and he couldn't help but feel guilty at having pulled Bilius away from the shop. And he couldn't help but feel *nervous* that Bilius was going to be really, really upset with him.

And on top of all that, he was quite sore.

Principal Gundersen had asked if he'd needed the nurse's office, but Oscar felt confident nothing was broken or severely hurt. His nose had bled a bit and his eye was still swollen and his body ached in a way it wasn't used to, but he was fine.

Or he *was* fine.

Until his father arrived and, just as he'd worried, started yelling at him.

"What in the WORLD, Oscar!" Bilius said, his voice getting higher and higher.

Principal Gundersen poked his head out of his office. "Hey there, Bill," he said. "Just a little scrap in the schoolyard. I've had a chat with all the kids."

"Your EYE!" Bilius hollered. "Oscar, what has gotten INTO YOU?"

"I didn't start it," Oscar muttered.

"You didn't...you didn't...Oscar, did you FINISH IT?" Bilius demanded.

"Bill, if you'd just keep your voice down, please," Principal Gundersen said calmly.

"No, I didn't really finish it, either," Oscar admitted. "I was just sort of in the middle for a minute."

Bilius sunk into a chair and ran a hand through his hair. "I'm sorry, Albert," he said to Principal Gundersen. "It's just a bit of a shock."

"Of course," Principal Gundersen replied. "I completely understand. Take all the time you need in here. I'll give you a bit of privacy."

He retreated to his office, shutting the door behind him.

"Oscar," Bilius said after a minute. "What were you *thinking*?"

His voice had gotten quiet, and Oscar found he missed the yelling. This was unnerving. This made his skin crawl.

"I don't know," he said finally. "I'm sorry. I don't know what came over me. I was angry. These guys, they're just... they're so mean to everyone. They threw my apple into the sea. I know that isn't an excuse, but... I don't know. I just lost my temper, I guess."

"We should have someone look at your eye," Bilius said.

"No, no, Dad, I'm fine," Oscar insisted. "I just want to go, if that's okay."

Bilius nodded. "Of course. I should get back to the shop."

But Bilius didn't move right away, and Oscar followed his father's gaze to the wall...

Where a framed photograph hung.

Elenore Buckle.

There was that pang of old sadness again.

Sadness for a person Oscar couldn't even really remember.

Elenore had been the principal of the school before Principal Gundersen. She'd totally reinvigorated the curriculum, and while the outside of the school was still kind of shabby, the *inside* was another story entirely. Oscar's floor, for example, had light blue walls, light green lockers, and an underwater tile motif in all the bathrooms.

When Principal Gundersen took over, he'd renamed the school in Elenore's honor, hung her portrait here and in the entrance hallway, and made sure things ran as smoothly as they had when she'd been alive.

Oscar wished he could say he *missed* his mother.

But that wasn't exactly true.

More accurately, he *wished* he missed his mother. He wished he *knew* his mother. He wished he had some memory he *could* miss, like a pair of warm hands tucking him into a crib or a soft cheek pressed against his or a wave of brown hair falling across his face.

But he couldn't remember anything like that at all.

The Umbrella
Collection

OSCAR AND BILIUS LEFT EBA a few minutes later and Bilius turned south, toward the umbrella shop. He kept up a swift pace and they made it in under ten minutes. It was still misting out, but the sky looked menacing and grayer than usual.

In Roan, you got to know rain. You knew when a sluice[44] was going to get lighter or heavier. You knew when you might have an almost-dry morning. You knew when the sky was going to open up and rour.[45]

Oscar predicted a good rouring in a couple hours or so. He just hoped it waited until after he went to bed, otherwise he might not be able to meet Saige in Fort Cleverbuckle later.

---

[44] A very cold, almost freezing rain.
[45] This is pronounced like *roar*, and it's basically a combination of *raining* and *pouring*. It's raining, it's pouring! You get the idea.

Bilius unlocked the shop door and they slipped inside. Oscar flipped the CLOSED sign to OPEN and took a deep breath.

The shop smelled so familiar to Oscar; it was instantly comforting. A little bit of glue and a little bit of metal and a little bit of oiled canvas and a little bit of rubber and a little bit of sawdust. Nothing that necessarily smelled good on its own (well, sawdust did, in Oscar's opinion), but when it all mingled and danced together, it made something that reminded Oscar of home.

Bilius turned the lights on and took a seat at a high work-bench, immediately fiddling with a half-completed umbrella that was lying there.

There were many parts to an umbrella.

The stretchers were thin metal rods that blossomed outward to keep the canopy open.

The ribs were additional metal rods that hugged the inner canopy, ending in points that were called tips.

The shaft was the sturdy center bar of the umbrella that started with the handle at the bottom and ended with the cap at the top.

The runner was the piece that ran along the shaft that you pushed up to open the umbrella and slid down to close it.

Oscar knew every single part of an umbrella and he could tell you, in an instant, where the umbrella had been made and how old it was.

Buckle Umbrellas was part shop and part museum, for Bilius Buckle collected umbrellas from all over Erde.

There were long, skinny, delicate umbrellas from Galla.

There were short, thick, square umbrellas from Dorn.

There were colorful, playful umbrellas with interestingly shaped canopies from Sun Island.

There were rudimentary, half-disintegrated umbrellas from eons[46] ago.

There were full-size umbrellas. Travel umbrellas. Telescoping umbrellas. Straight umbrellas. Bubble umbrellas. Foldable umbrellas. Automatic umbrellas. Child-size umbrellas. Paper umbrellas. There was even one umbrella made entirely of metal, which wasn't functional and couldn't be closed, but which looked nice hung upside down from the ceiling, fashioned into an umbrella chandelier.

There was basically every kind of umbrella you could dream up, and sometimes people came to the shop just to look at them, not intending to purchase anything at all.

Bilius never minded that much. He *wanted* people to see his umbrella collection. He was proud of it. He thought

---

[46] The oldest umbrella Bilius had managed to get his hands on was from the Polytoeic Era—years and years before either he or Oscar were born.

umbrellas were basically the coolest things ever. And he understood that not everyone could afford one of his umbrellas. He offered a generous layaway plan—take the umbrella home with you today, pay whatever you can each week until it was paid in full—but sometimes people weren't in the position to do that, either.

Every day he saw more and more people traipse by with their cheap Brawn umbrellas, some falling apart at the seams, held together by duct tape, reinforced with plastic sheets. You could make a Brawn umbrella last a bit longer with some simple home repairs, and Bilius had seen them all.

"Does it ever bother you?" Oscar had said once. "All these cheap umbrellas being slapped together by robots?"

"Oscar, human ingenuity is endless," Bilius had replied. "I do not blame the innovator nor the innovation."

But Oscar saw the way Bilius lit up when he spotted one of his own umbrellas on the street, a model he'd sold a decade ago, that was still as strong and sturdy as the day he'd made it.

Oscar looked at his father now. A semi-awkward silence had hung between them since they'd left the school, and Oscar didn't know what to say to break the ice.

But, as it turned out, he didn't have to say anything, because just then, Bilius cleared his throat and said, "Oscar, I owe you an apology."

Oscar was so shocked at this that his mouth dropped open. "You ... do?"

"The way I sprung all that on you last night..." Bilius trailed off, closing his eyes and shaking his head. "I was a jerk, and I'm sorry. I'd like to talk to you about it more tonight, if you'd be willing."

"That works for me," Oscar said.

"I'm grateful for you, son. Now ... is there anything *you'd* like to say to *me*?"

"Oh, um ... Yeah. I'm sorry I punched Gregory Fairmountain in the face."

Bilius actually chuckled a little. "Yes, well. I would ground you, but I think you've been punished enough." He gestured toward Oscar's swollen eye, and it was Oscar's turn to chuckle.

"Yeah," he agreed.

"You won't get into any more fights?"

"No, Dad. I promise."

"I believe you," Bilius assured him. He dug around in his pocket and pulled out a few skiffs. "Here—now that we've said our peace, why don't you run along to the market and pick up something for dinner. Whatever you want."

Oscar took the skiffs and slipped them into his own pocket, then headed back outside.

The Flyer

IT WAS NOT A bad deal, actually, being suspended for the afternoon.

Oscar whistled to himself as he made his way back through the Alley to East Market, happy for the misty reprieve from rain.

His dad's apology had dislodged a heavy feeling of dread from the center of Oscar's chest, and although he was feeling a little apprehensive for how the conversation would go at dinner that night, he was feeling better overall.

Except for his eye.

His eye still hurt.

Neko's stall wasn't open on Wednesdays, so Oscar walked around a little aimlessly, just browsing the different options, seeing if anything jumped out at him. He ended up buying a glamp and carrot pie from a sweet old woman named Shirley who always gave him a deal.

"Oh, Oscar," Shirley said when she saw him. "Your poor face."

"It's nothing," Oscar said, shooting her a swollen smile.

"Take this," Shirley insisted, handing him a small paper bag with an absolutely enormous cinnamon cookie inside it. "For dessert."

Oscar thanked her, then took the pie and the cookie and made his way back through the labyrinth of food stalls. He could smell the cookie and it made his stomach rumble a little. He hadn't gotten to finish his sandwich *or* his apple.

Poor apple.

It was probably fish food by now.

Oscar reached the southern edge of the market and paused, because there, just across the street, was Mr. Cleverer—Saige's father.

Oscar had never been a huge fan of Mr. Cleverer, to be perfectly honest.[47]

He was a tall, wide-chested man with a deep voice and the same brown skin and hair as his daughter. He always seemed like he was in a hurry, like he was half-distracted, like he didn't quite have time for whatever Saige needed from him. He was also a

_____

[47] And he was even less a fan of him now that he was taking Saige away from the Alley.

workaholic and believed everyone else should be, too, so when he saw Oscar, he gave a big wave, crossed the street, walked right up to him, and said, "Oscar, shouldn't you be in school?"

Oscar tried and failed to come up with an answer other than *I was suspended*, because he knew Mr. Cleverer wouldn't like that. His delay only gave Mr. Cleverer time to really look at him, and Oscar watched Mr. Cleverer's eyes narrow as he took in Oscar's bruised face.

"Oscar," Mr. Cleverer said, "what happened to you?"

"I tripped," Oscar said.[48] "They, um ... The nurse sent me home early. And said to ... rest."

It was clear from Mr. Cleverer's expression that he did not believe Oscar. But luckily for Oscar, Mr. Cleverer seemed, as he usually did, like he was in a hurry. He didn't press the matter.

"Yes, well. I guess you should be getting off, then," he said instead, glancing at his watch.

"Yeah, I guess," Oscar said. "Oh, um, congrats, by the way. On the new job."

One of Mr. Cleverer's eyebrows raised and he stared at Oscar just a beat too long, as if he were trying to decide something. Finally, thumping his hand on Oscar's shoulder, he said, "Yes, thank you. We are all quite excited. Well. It was nice to see you, Oscar."

---

[48] As far as excuses went, it wasn't his best work, but Mr. Cleverer always made him a little nervous.

Another shoulder thump, and then Mr. Cleverer had pressed on. Oscar turned and watched him march right alongside East Market to the East Door of the Wall. The guards didn't hesitate; they parted immediately to let him through.

Well, that made sense, Oscar supposed.

The Cleverers were moving north of the Wall, so of course Mr. Cleverer would be free to come and go as he pleased.

Feeling significantly grumpier than he had a few minutes ago, Oscar crossed the street, walking between two of the Alley's northernmost apartment buildings: Crow and Sandpiper.

Just outside Sandpiper was the Alley's only bus station. The bus made a loop of the Toe, making stops here, by the factories, and at Bleak Beach. There was nobody waiting for the bus now, and Oscar found himself pausing to admire some new graffiti that had popped up on the bus stop's small shelter. It was of a rat holding a bottle marked with the symbol for poison. A speech bubble had the rat saying, "Oh, no you don't! I smell a rat!"

Was it just Oscar's imagination, or did the rat look a bit like Mr. Cleverer? [49]

Oscar was about to move on when he saw a small piece of paper taped to the side of the bus shelter. Curious, he stepped closer—

_____

[49] This was maybe not a particularly *nice* thought, but we'll forgive him.

It was a flyer for the Night Market!

Oscar's heart skipped a beat as he balanced the pie and cookie carefully against his stomach. He unstuck the flyer from the wall with his free hand.

His fingers were shaking as he brought it closer.

THE NIGHT MARKET IS COMING...

That was all it said.

Under the text was an illustration of an enormous tent with a massive clock at its peak. Although Oscar had never seen it for himself, he knew it was the main tent that was erected in the center of each Night Market.

He folded the flyer as best he could with one hand, then slipped it into his pocket and walked quickly back to the shop.

Bills

By the time Oscar and Bilius closed up for the evening, someone had placed two Night Market flyers on the wall outside the shop.

They passed five more on the side of Finch, the apartment building between the shop and Dove.

And there were three on the front door of Dove.

"They *are* tricky," Bilius said as they waited for the elevator. "I'll give them that. Nobody ever sees who puts them up."

"Do you think it will be this weekend?" Oscar later asked excitedly as he slid the pie into the oven to warm it up.

"Probably next," Bilius said. "They like to time it well, and they'll know that all the schools in Roan finish at the same time."

"And where will it be?" Oscar asked.

"Just north of Commerce City, on the edge of Roan," Bilius replied. "It's the only place where there's room for it."

Oscar was so excited he couldn't stand still, and he bounced back and forth on his feet as they waited for the pie to get hot.

"And I can go, right? I can go this time?" he asked.

"I don't know, Oscar...We might not have the money for admission. And there's food to consider and transportation and—"

"But you could sell your umbrellas there, right? You could make money!" [50]

"Well, I *could*, Oscar, but...," Bilius said. "Still. I'll have to think about it."

Oscar tried not to show how disappointed he was.

He didn't want to make Bilius feel bad, especially after they'd just made up.

When the pie was hot, Oscar took it out of the oven and cut it in half.

Shirley made the best pies in the Alley. Just the smell of it made Oscar feel better, and he tried to push the Night Market out of his thoughts for now.

"Good choice," Bilius said after his first bite. "We haven't had a pie in a while."

Oscar practically inhaled his slice. The pie was *so* good,

---

[50] Bilius had a leather backpack that could fit about eight umbrellas. It looked a bit like an archer's quiver, which they use to carry their arrows. Bilius made it himself.

and when he was done he remembered the cookie and he felt even better. He pulled it out and broke it into two equal pieces, and they had that for dessert.

"Bless you, Shirley," Bilius said. "All right, let's get everything soaking in the sink, then we'll have our talk."

The impending talk seemed much easier to stomach on a *full* stomach, so Oscar took the dishes to the sink and submerged them in soapy water. Outside the window, he could see the Cleverers' apartment all lit up and Mrs. Cleverer walking around in their own kitchen.

He realized he hadn't yet told Bilius they were moving. He probably should.

When Oscar sat back down at the table, Bilius took a deep breath, folded his hands in front of him, and said, "Right. Oscar. I'm sorry. I know this won't seem fair to you. It *isn't* fair. But I just can't..." He paused, biting his lower lip as if he was trying to find the right words. "I wasn't sure how much to tell you. But I've thought about it, and I've realized that it's just the two of us, and I owe you the truth. The whole truth. And the truth is... things are getting tighter. Every year we're selling fewer and fewer umbrellas. I can only make one or two a week as it is, and I can't lower the cost any more with the price of materials and the time of labor. If I had you to help me, if we worked as a team, perhaps I could afford to bring the cost down enough so that we could actually sell more. Does that make sense?"

"Did you always want to be an umbrella maker?" Oscar asked quietly. "Or did your father make you do it?"

Bilius inhaled sharply and sat back in his chair. More biting of his lower lip. More pausing. "I don't know," he said honestly. "I knew that there was never another option for me, so I don't think I even bothered to *think* of another option."

"I really want to finish my Uppers," Oscar said.

"I know you do. And I know it's what your mother would have wanted...." Bilius trailed off and half closed his eyes. Oscar knew he was thinking about Elenore.

"Maybe I could do both?" Oscar suggested. "I could finish my Uppers and work in the shop every day after school? Before school? On weekends?"

"You wouldn't have time for anything else," Bilius said. "You wouldn't have time to *live.*"

"Can we at least think about it?"

"I've thought about it. Believe me, I've thought about it. I just don't see another way. I'm worried about paying the bills. I never wanted to bring you into any of this, but...I also don't want to lie to you anymore. I'm worried about paying *rent*, Oscar."

There was silence in the kitchen as Oscar took all of this in.

"But I don't want to be an umbrella maker," he said at last, his voice small and sad. "I want to be a wood-carver."

"I know, Oscar. And I'm so, so sorry. But I just don't see how that's possible."

And as sad and heartbroken and on the verge of tears as Oscar felt, he could tell Bilius was feeling the exact same way. His father's eyes were downcast and wet and Oscar found it hard to look directly at him. So instead he looked at his own hands, folded on his lap, and he wished he were anywhere in the entire world except sitting at this kitchen table, having this conversation.

But alas.

He didn't have a shooting star fruit.

So he was stuck, solidly, in this very moment.

Drawings of Fireworks

OSCAR FORGOT TO TELL his father about the Cleverers' plans to move away from the Alley. Even though their talk had gone much better than the previous night, it still left him feeling strange and empty, hollow and without hope. He just couldn't bear to talk about *more* sad things when it was over. Instead, he mumbled that he was going to meet Saige, gathered up his homework, and left for Fort Cleverbuckle.

Saige was already there, finishing up a math worksheet from the comfort of her green beanbag. Dot was next to her. She'd painted the wheelchair a pale pink sometime last year and stuck glow-in-the-dark stars all over it.

Saige had used a wheelchair for almost nine years now. When she was three, she'd contracted acute flaccid myelitis. The virus had mostly affected her legs, causing numbness, tingling, and eventually a muscle weakness that meant she couldn't put her whole weight on her legs anymore.

"Hey," Oscar said as he slipped into the fort. It was still misting outside, and he predicted it would begin rouring within the hour, so they didn't have much time to spend together.

"Hey, Oscar!"

And at the same exact time, they pulled something out of their pockets—

They both had Night Market flyers!

Saige started laughing. "I was hoping you'd find one, too!"

"There were so many when we walked home from the shop!"

"Was your dad super mad at you?"

"Not really. We talked about it. I think he knows Gregory and Tim are bullies."

"Good. I'm sorry that happened. But on the bright side— we get to go to the Night Market!"

Oscar's stomach fell.

"Well—*maybe*," he said.

"What do you mean, *maybe*?"

"My dad says we may not be able to go. Things are kind of…tight. With money. Actually, there's something I've been meaning to tell you. I just couldn't figure out a good time. But, um. I guess now it is…."

"Oscar?" Saige said, her voice quiet. "What's wrong?"

"Money is *really* tight. My dad says...well, he says I can't do my Uppers. I'm going to be an apprentice instead. I'm going to be *his* apprentice."

"At Buckle Umbrellas?" Saige asked, her eyes wide. "You aren't going back to school?"

"I guess it doesn't really matter, anyway, since you won't even be there...."

"Oscar, I don't know what to say. Your mom..."

His mom and Saige's mom had been best friends.

It's why he and Saige had known each other since they were babies.

He knew Saige didn't remember his mom any better than he did, but she knew Elenore had been principal of EBA, and she knew how much she valued education.

"Let's talk about something happier," Oscar said, to break the awkward silence in the fort. "What was your favorite part of the last Night Market?"

"The fireworks, of course," Saige said. "But to be honest, I don't remember much else." [51]

Saige loved fireworks. The walls of Fort Cleverbuckle

---

[51] She had been only five. The fireworks had been larger-than-life, brilliant explosions of color that she thought of often. Oscar had seen them, too, from Dove's roof, but they'd been far away, tiny pinpricks of light against the horizon.

were covered in her drawings, and they included many papers filled with brightly colored sky explosions.

He looked around at the drawings now and wondered, suddenly—what would Fort Cleverbuckle be when Saige left?

Would Oscar still come here?

Or would it be too painful to be here without her, too lonely, too sad?

Would she take all the drawings with her?

Would it be just an empty, depressing space?

He loved this fort.

He kept looking around, at the single light bulb hanging from the ceiling,[52] at the two beanbags, at the small table pushed against one wall, at the rug Saige had rescued from the side of the road. At Saige herself, who'd gone back to her math homework, quickly filling in the answers to questions that would have taken Oscar twice as long to answer.

He reached into his pocket and felt the smooth surface of Wib. It made him feel just the tiniest bit better. And then—

There was a tremendous crack of thunder.

"Uh-oh," Saige said.

They left Fort Cleverbuckle quickly, wanting to avoid the rour.

Back in his bedroom, Oscar watched the light come on

---

[52] Janet had helped wire it.

in Saige's room. He forced himself to do his homework, then he sat on his bed and took up a half-finished carving from his nightstand. It was a blue whale. He'd been carefully creating the lines on the underside of its enormous mouth, running his whittling knife along the wood to create smooth, shallow grooves.

He wasn't supposed to carve in bed, because he always got wood flakes and sawdust on his sheets, but he liked having the smell of the sweet wood all around him as he fell asleep. It was comforting, familiar. Like the smell of the umbrella shop.

Outside his window, it roured with a vengeance. The streets would probably be flooded tomorrow, ankle-high water splashing against his legs as he trudged his way to school. He'd have to wear his rain boots—otherwise, his sneakers would just end up soaking wet.

But he still wouldn't carry an umbrella.

More so than ever, he had no desire to do that.

The Best Umbrellas
in the Entire
Country

THE REST OF THE week passed by uneventfully, with no major life-changing announcements or fistfights.

Oscar was relieved about that.

He carefully avoided Gregory and Tim at school, keeping his head down, doing his homework, making sure not to go near the tree they'd claimed as their own.

By Saturday morning, he could open his eye, but it was still brilliantly bruised, an impressive palette of blues and purples and dark yellowy-oranges.

He went downstairs and made himself toast with flack[53] butter and jam, then joined his father at the table.

---

[53] A flack is a type of nut known for its creamy, buttery flavor.

"Are you still good to help at the shop today?" Bilius asked. "I have to make a trip to the factories to source those parts I need."

"Yup, no problem," Oscar said. He had a plan to bring all his homework to the store and get it out of the way for the rest of the weekend.

"And will you stop by the spice store? We're out of salt. Take the canister."

"Sure thing, Dad."

The spice store was called Rainy Season[54] and Mrs. Cleverer had worked there since Oscar and Saige were kids.

As he headed there now, he wondered if she would be sad about having to leave it.

She had always loved spices and cooking and baking so much.

But there was probably an even better spice store near Roan Piers, Oscar thought. Maybe she would get a job there.

That made him feel a little grumpy, although he tried to brush off the feeling as he reached Rainy Season and stepped inside its cozy, well-fragranced walls.

Mrs. Cleverer was sitting on a stool at the register. Unlike her husband, who had not a drop of warmth about him,

---

[54] The owner, an old man named Mr. Bumbleshire, was incredibly proud of that pun—and I don't blame him.

Mrs. Cleverer was a cheerful, short, chubby woman who always had a smile on her face (and a small sachet of sugar for Oscar).[55]

"Oscar!" she said now, adjusting Arthur on her lap. Saige's younger brother was almost a year old, and he was currently keeping up a steady stream of baby babble. "It's so nice to see you."

Mrs. Cleverer's face was smiley and warm as usual, but Oscar thought he also detected a shadow of...guilt? Regret?

Well, that made sense. Where Mr. Cleverer didn't give a hoot about yanking Saige away from the Alley and Oscar, Oscar was sure that Mrs. Cleverer felt badly about it.

Which was evidenced by how she immediately set Arthur down on the ground and filled a *very* large sachet of sugar for Oscar.

"Shh," she said with a wink, slipping it into his pocket. Then, for good measure, she stuffed a long, skinny paper bag with several cinnamon sticks and gave him those as well.

"What else do you need, Oscar?" she asked.

"Just some salt, please," Oscar said, handing her the empty canister.

"Are you excited for the Night Market?"

"Oh, yeah, totally," Oscar said. He didn't feel like telling Mrs. Cleverer he might not be able to go.

---

[55] Sugar is a delicacy they rarely have access to in the Toe.

"I love the Night Market," Mrs. Cleverer continued. "Those Farsouthians bring magic with them. Magic that doesn't exist in Terra anymore. One skiff forty for the salt. Will Bilius bring some umbrellas to sell?"

"I think so," Oscar said, digging around in his pockets for the money.

"Well, I hope to see you there."

Oscar placed the money on the counter. "Me too. And thank you for these." He patted his now-full pocket, where the sachet of sugar and bag of cinnamon sticks were safely kept. He'd make sweet cinnamon tea for dessert that night. Bilius would love that.

The Buckle Umbrellas shop was chilly and dark when Oscar arrived; he turned the lights on and flipped the CLOSED sign to OPEN and lit a fire in the small furnace, crouching down before it and rubbing his hands together to keep warm. It had been sluicing all morning and Oscar felt chilled to the bone.

Once he could feel his fingers again, he moved to the workbench and spread his homework out on the surface before him. He was an hour or so into an essay on Roan's industrial history when someone pushed into the shop, the bell above the door tinkling cheerfully.

"Hi there," Oscar said, looking up to find a person draped in many layers of brown fabrics, with an oversize brown hood pulled over their head, hiding their face. As it was currently freezing cold outside, Oscar didn't find this odd at all. "Welcome to Buckle Umbrellas. Feel free to browse around and let me know if you need help with anything."

The person nodded their head as if to say thanks, and Oscar watched as they moved slowly around the room, occasionally touching an umbrella or pulling it out of its barrel to get a closer look.

The umbrella finds the person, Bilius always said,[56] which meant that Oscar never had to be a pushy salesman. Bilius much preferred to sit back and let the customer browse on their own time.

So that's what Oscar did.

He went back to his essay and was engrossed in writing about the factory revolts of 1392 when the customer carefully set something on the desk in front of him.

It was the Gennal[57] model. All of Bilius's umbrellas were named after different types of rain, and the Gennal had a clear canvas so you might see through it to the lovely blue sky above you.[58]

"Great choice," Oscar said. He made a movement to take

---

[56] Which was incredibly nerdy, in Oscar's opinion.

[57] If you don't remember, a gennal is a type of warm rain that falls from a seemingly cloudless blue sky.

[58] Even though Oscar couldn't remember the last time he'd seen a lovely blue sky above him.

the umbrella, but the customer held up one hand in a gesture that clearly meant: *I'm not done yet.*

Oscar nodded and went back to his essay, leaving the Gennal where it was.

After a few more minutes, the customer set another umbrella next to the Gennal. This one was a Tranklumpet,[59] which was one of the stronger umbrellas Bilius made, with reinforced ribs and stretchers.

Before Oscar could even move, the customer held up a hand. *Still not done.*

---

[59] A reminder: This is a rain consisting of sudden bursts of heavy downpour.

This time, Oscar couldn't quite focus back on his essay. He watched the customer as they moved through the store, taking one umbrella from a stack of Wibs,[60] one from a barrel of Mists, one more from the Gennals, and one from a display of Blanderwheels (these were the most expensive umbrellas Bilius sold; they were virtually indestructible).[61]

The customer set these four new umbrellas down on the desk, studied their collection thus far, then nodded at Oscar.

There were six umbrellas in front of him.

Oscar couldn't move for at least ten seconds, but then, with shaky hands, he grabbed the receipt book and began to write down the purchases.

The customer's face was still hidden by their hood, and they waited patiently as Oscar tallied everything and, in a slightly astonished voice, read the total aloud.

"That will be three hundred and eighty skiffs, please."

The customer nodded, pulled a worn leather wallet from the folds of their robes, and counted out a number of bills.

They held them out to Oscar, who took the money, his hands still shaking, counted it (it was exact), and slid the bills into the drawer.

---

[60] And this is Oscar's favorite type of rain: a gentle sprinkle.

[61] I know what you're thinking—*Blanderwheel! Oh, right! I remember that! Hey— when is Oscar going to get trapped in the blanderwheel? Is he going to be okay? Should we go back and check on him? Did you forget about him?* The answers to these questions are: *Soon; Maybe; Not yet; No.*

"Let me wrap these up for you," he said, taking a few sheets of brown paper from another drawer. Once he had wrapped the umbrellas and slipped them into two long paper bags, he held them out to the customer and said, "Thank you. So much. We really appreciate your business."

"Your father makes the best umbrellas in the entire country," the customer said. "I am honored to be here. Thank *you*."

And then they left the store.

And Oscar did not move for at least a minute.

And then he let out a joyful yelp and danced around the shop for the next five minutes.

They would *definitely* be able to go to the Night Market now!

Just a Couple

Two more customers came to the store before Bilius returned, and Oscar sold one more umbrella, another Wib. He added fifty-five skiffs to the till, bringing the day's total to four hundred and thirty-five skiffs.

When Bilius returned to the shop that afternoon, tired and a little grumpy from taking the bus all over the Toe, Oscar struggled to keep a straight face.

"Any sales?" Bilius asked, dumping his parcels on the floor in the back of the shop.

"A couple, actually," Oscar replied.

"A couple? Nice job, Oscar!"

"Yeah, no big deal," Oscar said. "Couple of Wibs."

"One of my most popular," Bilius said, nodding.

"Couple of Gennals, too."

"Really?"

"A Mist," Oscar continued.

Bilius moved toward the workbench, looking at Oscar carefully. "Oscar. How many umbrellas did we sell today?"

"Oh, just a couple," Oscar repeated. "Like, you know, seven."

"Seven!" Bilius said. "We sold *seven* umbrellas?"

"Including a Tranklumpet. *And* a Blanderwheel."

Bilius took one step back, then one step forward, then he put both of his hands on the workbench and stared at Oscar intensely.

"Oscar. Are you joking?"

Oscar took the stack of skiffs from the till and spread the bills out in front of his father.

And Bilius had basically the same reaction Oscar had.

He stared.

He yelped.

And he danced.

A Feast

THAT NIGHT, BILIUS SPREAD the skiffs on the kitchen table and divided them into three piles. He slid the largest pile to the side.

"This is for bills," he said.

The remaining two piles contained fifty skiffs each.

He pushed one of these piles toward Oscar.

"And this is for the Night Market," he said.

"What! Really?" Oscar exclaimed. "So we can go?!"

"Really. You earned it today, Oscar."

Oscar was so excited that he was shaking, and Bilius couldn't stop smiling. They had a feast for dinner, two different kinds of pies and a cookie apiece for dessert. Both of them smiled for about six hours straight. They played flock with their bellies full, a mug of sweet cinnamon tea for each of them.

"And what did they look like again?" Bilius asked for the third or fourth time.

"Dad, I told you! They had a hood on. I couldn't really see their face."

"And brown robes, you said?"

"Brown robes, yup. Lots of layers. Kind of cool-looking."

Bilius made his move, then looked up at Oscar. "I can't say for sure, but I *think* you might have sold six Buckle umbrellas to a Farsouthian."

"Really?" Oscar asked. It was the first time Bilius had suggested it, and just the idea alone sent a thrill through Oscar.

"It just doesn't sound like anyone from around here," Bilius said. "And the Farsouthians will have started to arrive by now, I think. At least some of them."

"Wow," Oscar said. "A Farsouthian. I can't wait to tell Saige."

But Saige wasn't around that weekend, he remembered; her family had gone to Roan Piers. They were looking at their new house and starting to get acquainted with their neighborhood and buying new furniture and doing all that boring stuff Oscar couldn't care less about.[62]

---

[62] Obviously he *did* care about it, he cared about it very, very much, but he thought if he kept pretending he *didn't* care about it, he might manage to convince himself it was true.

"How is Saige, anyway? Haven't seen her in a few weeks," Bilius said.

Oscar still hadn't told his father that the Cleverers were leaving the Alley, and he guessed that now was as good a time as ever. He made his move in flock, crossed his hands on the table, and said, "She's moving."

"Oh? Moving where? Cardinal? They've just had a lovely remodel, I hear."

"Roan Piers," Oscar mumbled.

Bilius looked up, his eyes suddenly narrowed, his mouth tight. "Oh, Oscar. I'm so sorry."

Oscar shrugged. "It's okay. It's better for her. It's better there."

"Not better, Oscar," Bilius corrected gently. "Just different."

"Yeah, well. Either way. I'll probably never see her again."

"Nonsense," Bilius said. "We can go visit her whenever you'd like. Once a month. It's a nice trip. We should get out of the Toe more often, anyway. We're a regular pair of homebodies."

Oscar didn't mention that they were *supposed* to leave the Toe for his birthday, which was now just three weeks away, but he didn't want to make his father feel bad, so he didn't say anything at all.

Plus, next week they were going to the Night Market!

He'd take that over Commerce City any day.

Last Day

Isn't it always the case that when you are absolutely *dreading* something, time seems to speed up and move much more quickly than it ever has before, so that the thing you're dreading seems to fly toward you with superhuman speed?

And similarly, when you are *so excited* for something that's coming up, time seems to slow down to a painstaking crawl, so that the thing you're excited for seems impossibly far away, like it might never arrive at all?

That next week was something of a constant battle between the two extremes, because Oscar was both *dreading* the end of school (because it was the end of school for him forever *and* because Saige was moving) and *desperate* to reach Friday night, to visit the Night Market. As a result of these two very different emotions, it seemed that time couldn't figure out what to do with itself. Monday seemed to never end, Tuesday and Wednesday were gone in a flash, Thursday lasted for at least a year, and Friday happened *much* too quickly. Before Oscar was really prepared for it, their fourth session teachers had dismissed them all and Middles were officially over.

The hallways were alive with energy. Every kid in the Toe was ecstatic that school was over and summer had started and the Night Market was just a few hours away.

Well.

Every kid except Oscar.

And Saige.

Saige had been quiet all week, and more than once Oscar had to say the same thing to her multiple times before she properly heard him. She kept dazing off, getting solemn and somber, then snapping out of it and going almost back to normal.

He found her at her locker now, dutifully cleaning it of all books, paper, pencils, pens, and other detritus that had accumulated over the school year. She was sliding everything carefully into her backpack.[63]

Oscar stood behind Saige, just watching. One of the last things she removed from her locker was a photo of the two of them, which had been held to the door of the locker with a

---

[63] Except for a very brown and old banana peel, which she had dropped on the floor and was fastidiously ignoring.

small magnet. She took it down and held it in her hand, just looking at it. Then she slipped that, too, into her bag.

"Hey," Oscar said, finally making his presence known.

"Oh. Hey."

"Want to go to the market with me?" he asked, then clarified, "East Market. Just need to see Neko."

"I have to get home," she said, not quite meeting his eye. "You know. The movers will already be there."

"Right," Oscar said. "Okay. Well...See you tonight?"

Oscar had told Saige he was going to the Night Market, and they'd made a plan to meet in front of the Ferris wheel[64] at ten o'clock that night.

"Yeah," Saige said. "Sounds good."

"Are you..." But he let his voice trail off. Because he'd been about to ask her if she was okay. And of course she wasn't okay.

"Excited for tonight," she said, forcing a smile. She shut her locker, looped her bag around the back of her wheelchair, and picked up the banana peel with two fingers. She tossed it in a trash can one of the teachers had set in the middle of the hallway, and started for the elevator.

It had been...

A week.

Oscar felt exhausted and miserable.

---

[64] A real-life Ferris wheel! Oscar would have never dreamed he'd actually see one!

But he also felt excited, eager, and *really* happy about riding a Ferris wheel.

It was a lot of emotions for one person to have, and as a result he felt almost *stuffed*.

A bit swollen and heavy.

And when he reached Neko's stall at East Market, Neko noticed immediately.

"My small friend, why the long face?"

Oscar shrugged. "Last day of school."

Neko softened. He knew all about Saige leaving, and about Oscar not continuing on to his Uppers. Oscar told Neko everything, pretty much, and he listened closely, usually while sharing a midnight orange or slicing an apple in half.

"This is a big day, Oscar," Neko said now, patting Oscar heavily on the shoulder. "Feel those feelings."

"I don't think I have another option," Oscar replied dryly. "I've tried *not* to feel them, and they just keep coming."

"I know how that goes," Neko said, laughing loudly, a comforting, friendly laugh that made Oscar smile. "Can I get you anything to eat?"

"No, that's okay, Neko. My dad just wanted me to make sure you can still drive us tonight."

"Of course I can. I'd do anything for old Bill," Neko said. Then, winking, he added, "And you."

"Meet you here at eight?"

"Perfect."

"We'll bring you dinner, okay? I'm making a flatbread."

Neko clapped his hands together. "You know the way to my heart is through my stomach."

"It's the least we can do," Oscar pointed out.

Neko was one of the lucky few in the Toe to own a truck; most people would get to the Night Market by walking. It would probably take them close to two hours each way, and a good number of them would carry tents on their backs, sleeping in the open fields to the north of the fairgrounds so they wouldn't have to make the trek twice in one day.

Neko's business at the Night Market was, of course, fruits. But not just any fruits. He only brought the things he wouldn't even sell at Central Market—that's how rare and pricey they were.

Neko looked around now, checking to see if anyone was watching, then he slipped his hand underneath a canvas curtain and withdrew a small rock.

"Stonefruit," [65] he whispered. "Careful with it. If anybody sees you with that . . . just put it in your mouth, quick."

"I'm not eating a *rock*," Oscar said, shocked.

"Put. It. In. Your. Mouth," Neko hissed back, and if it was

---

[65] In our world, a stonefruit is a fruit, such as a peach or a plum or a cherry, that has sweet, pulpy flesh surrounding a hard, stonelike pit. In Oscar's world, a stonefruit is a very rare fruit that, true to its name, looks and feels exactly like a stone.

anybody else, Oscar would have tossed the stone right over his shoulder, but because it was Neko, he popped it into his mouth, expecting to taste dirt and grit and, well, rock.

Because it *was* a rock.

But...

But what...

The stone—which for a moment felt and tasted exactly how a stone would feel and taste on your tongue—melted almost instantly, liquifying in Oscar's mouth, pouring over his teeth and tongue and tonsils. It was chocolatey and sweet with just the perfect amount of tartness. Oscar's eyes grew wide. When he swallowed, it was like hot chocolate gliding down his throat. It was the most delicious thing he had ever tasted in his entire life.

"I told you," Neko said, smirking.

"Is that...is that *illegal*?" Oscar asked. "What do you mean *if anybody sees you with that*? Is it not allowed? Can I have another one?"

"These go for ten skiffs apiece, Oscar, so as much as I love you, no, you may not have another one," Neko said.

Oscar briefly debated whether he should spend his fifty skiffs on five more pieces of stonefruit. That was how good it was.

But before he had a chance to decide either way, Neko shooed him off. Oscar spent a few more minutes at the market collecting the ingredients for his flatbread, then set off toward Dove.

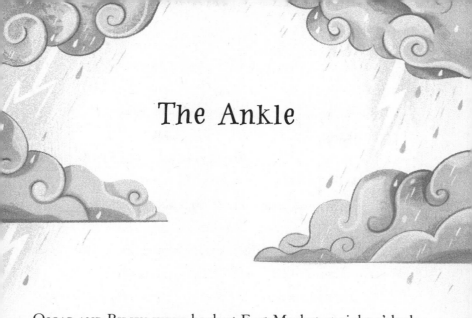

The Ankle

Oscar and Bilius were back at East Market at eight o'clock sharp, Bilius with his quiver of umbrellas and Oscar with the flatbread he'd made for Neko, a small round of dough with ollins, cheese, tomato sauce, and olives. Neko and his niece and coworker, Pietra, were loading up Neko's truck when they arrived. Pietra usually worked Central Market while Neko worked the East, so Oscar didn't see her that much. She gave him a big hug now, ruffling his hair and cooing loudly about how big he was getting. Which was kind of funny, because she was young herself, barely twenty-five, and wouldn't have been taller than Oscar if it weren't for her wild head of curls that bounced and jiggled with her every movement.

"I didn't know you were going to be here, Pietra, or I would have made a flatbread for you, too!" Oscar said.

"I already ate," she replied, waving a hand through the air to mean *no sweat*.

"Almost ready," Neko said, sliding one final case of fruit into the cargo bed of the truck. Neko set a blanket out on the bit of space that was left in the bed (Oscar and Pietra would have to ride in the back), then slipped his hand into one of the crates, fished around, and withdrew another stonefruit. "My friend," he said, handing it to Bilius.

"I can't take this," Bilius said, stepping back, his hands held up in front of him. "Neko, this is too much."

"Don't be ridiculous," Neko said. "Look at what I've got in return!" He took the flatbread from Oscar and took a big bite. "Best cook in the Toe!"

He tossed the stonefruit into the air, leaving Bilius with no choice but to catch it or let it drop.

He caught it.

He looked at it for just a moment before closing his eyes and placing it gently on his tongue.

His face melted into an expression of utter joy.

"My sun," [66] he said quietly. "Absolutely perfect."

"It's a good batch," Neko said, laughing thunderously. He finished the flatbread in a few more enormous bites, then banged his hand against the side of his truck. "And we're off!"

---

[66] Since the people of Roan rarely saw the sun and longed for it daily, this expression was reserved only for things that were *really* good.

Oscar and Pietra climbed into the back of the truck and Bilius shut the tailgate behind them. In another minute, they were rolling down the road. Only Central Door was big enough for a vehicle, so they headed there. Because of the Night Market, the guards were letting everyone and anyone through the gates. Oscar and Pietra waved to them as they drove through. One of the guards, a young woman with short red hair and cheeks full of freckles, winked at Pietra.

"Who was *that*?" Oscar asked teasingly.

"Never you mind," Pietra said, but Oscar saw her glance back at the guard several times, a big smile on her face.

Oscar found himself thinking about the last time he'd been through the Wall. It had been for his ninth birthday, almost three years ago. Bilius and he had stayed in Commerce City, just like they were supposed to do this year. It had been a beautiful weekend. Actually... wasn't that the last time it had stopped raining for any significant amount of time? They'd enjoyed blue skies, fair weather, lots and lots of sunshine...

"What's going on up there?" Pietra asked, tapping Oscar on the side of the head. She had to raise her voice to be heard over the roar of the truck's engine and the rush of the wind. It was shlinking out, but Oscar of course never used an umbrella and if Pietra tried to open one, it would have simply blown away.

"Oh, just thinking about the last time I came to the

Ankle," [67] Oscar said. They were passing Central Market. It was bigger than he remembered, an endless sea of colorful tents. But it was basically deserted now; everyone was on their way to the Night Market.

"I remember that," Pietra said. "You stopped by my apartment!"

Pietra lived in a small studio apartment in Commerce City. Oscar had loved how bright it was, how happy it seemed. Every wall was painted a different color, and Pietra's own artwork decorated the small space.

As they continued north, Oscar noticed that the rain got a little lighter, sliding from a shlink to a wib before stopping altogether. The skies grew slightly less gray, too, slightly less cloudy, so that Oscar could actually see the moon shimmering high above them.

"It rains less here," Pietra explained. "Geographical anomaly."

"I remember the sun," Oscar said. "The last time I was here."

"Sometimes the sun comes out," Pietra said, nodding slowly, careful not to sound like she was bragging, trying to downplay it as much as she could.

"The sun never comes out in the Toe anymore," Oscar continued. "Not for years."

---

[67] This is what people from the Toe sometimes call Roan Piers and Commerce City, although most people from Roan Piers and Commerce City would never refer to it as such.

The climatologists talked about changing air patterns, shifts in the tectonic plates, weather anomalies they had many big, complicated words for but could never quite explain in simple terms.

But here...

How come he didn't know that it was sometimes sunny in the Ankle?

How come he didn't know that it rained less here, that even while it shlinked in the Toe, it was mild and almost dry as they drove past Roan Piers?

He thought again of his trip to Commerce City three years ago. It had been so nice north of the Wall.

It didn't feel fair.

It *wasn't* fair.

The only thing that separated the Ankle from the Toe was one manmade, twenty-foot-high wall.

So why was the weather so different?

When Commerce City came into view to the east, Oscar leaned over the side of the truck and stared at it. Pietra had a bike, he knew, and would ride it from the city to Central Market and sometimes to the Toe. It had a wicker basket on the front and a bell attached to the handlebars.

He'd always wanted a bike.

He patted his pocket now, where the fifty skiffs were tucked safely inside an old wallet of Bilius's.

Maybe he would budget, spend just ten skiffs at the Night Market and use the remaining forty to buy himself a used bike.

He shook his head.

His thoughts were spinning about a mile a minute, and Pietra was still looking at him, like she could tell.

"Everything okay, Os?" she asked.[68]

"Wondering what to get at the Night Market," Oscar said, trying to snap out of the weird mood he suddenly found himself in.

"I've saved up all year for an Ocspectrascope," she replied.

"What's that?"

"Coolest thing ever. You fit it over your eyes—it's sort of like a cross between eyeglasses and a monocle—and you can see *more colors*! The human eye can only perceive, like, a million color variations. But there are colors we can't even see! I learned about it in art class."

"Wow," Oscar said. He knew Saige would love one of those. "How much are they?"

"About two hundred, I think," Pietra said.

Oscar frowned. He wouldn't be able to buy one for Saige, then.

He looked back out toward Commerce City. All lit up at

---

[68] She is the only person in the world who calls him Os.

night, it looked almost like a faraway ship on the Gray Sea, surrounded by darkness and water and waves.

On either side of the truck, the people of the Toe (and some from the Ankle, too) were making the long journey to the Night Market.

Oscar felt bad they had to walk so far and grateful that Neko was able to drive him and Bilius.

Neko wasn't technically allowed to have his own booth,[69] but he was old friends with a Farsouthian who let Neko share his space. The Farsouthian's name was Innis, and although Oscar had never met him, he knew Innis was a wood-carver, too. Neko had brought back a few pieces Innis had carved over the years, and they held special places on Oscar's shelves. What was weird was that every so often—out of the corner of his eye—Oscar swore they moved.

On Neko's urging, Oscar had brought Innis a wood carving in return. He pulled it out of his pocket now. It was a pig. He'd chosen it for no reason in particular, but he was rather fond of the way the nose had turned out, as well as its delicate, slender cloven hooves.

"May I?" Pietra said, holding her hand out.

Oscar placed the pig in her palm.

"Did Innis make this?" she asked.

---

[69] Only Farsouthians can operate their own booths at the Night Market, but anybody can sell wares on foot—like Bilius with his quiver of umbrellas.

"No," Oscar said, suddenly embarrassed and a little squirmy.

Pietra looked up at him, her face soft. "Oscar...*you* made this?"

Oscar shrugged, feeling even squirmier. He took the pig from her and put it back in his pocket. "Yeah."

"I wish I could get you in front of one of my art professors," Pietra said. "Maybe one day, huh?"

"Maybe one day," Oscar agreed.

But of course there wouldn't be a one day.

If he didn't complete his Uppers, he couldn't go to university, like Pietra.

In danger of getting sad again, Oscar blinked rapidly, then turned to the front of the truck.

And any sadness he felt dissolved at once.

Because there it was.

There it was!

The Night Market!

The Night Market

It loomed out of the darkness in front of them, taking Oscar's breath away.

Beside him, he felt Pietra turn, falling silent herself.

They had passed Roan Piers and Commerce City and arrived at the northern edge of Roan, which gave way to the Northern Wastelands and the rest of Terra beyond that.

Rising out of the miles of nothingness before them was one enormous pitch-black tent, soaring at least five stories high. There were openings all over it with a lantern set inside each, so it felt as if you were looking at the night sky, ablaze with stars. Surrounding this main tent were four smaller ones (but each still about the size of Oscar's school). And surrounding *these* were hundreds and hundreds of smaller tents, about the size of the stalls in East Market.

To the right of everything were the rides, and Oscar's heart leaped in his chest when he saw the Ferris wheel.

It was *enormous*.

How had they built this entire thing in one day? And how would they possibly take it down again when it was all over?

But the Farsouthians had magic. They moved faster than the people of Roan, the people of Terra. They were nimble and light on their feet and quick with their hands.[70]

"Wow," Pietra whispered.

"How many times have you been?" Oscar asked.

"This is my fourth," she said. "And it never gets old."

People were parking cars and setting up tents and make-shift shelters all over the place; there seemed to be no rhyme or reason to it. They passed a two-story tent with electric lights, a lean-to–type thing built into the bed of a truck, and a car that pulled a wheeled shed behind it.

Everything was lit up by crisscrossing strands of white, flickering fairy lights, strung up on ten-foot poles. There were long strands of lights starting at the top of the biggest tent, too, as well as old-fashioned lanterns set on high poles throughout the fields and the market itself.

It was almost too much to take in, but Oscar did his best to keep his eyes open. He didn't want to miss a single thing.

---

[70] And yes, of course, there were rumors that elf blood still ran in their veins, that elf magic still thrummed in their fingertips, that elf light still blessed their footsteps, and certainly they *looked* a bit like elves, with their slender, pointed ears and their sharp, clever smiles.

Neko drove the truck past the fields, past the tents, past the people still walking in from the south. He kept going until they got to the boundary of the market, which was marked by a low, wooden fence.

"This won't keep many people out at all," Oscar observed. He was used to the Wall, after all, and he could easily hop this fence.

"I wouldn't be so sure about that," Pietra replied. "There's more to this fence than meets the eye."

The main entrance to the Night Market was in the middle, but the gate before them was toward the side and manned by just one Farsouthian. Oscar sucked in a sharp inhale, because just like Bilius had said, the Farsouthian was wearing robes *exactly* like the person who had come into the shop and bought six Buckle umbrellas. That customer had definitely been a Farsouthian. There was no doubt left in Oscar's mind.

This Farsouthian had her hood down, and Oscar was struck by just how *beautiful* she was. She was tall and fat, with pale, almost shimmering skin and light brown eyes that perfectly matched her light brown hair, which hung down her back in an intricate and complicated series of braids. And her ears. They were pointed![71] Oscar tried not to stare, but the woman was practically glowing with beauty and stature, and

---

[71] Of course Oscar *knew* Farsouthians had pointed ears, but he had never actually seen them before!

it was hard to look anywhere else. The Farsouthian took one look at Neko and waved the truck onward. Neko nodded in thanks and continued past the fence.

The Night Market was a maze of stalls and tents and booths and pathways, and there were many roads that branched off to different parts of it. Neko seemed to know exactly where he was going, though, and turned right, then left, then left again, and then Oscar lost track of where they were and how many skinny roads they'd driven down. But he could just see the top of the main tent to his right, which gave him a comforting feeling of orientation.

"You can see it from everywhere," Pietra said, as if reading his mind. "It's like a compass."

The Night Market had not yet opened to the public; it would do so at nine o'clock exactly. Each night—Friday, Saturday, and Sunday—it would open its doors from nine to midnight. Just three hours at a time.

Neko brought the truck to a stop in front of an open-air booth. It was much larger than his stall at East Market, and most of its shelves were already filled with exotic fruits and vegetables. The low walls were arranged to form an entranceway that led to the booth and its two rows of goods. And standing there was another Farsouthian—Innis, Oscar presumed.

Innis was tall and dark-skinned, with finely braided hair that was looped into a chignon at the nape of his neck. His eyes were a dark, enchanting brown, and his ears were more pointed than the guard's had been. He had a serious face, but when he saw the truck and Neko in the driver's seat, his mouth turned up in a smile of pure joy. He opened his arms as Neko got out of the truck, and the old friends embraced, laughing and smiling.

"My friend," Neko said, pulling away but keeping hold of Innis's hand. "You look as well as ever."

"It brings me great joy to see you," Innis replied, placing one of his hands on Neko's cheek. "And your friends!" He turned to the rest of them. Bilius had gotten out of the truck, and he walked around the front now to hug Innis himself. Then Pietra danced over and *she* hugged Innis. Oscar felt a little awkward as he hopped off the back of the truck and stood there waiting. It seemed he was the only one who didn't know Innis.

"And you must be Oscar," Innis said. "Neko speaks highly of you."

"Um, hi," Oscar said. "It's nice to meet you."

"An honor," Innis said, holding out his hand.

They shook, then Oscar pulled the pig out of his pocket. It suddenly seemed like the weirdest choice of animal; why hadn't he gone with something cooler, like a lion or a wolf or an eagle or even the woolly mammoth that he'd fixed the other night!?

But that couldn't be helped now—the pig was all he had. He offered it to Innis.

"Neko has brought me a few of your carvings over the years. They're wonderful. I…well, I'm sort of a carver, too. It's just a hobby. Nothing serious. I wanted to bring you something. As a trade, I guess."

Oscar noticed that his father looked down at the ground at that, almost like he was…sad? Irritated? Disappointed that Oscar was still talking about wood carving?

Innis took the pig from Oscar's hand and gently set it on his own palm. He brought it up to eye level and studied it carefully, first from one angle, then another. It was a long few moments before he spoke, and Oscar was beginning to feel *really* self-conscious.

Did he hate it?

Should he just take it back?

Should he find a shovel somewhere and dig a hole and then crawl into it and bury himself so he never had to face the Farsouthian again?

Finally, Innis lowered the pig. He covered it with his other hand, gently cradling it between his palms.

"You are quite talented, Oscar," he said. "Who taught you this craft?"

"I guess I just taught myself," Oscar replied.

"This is a truly remarkable rendering," Innis continued. "I will treasure this. Thank you for gifting it to me."

Oscar's cheeks were practically on fire now, and Innis seemed to sense this, so he slipped the pig into the deep pockets of his robes and turned back to Neko, letting Oscar have a moment to be embarrassed in peace.

"Shall we unload?" Innis asked.

They formed something of an assembly line, with Neko in the bed of the truck handing boxes down to Pietra, who handed them to Bilius, who passed them to Innis, who placed them on the floor of the stall. Oscar tried to stay out of the way, but he couldn't resist wandering just a bit. Next to Innis and Neko's stall was a booth that sold thousands of spices in small glass jars.[72] On the other side of that was a booth that sold dried beans in deep, wide barrels.[73] And across from the booth was a stand that sold only leaves of lettuce, in every shade of green (and some purples, reds, and blues, too) you could imagine. It seemed like this part of the market was devoted entirely to food and produce, and Oscar couldn't *wait* to see what other sections there were!

When the truck had been completely unloaded, Neko climbed back into the driver's seat and went to park in the

---

[72] Mrs. Cleverer would have loved to see that, Oscar thought.
[73] Oscar had to resist the urge to stick his hands into them.

vendors' lot. Innis, Bilius, and Pietra started arranging the new produce Neko had delivered, and pretty soon the booth was set up perfectly, with everything nestled into its rightful place. The shelves were overstuffed with bright-yellow butter lemons,[74] pale green bite-size apples, and burning-hot baskets of shooting star fruit. Some of the crates had glass lids fit over them. These locked with tiny silver deadbolts.

"The more expensive the fruit, the more appealing to the thief," Innis explained.

The stonefruits were one of the fruits that had been safely locked away, and next to them Oscar noticed a small, baseball-size fruit with vicious-looking spikes growing from its red-black skin. These were also kept under lock and key.

"What are those?" he asked, pointing.

"Devil's apples," Innis said. "A single poke from one of those spikes will send a grown man to sleep for a full day. A devil to eat, they are, which is probably how they got their name." He chuckled softly at his own joke, then went to fix a display of pale purple bananas.[75]

"Just ten minutes until the gates open," Bilius said, patting Oscar's shoulder. "Are you excited?"

---

[74] Much like a regular lemon, although less tart and more of a buttery and smooth flavor.

[75] These are known as lavender bananas; they taste exactly like regular yellow bananas, except they *look* a lot cooler.

"I can't wait!" Oscar exclaimed.

He was going to spend the first hour walking around with his father, getting the lay of the land and a feel for everything, and then he'd meet Saige by the Ferris wheel at ten. He knew there were other rides in the fairgrounds part of the Night Market, but the Ferris wheel was what he was most excited for.

Neko got back to the booth five minutes later, and by that time, Oscar was basically quivering with excitement. The start of the market was marked by a cannon's boom each night ("Do they actually shoot a cannonball?" Oscar had asked Neko, who assured him that, no, the cannon wasn't loaded), and Oscar couldn't *wait* to hear that sound.

Innis and Pietra were putting the final touches on the booth, making sure everything looked perfect.

"Bilius, will you stay and help out for the first hour? I told Pietra she could have that time to wander around herself," Neko said.

"Oh," Bilius replied, "I promised Oscar I'd walk around with him first."

"I'm sure Pietra will watch him, if you don't mind?" Neko said.

"No way," Pietra called over jokingly.

"Oscar, is it all right with you?" Bilius asked.

"We have all weekend to walk around, Dad," Oscar reassured him.

"Pietra? You won't lose him?" Bilius said.

"Lose him? No. Sell him to a pirate raider from the north? Potentially," Pietra said, joining them and looping her arm around Oscar's shoulders.

"Don't look so worried, Bilius. There haven't been reports of pirate raiders for at least a decade!" Neko joked, then he laughed his deep booming laugh—

At the same exact time the cannon fired.

Magical Artifacts

PIETRA AND OSCAR MADE their way through the farmer's market section of the Night Market ("I mean, you can get some truly wild things here, but we're on a mission," she said as she hurried him past a display of floating apples[76]) and emerged from a row of booths to find themselves in an open space just left of the five main tents. Pietra named each of them as she pointed, starting with the four smaller ones and ending with the biggest.

"Agriculture. Horticulture. Magical Artifacts. Arts and Textiles. And, of course, the Stage."

"The Stage?" Oscar asked.

"There's one show a night. It starts at eleven. You have to

---

[76] Totally normal apples with a tiny hovering enchantment that doesn't affect the taste at all.

get your tickets early—see that line?" She pointed to where there was already a vast line of people forming (and it was only getting longer by the second). "They're all waiting for tickets."

"Should we get tickets?"

"We have them already," she said. "For tomorrow night. Perks of being a friend of Innis's."

"How *do* Neko and Innis know each other?" Oscar asked as Pietra took his arm and steered him to the Magical Artifacts tent. "I tried to ask him about it but he changed the subject."

"Right, of course he did, because you're young and impressionable. And because Bilius asked him not to tell you." She looked over at him and winked.

"Why would my father ask Neko not to tell me something?"

"I don't know. Parents are weird," she said. "Sometimes they think they have to protect their kids from the truth. I can't explain it, Os."

"So what *is* the truth? Will you tell me?"

"Sure, because your dad didn't make *me* promise anything, and I'm nothing if not a bad influence. Neko and Innis used to be runners together."

"Runners?"

"Smugglers. Bootleggers. Moon cursers. Moonshiners. Moon—"

"They were *thieves*?" Oscar squeaked.

"*Thieves* is *not* a word I'd use to describe them. A thief is someone who picks a wallet out of your back pocket. Which reminds me, pay attention to your wallet. There are a lot of people about. You don't have to worry about Farsouthians, but folks come from all around Terra to visit the Night Market, you know? The good *and* the bad."

Oscar patted his pocket instinctively, relieved to feel that his wallet was still there. He buttoned his pocket and struggled to keep up with Pietra, who had much longer legs than he did.

"Smugglers. Really?" Oscar said.

"A million years ago," Pietra said. "And they prefer *runners*. There's a negative connotation to smugglers that isn't quite fair. They weren't stealing from the *people*. They were taking back what rightfully belonged to those people. They were redistributing the wealth. It's the government who steals, Oscar, who *smuggles*. And don't you forget it." They'd almost reached the entrance of the Magical Artifacts tent. "Oh, and most of the stuff they were running was purchased legally. It just wasn't strictly legal to *run* it."

"How could something be legal to buy but not legal to run?" Oscar asked.

"It's all politics," Pietra said. "Different countries have different import laws. Different cities, even. Like Roan. You can't import umbrellas to Roan. Did you know that?"

Oscar did know that, of course. He nodded.

"Do you know *why?*" Pietra pressed. She stopped just outside the entrance to the tent and turned to face him.

Oscar shook his head.

"It's because of Brawn Industries," Pietra said. "They have *endless* money. When they started making umbrellas, they paid off the politicians of Commerce City. They made it illegal to import umbrellas into the city. Then they systematically started choking out every umbrella maker *in* the city. And now there's just..." She trailed off, waiting for him to catch up.

"My dad," Oscar said.

"Your dad," she agreed.

"Wow."

"Yeah. They're not good people, Os. And your dad is the *only* one they haven't managed to crush into oblivion."

"Why is that?"

"Simple," she said, smiling. "He makes *really* good umbrellas. *And* he's just one tiny fish in the sea. He doesn't present much competition. They probably figure it would take more effort to really squash him than it would take to just leave him alone, at this point." Pietra looked around, then took a step closer to Oscar. "Don't you think it's weird that the weather here got really bad as soon as Brawn started making umbrellas? Do you know what they made *before* they made umbrellas?"

"Tires," Oscar said.

"Yup. And before that?"

"Um. Jump ropes, I think."

"And before that?"

"I dunno."

"A long list of things. Nothing ever really took off. And then they switched to umbrellas and *bam*—" She snapped her fingers about two inches from Oscar's nose.

"Are you saying..."

"I'm saying it's weird," Pietra replied. "That's all. All right—let's go find me an Ocspectrascope. And don't tell your father I told you any of this. Got it? Or Neko. Or Innis. Actually, don't tell anyone. Especially not Saige."

"Why *especially not* Saige?"

"Just trust me. Okay?"

"Okay," Oscar promised, and he didn't have even a second to process everything she'd just told him (why couldn't he tell Saige?) before Pietra grabbed him by the hand and pulled him through the small mob of people currently entering the Magical Artifacts tent.

Oscar's eyes widened and he almost forgot to even breathe. He was thankful that Pietra still kept hold of his hand; she led them away from the entrance and off to the side, where there were fewer people and Oscar had a second to take it all in.

The inside of the tent was a rich, dark amethyst color, and

the same fairy lights were strung along the ceiling, zigzagging across the entire space. At the top of the tent was an enormous chandelier. It was made up of what looked like hundreds of clear glass bubbles, all crowded around each other and piled on top of each other, like if you took a spoon and scooped off a layer of bubbles from a bubble bath. Each bubble burned a different color—blues and purples and silvers and golds and yellows and lavenders and pinks and greens. Pietra followed his gaze and beamed.

"Now *that* will look incredible through an Ocspectra-scope," she said. "See the clear bubbles throughout the chandelier? Those aren't clear at all. Those are colors the human eye can't see. Well—Farsouthians can probably see them. They have those magical elf eyes."

She continued her excited stream of consciousness babble, but Oscar barely heard her. There was just too much to *see*. It was like if you smashed together a massive magic shop (he'd been to one once in Commerce City) and the biggest bookstore you'd ever seen (one side of the tent was covered in bookcases from the floor to the ceiling) and swirled everything together with a mechanic's workshop, a natural history museum, and a toy store. There were booths set up everywhere, and each of them was like its own separate shop. Some of these even had roofs and doors and little windows you could peek through. The floor was cobblestoned in places and brick in other places and packed dirt in other places. Not for the first time, Oscar wondered how all of this was *possible*. Even if the Farsouthians had magic, how could they possibly manage all of *this*?

It was unlike anything he'd ever seen.[77]

"Os?" Pietra said, and Oscar had the impression it wasn't the first time she'd said his name. He smiled sheepishly and looked at her.

"Sorry."

"It's a lot, I know."

"It's so..."

"Cool."

"I mean, that's an actual...*cottage*."

He pointed at a stone building just twenty or thirty feet in front of them. It had a thatched roof, a rounded door, and a chimney with *smoke coming out of it*!

"Yeah, we should definitely go in there," Pietra agreed. "She sells these candles with flames that burn different colors. Oh! *Those* would be amazing with an Ocspectrascope!"

"Let's get your Ocspectra-thingy first," Oscar said, laughing, knowing how excited she was. "We can look around after that."

Pietra gave a little squeal and, although she wasn't holding his hand anymore, made sure to look back every few feet so as not to lose Oscar in the crowd.

---

[77] It's unlike anything *I've* ever seen, too, and it's probably unlike anything you've ever seen as well.

Oscar tried not to look around him; there was just too much to *see* and he didn't want to lose Pietra, either. He focused on keeping up with her, and after a few minutes of walking, she paused in front of a nondescript folding table with an impossibly old Farsouthian sitting on a chair behind it. She had pale, paper-thin skin covered in wrinkles, and she wore a pair of eyeglasses with the tiniest lenses Oscar had ever seen. The table in front of her was filled with what Oscar assumed were Ocspectrascopes. They had one arm that hooked over your ear, like a regular pair of eyeglasses, but the second arm was designed to fit over your head. And they only had one lens. It fit over the right eye. To be honest, they were kind of... boring-looking.

"Two hundred skiffs," the Farsouthian announced tiredly. "But I like your hair. So one ninety for you."

All of the Ocspectrascopes looked exactly the same, with not so much as a different screw or color among them. But still, Pietra took her time choosing. She picked up each one, examined it carefully, turned it over in her hands, and finally put one on her head.

Wordlessly, she took her money out of a flat, small purse Oscar hadn't even noticed before, handed it to the Farsouthian, and whispered, "Thank you."

"Enjoy the rest of the Night Market," the Farsouthian replied, bowing her head in farewell.

Pietra wandered away, apparently forgetting all about Oscar as she looked through her new Ocspectrascope. Oscar followed her silently, smirking, happy that she was so happy.

And then he saw a little shop made of red brick, with two small windows, the glass marked by air pockets, through which he could see...

Wood carvings.

The shop was filled with wood carvings.

He whirled around to tell Pietra to wait, but she was already gone, swallowed up by the crowd in the few seconds Oscar had taken his eyes off her.

He knew he should try to find her, but the pull of the shop was too much to ignore, and before he could talk himself out of it, he opened the door and slipped inside.

The interior of the shop was dark, lit only by a few taper candles set into nooks in the wall.

There were two wooden tables, and each of these was completely filled with wood carvings.

Oscar took a deep breath—it smelled like his bedroom. Like his favorite smell in the entire world. The smell of sawdust.

But this wood was something he'd never seen before. He bent down to examine one of the carvings more closely. The wood was dark, practically black, with almost no grain at all. The carving was of a curled up, sleeping cat. Its tail was tucked under its chin and its paws were hidden underneath its body. Its fur was carved so expertly that it seemed like each hair was a separate, individual knife stroke. As Oscar watched, one of its ears twitched in its sleep, and the gentle rise and fall of its chest became more noticeable.

Wait.

One of its ears twitched...

The rise and fall of its chest...

The cat was *breathing*?

Oscar took an awkward step backward, still hunched over, and immediately tripped, landing hard on his butt on the wood floor.

In the shadows at the back of the shop, someone laughed amicably.

A Farsouthian.

Oscar hadn't seen her before, but she moved into one of the circles of light now. She had light brown skin and warm, red hair and sharp green eyes. Her face was friendly and she had one beauty mark under her left eye. She was beautiful, just like all the Farsouthians he had seen so far, and Oscar suddenly felt self-conscious, sitting on his bum in the middle of her shop. He quickly scrambled to his feet.

"Um. Sorry," he mumbled.

"It can be a bit of a shock," she said. "They do move a little."

Which was exactly when Oscar noticed that all of the wooden carvings—not just the cat—were moving.

There weren't just animals. There was a one-foot-tall wooden ship that perpetually rocked forward and backward, as if sailing along on high seas. There was a windmill with its four wooden sails spinning slowly clockwise. And there was a tree, the tallest carving there, three feet high with many branches and individual leaves. It swayed gently in an invisible breeze.

All of the carvings were done in the same dark, almost-black wood. It was as smooth as blown glass and Oscar wished desperately to touch it (but he thought that would probably be rude).

"Are they . . . enchanted?" he asked.

"No," the Farsouthian replied. "Not by any spell or charm. It's the wood itself. This is monkwood. It grows in the swamps of Monkland. It drinks the magical waters around it and becomes infused with its magic. Just a little bit infused, though. The cat will sleep forever, although occasionally it will twitch an ear or breathe or peek open one eye. The ship will rock back and forth but never set sail."

"Monkwood," Oscar repeated. He had never heard of it.

"Please," the Farsouthian said, gesturing to a table. "Feel free."

Oscar stepped forward again and picked up the sleeping

cat. The wood felt warm underneath his hand, and he could feel the low purr of the cat's breathing, the gentle thrumming of its small body.

"And you're sure it's not..."

"Alive?" the Farsouthian guessed. "I assure you. The monkwood takes on certain characteristics of the carving, but the carving is still just wood."

"The grain is so smooth," Oscar noted. "And the weight, it's so much heavier than it looks."

The Farsouthian raised an eyebrow. "Are you familiar with wood, then?"

"Sort of," Oscar admitted. "I carve a little."

"How lovely," she replied. "In that case, I would like to offer you a gift."

"Oh, no," Oscar said, setting the cat back on the table. "I couldn't."

"I will give you *two* gifts," she amended. "The first is a bit of advice. Never refuse a gift offered by a Farsouthian." She smiled and Oscar felt his cheeks flush with warmth. "The second is this—" And she turned around for a moment, then faced Oscar again with a small block of wood in her hand. An uncarved piece of monkwood. "From one carver to another."

She handed him the block of wood. It was about two inches by four inches, and it was deliciously solid and warm in his hands.

"Thank you," he said. "Truly."

"You are very welcome," she said. "Come back and see me one day. I'd love to know what you find in that wood."

Oscar promised that he would, then he slipped the block of wood into his pocket and left the shop.

The Magical Artifacts tent was much more crowded now, and he gave up any hope of finding Pietra. But it was probably about time to head to the Ferris wheel, anyway, so he made his way back to the entrance of the tent, trying not to get distracted by everything there was to see.

He felt like he'd just barely scratched the surface of the tent, and he wanted to come straight back after he rode the Ferris wheel with Saige. She would *love* it here. He wondered what she'd been doing so far, and then he remembered what Pietra had said—*Actually, don't tell anyone. Especially not Saige.* It was just kind of weird, wasn't it, that Pietra had singled Saige out?

Well, she'd *also* mentioned Bilius, Neko, and Innis. So maybe it wasn't so weird after all. She probably knew that Oscar told Saige everything, and that was her way of covering all her bases.

Although.

It didn't *feel* like that, did it?

Pursuit

Oscar slipped out of the Magical Artifacts tent, took a second to get his bearings, and turned toward the direction of the Ferris wheel. There were so many more people around now, and he kept patting his pockets nervously, making sure both the wallet and the block of monkwood were safe. When he passed around the front of the largest tent, he noticed it had an enormous clock over the entranceway (which was currently closed). This was the clock that he'd seen on the Night Market flyers. It was five minutes till ten; he picked up the pace.

The area to the immediate right of the five main tents was filled with rows and rows of food stalls and food trucks and food tents, and Oscar felt his stomach turn over eagerly as he smelled all the rich, enticing options. But still, he forced himself to ignore all of them, because he didn't want to keep Saige waiting.

Past the food area, the ride area began. The Ferris wheel sat in the center of all the other rides, and Oscar dutifully planted himself in front of it after scanning the area and determining that Saige wasn't already there.

All around him were the shouts and squeals and happy voices of the market-goers.

Aside from the Ferris wheel, there was a ride that lifted you into the air and spun you around at a million miles an hour (no thank you, thought Oscar), a ride that was shaped like a great sailing ship and rocked back and forth with giant heaves (also no), and an area for the younger children that included a swing ride that lifted you gently into the air and swung you around, a long dragon-shaped roller coaster that breathed real fire, and a beautiful merry-go-round, each animal so realistic that it almost looked alive.

Oscar waited for about five or ten minutes, getting more impatient by the second. But the market was huge, and if Saige had lost track of time, it could take her quite a while to reach him. So he continued to wait, and finally, when he couldn't ignore the sweet smells of the food area anymore, he backtracked to find himself something to eat.

He settled for a thick round of fried dough, dusting it with plenty of powdered sugar.[78] He sunk his teeth into the hot bread and actually moaned, it was that good.

He walked slowly back toward the Ferris wheel, taking small bites of the dough, trying to savor it as long as possible. He had forty-eight skiffs left, and he'd buttoned them carefully back into his pocket.

He ate exactly half of the dough, intending to save the rest

---

[78] We already know sugar is hard to come by in the Toe, and *powdered* sugar is even rarer. Oscar had never had it before.

of it for Saige, but after another five minutes or so, he decided to eat just half of *that*, and five minutes after that he ate the rest of it, reasoning that he didn't know if Saige would be hungry, anyway.

And where *was* Saige, he thought, somewhat annoyed now that the food was gone. He found a trash can and wiped powdered sugar off his hands and face, then dropped the plate and napkin into the barrel.

Back in front of the Ferris wheel, he stopped an older woman and asked her what time it was. Ten-thirty.

There was only an hour and a half left of the first night of the market and Saige was still nowhere to be found. He could leave and do something else, but what if she arrived in a few minutes? Then again, she was pretty late now. Maybe she'd gotten busy and couldn't get away from her family, and Oscar was waiting for nothing?

He brushed some leftover powder from his shirt and decided to wait another five minutes when something knocked into his shoulder, hard. He whirled around to see—

Gregory Fairmountain and Tim Klint.

His stomach flipped over uncomfortably and he took a step backward, away from the bullies.

"Oscar, Oscar, Oscar," Gregory said in an annoying, sing-songy voice. "What a fun surprise seeing *you* here."

"I was just leaving," Oscar said. "My dad's waiting for me right over there. I have to go."

"Now that's a lie, isn't it?" Tim said. "We've been watching you for a few minutes, and we think you're all alone."

"I'm not," Oscar insisted. "So you better leave."

"I actually don't *want* to leave," Gregory said, his singsongy voice gone and his words full of nothing but deep anger. "What about you, Tim?"

"Oh, I don't think I want to leave, either," Tim said. "This seems like the perfect place to have a little chat. No annoying cousins here to save the day. No Principal Gundersen. No one at all except a market full of people who couldn't care less about one little scumbag getting his face bashed in."

Oscar took another step back. "I'm *telling* you," he said. "My dad's right over there. He's just getting a coffee, and when he gets back—"

"I thought he was waiting for *you* to go back to *him*?" Gregory said. "Getting your story confused, are you? Well, how about this: How about we go find him together? The three of us. And if he's there, Tim and I will say hi and go on our way. And if he's *not* there..."

"We'll bash your face in," Tim finished happily.

"All right," Oscar said, his heart beating faster now, his palms feeling a little sweaty. "Sounds great. Follow me."

Gregory and Tim kept a close tail on Oscar as he led them over to the food area. He could see a wooden stall with a neon-blue light on the side that said COFFEE! He walked slowly, feeling all of the muscles in his body tense up.

Standing at the side of the stall, adding creamer to his cup, was a man with his back to them. Oscar pointed, hoping they wouldn't notice his hand shaking, and said, "See? There he is."

He looked over his shoulder and saw Gregory and Tim exchange a wary look—

And as soon as their eyes were off him, Oscar started running.

He heard Gregory and Tim shout behind him as he darted around the side of the coffee stall, then looped around and ran between a candy apple place and a roasted-nut stand. He kept making erratic turns, knowing that Gregory and Tim were both faster than he was, not daring to look behind him as he pumped his arms faster and faster.

In just a minute, he shot out from the edge of the food area and his heart sank when he saw how out in the open he was. He spent a split second deciding whether to run for the nearest tent—Agriculture—but in the end he decided to try to make it to the other side, back to his dad and Neko and Innis, who could protect him.

He heard more shouting behind him but he didn't stop to

look. He simply willed his legs to move faster, forcing himself to keep running even as a painful stitch developed in his side.

He passed the Stage tent, then rounded the Magical Artifacts tent and kept going. His lungs were burning now, his vision was going a little wonky, and he finally chanced the quickest look behind him and saw how close they were, their faces twisted into expressions of pure rage....

Neko and Innis's stand was too far away. He'd never make it. He veered right, toward the back of the market, and broke into a line of tents he hadn't yet been to.

It seemed darker back here, as if the fairy lights of the market couldn't quite reach the densely crowded grounds. The aisles were thinner here, too, and Oscar had to pivot quickly to avoid running someone over.

"Sorry!" he called, still running. A moment later, he heard a crash and a chorus of shouts from behind him. He turned to see a jumble of bodies on the ground—Gregory and Tim had just run into a group of people.

Smirking, Oscar turned back around—

Just in time to smash face-first into someone or something.

And then everything went black....

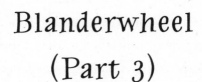

Blanderwheel
(Part 3)

AND THEN EVERYTHING WENT black....

His ears roared with sound.

Was he dead?

No.

You probably couldn't hear things if you were dead.

And he could *feel* things, too.

His cheek and chest and hips were pressed against something hard.

The ground! He had fallen to the ground.

Ouch.

The wind was violent, whipping his hair around his face.

He struggled to open his eyes, to push himself up. He needed to find Saige. He needed to keep going. If he stayed out here in the storm for much longer...

Well. Then he really *might* die....

The Teller

BUT AT LEAST FOR now—he was definitely *not* dead.

And he was still at the Night Market.[79]

Oscar opened his eyes to darkness. He moaned and grabbed for his head, but he didn't seem to have complete control of his body, because he ended up smacking himself in the nose instead. He tried to sit up but a pair of gentle—though firm—hands held him down.

Gradually his eyes adjusted to the dim light, and he could just make out the inside of a bare tent. He was lying on a rug that felt scratchy on the back of his arms. Next to him was a small table with two chairs, and on the table was a lone candle and some sort of crystal globe.

---

[79] But don't worry—we'll get back to the blanderwheel soon!

He closed his eyes again.

His head was throbbing.

"Are they…" He tried to talk but his tongue wasn't quite working yet. The words were thick in his mouth.

"They won't find you here," said a voice, and Oscar was surprised to find that it sounded like…a girl?

He tried to sit up again, and this time the hands let him, and he caught a glimpse of the person they were attached to, of their face, and it *was* a girl, about his age, dressed in the robes of the Farsouthians, her blond hair braided into two plaits, her pale white face dotted with freckles.

"I'm being chased," Oscar said dully, and he pointed to the flap of the tent, which was open by just an inch or so, enough to see a sliver of the night sky outside it.

"They're gone," the girl said calmly. "They caused a bit of a ruckus, and they've been removed."

"Removed?"

"Escorted off the grounds. I dragged you in here so they wouldn't see you."

"My face feels…"

"You ran into a pole," she said, her voice sympathetic. "But I put some alder[80] cream on you. You won't bruise."

Oscar felt his face again; it did feel a bit sticky and warm.

---

[80] A tree that, in Oscar's world, has certain healing properties.

"Ow," he said.

The girl smiled. "Yeah. Face-first into a pole will do that."

Oscar smiled back (it hurt). "I'm Oscar," he said. "Thank you. Those guys are . . . well, I'm just glad they didn't catch me."

"Eunice. And you're welcome. Why were they chasing you?"

"We go to school together. They're just jerks."

She nodded. "Yeah, I picked up on that."

Oscar looked around the tent again. "What part of the Night Market is this?"

She brightened. "Oh, welcome! This is the Others."

"The Others?"

"Everything that can't be neatly categorized. The guy next door can make your hair any color of the rainbow. Lady over there can turn all your teeth into wood."

"But why would you want—"

"I have absolutely no idea," Eunice said, laughing.

"And what about you?" Oscar asked. "What do you do?"

"I'm a Teller."

A Teller.

It sounded familiar, tugging at the edges of Oscar's memory. But his head still hurt, and it was difficult to find the information he knew was in there.

Eunice hopped to her feet and held her hand out to Oscar, then helped him up.

She was surprisingly strong for someone about three inches shorter than Oscar himself.

"I don't think I know what that is," Oscar said apologetically.

"I can see futures," she said. "But my powers are really... specific. It's not like palm reading or anything. I can't just do it to anyone. I have to have some kind of a connection to them. So it's kind of... Well, let's just say that business has been slow. Not a lot of people want a reading from me, because I can't really guarantee beforehand if I'll see anything. But I offer a partial refund if that happens! I just can't give you your time back, you know. People get really protective of their time. I guess that makes sense. Oh, wait—I'm rambling, aren't I? Sorry!"

"I want a reading from you," Oscar said at once. It was the least he could do, he thought. She *had* just saved him from Gregory and Tim (even if she hadn't managed to save him *before* he'd run into the pole).

"Really?" she said, looking so hopeful that Oscar couldn't help but smile.

"Yeah. Absolutely. How much?"

"Oh, I couldn't charge you," she said quickly. "It wouldn't feel right. With all your recent facial injuries."

Oscar touched his hand to his face, feeling the sticky warmth of the alder cream.

Wait—

What did she mean *all* his recent facial injuries?

His black eye had mostly faded; he didn't even think it was noticeable anymore.

"How did you—"

"So what do you say?" she interrupted, her eyes widening. "Should we do it?"

Was she trying to change the subject?

No, no.

He was just being paranoid.

She was perfectly nice and Oscar had just had his skull knocked pretty hard.

He wasn't thinking straight.

"Can't I give you *something*?" he asked.

"Nah. This will be fun."

She gestured to a small table and they took seats on opposite sides of it. The crystal globe was between them.

The shadows in the tent seemed to darken as Eunice motioned for Oscar's hands. She gently arranged his palms so that both were flat on the table. Then she sat back, regarded him with an almost sad expression on her face, and closed her eyes.

He realized—after about two very long, very quiet minutes—what she meant about people getting protective of their time.

It was hard to sit still.

It was hard not to fidget, not to remove his palms from the table, not to cross his legs or get up and pace around the room.

Eunice, for her part, sat perfectly motionless.

She might have been a statue.

It was hard to look at her face, it was so frozen.

Oscar closed his eyes for a while, then opened them again, then closed them and counted to one hundred, then opened them again—

And jumped an inch off the chair when he found Eunice was staring at him, her eyes wide and bright.

"This isn't going to be easy," she said.

"Easy?"

"Your task."

"My . . . task . . . ?"

"She didn't meet you tonight, because she's ashamed," Eunice said. Her eyes had a vague, faraway look to them, like she wasn't seeing Oscar, really, but instead seeing *past* him.

Her words sent a chill through his body.

She was clearly talking about Saige.

"But none of this is *her* fault," Eunice continued. "You have to remember that, okay? Promise me."

"I promise?"

"Right. Here's what I can see. Your birthday is coming up, right? Two weeks?"

"That's right . . .," Oscar said.

"She'll invite you over to spend the night. She'll apologize for not meeting you in front of the Ferris wheel. You will go. There will be a locked door. You must open it."

"You want me to break into a room in my best friend's new house?"

"I'm just telling you what I see. And I see a *lot*. Your path, your future . . . It is intertwined with the lives and the futures of all the people of Roan." She paused, then nodded. "That's it."

"That's it?"

"That's what I see."

"You see my entire future somehow connected with the

future of everyone in Roan and because of this I have to break into a locked room in my best friend's house," Oscar said, his voice strangely emotionless.

Eunice nodded enthusiastically. "Yes, that's exactly it. Oh! And there's one more thing."

"One more thing."

"All of this has to do with the rain."

"The rain."

"The rain, Oscar," Eunice said, leaning forward. "Got it?"

"I guess?"

"Good."

She looked like she was about to say more, but at that moment, someone entered the tent. It was a boy about Pietra's age, maybe in his early twenties. He was tall and he also wore the robes of the Farsouthians. There was something vaguely familiar about him, but he was the spitting image of Eunice, so it must have been that.

"This is my brother," Eunice said. "Garner."

Garner nodded at Oscar but seemed hesitant to stick around for any amount of time; he slipped out a back opening of the tent that Oscar hadn't noticed before and was gone.

"He's, um, shy," Eunice said, and flashed a smile so suspicious that Oscar had to laugh.

The tension in the tent seemed to break at that, and somewhere far off Oscar heard a clock strike eleven.

"I'd better get going," he said. "Thanks again."

"Thank *you*!" Eunice said. "You're my first customer of the whole Night Market."

"I don't know if you can technically call me a customer, since you didn't let me pay," he pointed out.

"Eh, details," she said with a wave of her hand.

"But I'll spread the word. And I'll come back and see you tomorrow."

"Sure!" she said, wiggling slightly in her chair, suddenly uncomfortable. "That sounds great."

"Thanks again, Eunice," he said, standing up. He waved clumsily at her as he stepped out of the tent, back into the chaotic energy of the Night Market.

And he did go back to see her the next night.

Or at least, he *tried* to.

But he couldn't seem to recreate the path of his late-night chase; he couldn't retrace his steps from the Ferris wheel to Eunice's tent.

And when he stopped to ask someone, a tall Farsouthian woman in robes that fell down to her ankles, she only smiled at him curiously, tilting her head as she asked, "The Others? I've never heard of that section of the Night Market. I'm sorry about that, son, but you must be mistaken."

Bleak Beach

On Monday morning, Oscar woke up at his usual time, brushed his teeth, washed his face, got dressed in the pale half-light of morning, then dutifully followed Bilius to the umbrella shop for his first day as an official apprentice.

The rest of the Night Market had passed without incident.

If you could call never finding Eunice's tent—or the entire section of the Others—a nonincident.

To Oscar, it had felt deeply unsettling.

After his conversation with the Farsouthian woman who claimed to have never heard of the Others before, he worked up the courage to ask Innis, who studied Oscar before he said, "I simply can't recall."

I simply can't recall.

Oscar had known, just *known* Innis had been lying.

But why?

Why would he have lied about something like that?

Was the other Farsouthian woman lying, too?

He asked Pietra about it as they walked together to find a snack on Saturday night, and she, at least, looked entirely truthful when she said she'd never heard of anything like it.

"But they hand out maps at the main entrance," she'd said helpfully, then waited for him as he sprinted to get one.

There was not so much as a whisper of the Others on the map.

But Oscar knew he hadn't made it up.

Eunice had been real. Her brother, Garner, had been real.

The whole thing was just weird.

Bilius unlocked the shop when they arrived and put Oscar to work immediately, measuring and cutting fabric for canopies. Everything was done by hand at Buckle Umbrellas, and as a result, the process went rather slowly. By lunchtime, Oscar had only managed to cut out one half of one canopy. His eyes hurt. His fingers hurt. His brain hurt. And he wasn't even sure he'd done that good of a job.

"My lines are all crooked," he complained to Bilius.

Bilius pressed his fingers against the edge of the canopy, then tucked the fabric under itself.

"This will get sewn here," he explained. "So any imperfections won't show, and they won't impact the function of the umbrella."

"So you agree it's imperfect?" Oscar grumbled.

"Oscar, you've been my apprentice for three hours. Give yourself some time to learn." Bilius took a long look at his son, then added, "That's about enough for today, I think. We'll do half days this week, to ease you into everything. Sound good?"

Oscar nodded eagerly. "Thanks, Dad." He pushed out into the bliggoting[81] rain before Bilius could change his mind.

Oscar had a sandwich in the pocket of his coat, and even though it was raining quite a lot, he decided to go and eat at Bleak Beach. The beach was bound to be deserted in this weather, and Oscar just wanted to be alone.

He hadn't seen or heard from Saige after she hadn't shown up at the Ferris wheel. Was Eunice right? Was Saige ashamed? But what did she have to be ashamed about?

None of this is her fault, Eunice had said.

None of *what*?

Moving to Roan Piers?

Of course Oscar was sad that Saige had moved, but he didn't blame her. That wouldn't make any sense. It wasn't *her* decision to move.

---

[81] It hasn't bliggoted in a while, so as a reminder this is quite a lot of rain, and particularly unexpected.

Maybe she hadn't shown up at the Ferris wheel because she'd figured out what Oscar already knew.

People who lived in Roan Piers just weren't friends with people who lived in the Alley.

Maybe she'd decided not to come because she could feel—like he could—that their friendship was doomed.

Oscar groaned. He didn't want to think about Saige anymore. He wished he could turn his brain off for the rest of the day, just for a bit of a break.

He made it to the beach in about twenty minutes. The bliggot had let up a little but Oscar was still thoroughly soaked as he took a seat on a bench at the edge of the sand. He removed the sandwich from his pocket and took a bite of the waterlogged bread.

He felt miserable.

He'd tried to go into his first day of the apprenticeship with an open mind, he really had, but all his feelings of goodwill had seemed to vanish when Bilius handed him the measuring stick, the pencil, and the overlarge pair of scissors.

And things had only gotten worse from there.

Oscar finished the sandwich quickly, tucked the wrapping back into his pocket, and examined his hands.

They were red and sore and covered in small cuts.

How was it that he could whittle an entire elephant without so much as a scratch, but give him a pair of scissors and he'd manage to massacre his fingers?

He put his hand into his other pocket and felt his fingers close around a block of smooth, solid wood.

The monkwood.

He'd been carrying it around with him since the first evening of the Night Market. He liked the weight of it in his pocket, and it might have been his imagination, but he felt, sometimes, like it *hummed*. A soft, gentle hum that felt comforting against his fingers.

He hadn't decided what to carve.

It felt daunting, figuring out what to make with something so special. Every time he thought he'd decided on something, he changed his mind almost instantly.

But there was no rush.

He withdrew his hand from his pocket, stood up, and walked across the sand. Since it rained so much, the sand was pretty much always wet and, as a result, solid and firm. Oscar left a lonely pair of footprints behind him as he walked down to the edge of the gray water of the Gray Sea. Out in the bay, he could just make out the outline of Gray Lighthouse. Its beam had been dark for years; it no longer rotated or helped to guide any sailors home.

To be fair, there hadn't *been* sailors in ages. The Gray Sea was notoriously treacherous to navigate. Where the factories were now, in the western part of the Toe, used to be a bustling port, with ships docking every hour to deliver their trades and wares.

But the weather had turned, and too many ships had

gone down into the dark waters, and no sailor now dared to travel this way. All trade came in from the north, over land. It passed through Commerce City and Roan Piers and whatever was left over eventually made its way to the Toe.

Behind him, Oscar heard the rumbling engine of the bus that stopped at Bleak Beach five times a day. He heard its door open and he wondered idly who *else* would want to come to the beach on a day like today. The clouds were heavy above him; no doubt it would caterwhail[82] later. He ought to get home before it did, or else Bilius would inevitably worry.

As if a little rain ever hurt anybody.

Oscar heard the bus pull away from the curb, grunting as it got back up to speed and continued on its endless loop of the Toe. He turned around to see who'd been foolish enough to come to Bleak Beach in this weather, and his breath caught in his throat as he saw—

"Saige?"

She wore a new raincoat and matching rain boots, both of them a bright kelly green that stood out in stark contrast to the gray of the landscape. She had her hood up. Dot had a custom-made attachment that held her umbrella over her head. It was a Spillen,[83] from Buckle Umbrellas.

---

[82] We mentioned this a while ago, but just in case you've forgotten, a caterwhail is a summer thunderstorm.
[83] And a spillen is a steady shower.

She smiled shyly when their eyes met. There was a concrete boardwalk that extended all the way to the water, and she made her way over to it so she didn't have to put her wheelchair in the sand. When she and Oscar were just a couple feet away from each other, she said, "Hi."

"How did you... What are you...?"

"Your dad told me you were done for the day," Saige explained. "I just guessed you might be here."

"What are you doing in the Toe?"

"My parents had a few last things to pick up from the apartment," she said. "I only have a little while. I wanted to apologize. For Friday night."

"Oh, it's okay," Oscar said. "It's no big deal."

"It *is* a big deal," she insisted. "I told you I would be there, and I didn't show up. I'm sorry. There's..." She paused and took a deep breath, steadying herself. "There's something I want to tell you, Oscar. Something I only just found out. The reason why we moved. But I don't know... I don't know how to tell you. I'm scared you're going to... well, I'm scared you're not going to want to be friends with me anymore."

Oscar heard Eunice's voice in his mind: *None of this is her fault.*

"You can tell me anything," he said. "I promise I won't get mad."

"Will you come and stay with us? For your birthday?

We can pick you up, and you can spend the night at our new house. Will you just promise me that, and then I'll tell you?"

Oscar's stomach twisted uncomfortably. It was coming true. Exactly what Eunice had said would happen...

"Of course," he said. His voice sounded like a stranger's. He didn't quite recognize himself.

Saige looked like she was about to cry.

"I didn't know before," she said. "I promise. I only found out on Friday. He told me right before the Night Market."

"Saige, whatever it is, it's okay. We're friends. Nothing can change that."

Saige nodded, her eyes welling up with tears. "The job my dad got... The reason we moved to Roan Piers... He took a position with Brawn Industries. He's their new chief engineer. I just feel so... *sick* about it all. He should have told me before."

Oscar couldn't speak.

Whatever he might have been expecting Saige to say, this was certainly not it.

Brawn Industries, of course, made Brawn umbrellas.

And Brawn umbrellas were the reason Buckle Umbrellas was almost out of business.

Brawn umbrellas were the reason Oscar couldn't go back to school in the fall.

Brawn umbrellas were the reason Oscar had to do this apprenticeship.

Brawn umbrellas had ruined his *entire life*.

But still.

Eunice had been right.

None of this had anything to do with Saige. None of it was her fault at all.

Oscar tried to remember that.

Saige was crying openly now, tears running down her cheeks as the sky gave a dramatic rumble overhead. The caterwhail was coming. The bus wouldn't be back for another hour or so. They'd have to make it to the Alley on their own.

Oscar took Saige's free hand.

"It's okay," he said. "I understand."

"I'm so sorry, Oscar," she said. "My father wasn't even going to tell me. I went into his office, in the new house. And I saw this manual. These weird plans. And there were sketches of umbrellas everywhere and... He got really mad at me for snooping. And he told me he didn't have a choice. *What else could I have done*, he said. *A job is a job.*"

"Saige, really," Oscar insisted. "This has nothing to do with us. I mean, yeah, I wish you'd met me at the Night Market, because I probably wouldn't have almost gotten my butt kicked by Gregory and Tim—"

"Gregory and Tim were there?" Saige asked just as a massive flash of lightning streaked across the sky.

"We better head back," Oscar said as they both looked up.

Saige turned Dot around, and Oscar gripped the wheel-chair's handles, helping Saige move back up the sandy boardwalk.

Once they'd crossed the street and reached Piteous Park, they went side by side, Oscar with one hand sometimes resting on Dot, sometimes not. They didn't talk until they reached the northern end of the park and the first building of the Alley came into view. The heavier rain was hanging above them. They could both feel it, just as every person born and raised in the Alley could feel it. You learned to sense the rain above you, envisioning it as if the sky itself were a water balloon ready to burst at any moment.

Something Pietra said came back to Oscar then, when they'd been walking through the Night Market to get her Ocspectrascope.

Don't you think it's weird that the weather here got really bad as soon as Brawn started making umbrellas?

Oscar glanced quickly over at Saige, who looked as miserable as he felt.

They pushed into the Alley just as a truly enormous crash of thunder echoed overhead.

Oscar was glad for the noise.

It meant he didn't have to think of anything to say.

Apprenticeship

THERE WERE TWO WEEKS until Oscar's birthday and his sleepover with Saige.

Two weeks in which time did that weird sometimes-fast, sometimes-slow thing again.

Like, the time he spent in the shop passed excruciatingly slowly.

And whenever he wasn't in the shop, time zipped by, faster than a drop of rain in a blanderwheel.

It wasn't that Oscar really minded working at the shop *that* much. Especially during the first week, when he'd had the afternoons off. He liked the quiet of the workspace, the gentleness with which Bilius moved about the shop, the patience he used whenever he showed Oscar a new task.

Oscar had always enjoyed being with his father.

He thought it might be because his father was the only parent he had.

He often wondered what it would have been like if his mother hadn't died.

What would *she* be like? What sort of a relationship would they have?

"Oscar, you're dripping glue," Bilius said on Tuesday afternoon. It was only Oscar's second day of full shifts, and he was having trouble keeping his mind from wandering. He stifled a yawn and looked down at his workspace.

Bilius was right, of course. He had dripped glue everywhere.

He took a small rag, dipped it carefully into a container of paint thinner, and wiped the excess glue from the Wib he was currently assembling.

It made him think of Wib the dog.

Last week, he'd been able to work on his carvings during the afternoons.

Yesterday, after his first full day at the shop, he'd been too exhausted to carve anything.

He had a feeling today would be the same.

Oscar finished wiping up the glue and set the rag to the side.

The Wib was almost finished. The canopy was completed and open on the workbench in front of him, and Oscar was currently working on gluing the handle together. It would need to dry for a full day before the separate pieces could be assembled.

"You did a good job with that," Bilius said, coming over to examine the work more closely. "Let's get it in the vise and tighten it up. Then maybe we could take a little walk together? Get some fresh air?"

It hadn't been *too* rainy of a day; it was currently only flinnering.[84]

"Fresh air sounds great," Oscar said, so Bilius showed him how to set the handle into the vise, tightening the crank until the two glued-together pieces were fit snugly against each other. Then they turned the OPEN sign to CLOSED and headed outside. Bilius didn't even bring an umbrella.[85]

They made their way to East Market, which was busy with people taking advantage of the fair weather. Neko was working and tossed them each a shooting star fruit.

"I don't actually love these," Oscar whispered to Bilius.

"Me either," Bilius admitted. "But I know someone who does."

---

[84] A flinner is a rain that doesn't appear to really want to fall at all. It is sort of a hesitant, reluctant, mediocre drizzle.

[85] And, of course, Oscar didn't have one *to* bring.

And that is how they ended up trading their two shooting star fruits for two steaming cups of hot chocolate from Mrs. Flanders, who practically squealed with delight over the fruit.

"My *favorite*!" she announced.

"Neko would understand," Bilius said as he took his first sip of the hot chocolate. Then, with a wink, he added, "But we're not going to tell him."

They ambled slowly around the Alley, not headed in any particular direction. They paused on the far side of Finch and looked west across the Toe, to where the factories were. The smoke they belched into the sky looked particularly gray and dreary today.

"So," Bilius said. "How are you liking being my apprentice?"

Oscar had sort of known this conversation was coming, and he didn't exactly know how to answer. The truth was somewhere along the lines of "It's fine, Dad—it's not the most miserable thing in the world but I don't want to be an umbrella maker, and to be honest, I wouldn't want to work in the shop ever again if I didn't have to," but he didn't want to hurt Bilius's feelings. Because the truth was—he understood. Bilius didn't *want* to force Oscar into the family trade. But he *had* to. Otherwise, they wouldn't be able to pay the bills.[86]

So Oscar settled for the easiest answer.

---

[86] Even though the money from that mysterious Farsouthian *had* taken a bit of the immediate pressure off, those skiffs wouldn't last forever.

"It's good, Dad. Really good."

He watched as Bilius exhaled a sigh of relief.

And he felt relief himself.

Because the last thing he ever wanted to do was give Bilius *more* stress.

Roan Piers

THE REST OF THE week passed slowly. Oscar was exhausted by the time he got home in the evenings. He didn't have the energy to work on any of his carvings, and he still hadn't touched the block of monkwood.[87] He didn't visit Fort Cleverbuckle—should he rename it, anyway, to Fort Buckle?

In short, he was tired and depressed.

And he didn't have any idea what he could do about it.

He was stuck in an apprenticeship he didn't want.

In a routine he didn't want.

In a loop he didn't want.

In a *life* he didn't want.

And he didn't have any choice in the matter. All he could

---

[87] But he kept carrying it around in his pocket, hoping the perfect carving inspiration would hit if he kept it close to him.

do was continue on, helping his father make his umbrellas even when six straight days passed without a single sale.

It all would have been different if Saige and her family still lived in the apartment across from his.

Whoever had moved into her old bedroom had painted the walls a truly awful shade of green (Saige's walls had been robin's-egg blue).

They'd hung terrible curtains with polka dots.

They stayed up far too late; their lamp shone directly into Oscar's bedroom.

He'd started keeping his curtains closed.

You might think that the visit to Roan Piers and Saige's new house would have been a bright spot to look forward to, but Oscar had almost canceled at least fifteen times in two weeks. There was a knot of dread in the pit of his stomach that only grew larger and larger as the days passed. And then it was Saturday, and Oscar's birthday was the next day, and it was too late to cancel, so he packed his overnight bag and waited in front of Dove for Saige and her family to pick him up.

Which they did, right on time, in a brand-new, jet-black, very fancy, very big car, large enough for a hydraulic lift on the right side and a third row where Saige's wheelchair fit perfectly. There was a little rise in the roof so she had plenty of headroom, and the best part was she could get in and out without any help. She demonstrated this to him when they reached the house in

Roan Piers, though Oscar was having a difficult time concentrating on her as he tried to *also* take in their surroundings.

He had never been to Roan Piers before, and he was unprepared for just how *perfect* everything was.

Saige's new house was shaped like a big box, with pristine white siding, black shutters, a spotless black roof, a crimson front door, a matching crimson mailbox, a jet-black driveway, a buzzball[88] hoop set over the garage doors, and two flawlessly manicured flowerbeds, so perfect they almost looked fake. The sky above the house was a pale, light blue; there were white, puffy clouds floating overhead; and the sun was shining down on them.

It had been rouring in the Alley.

It had been rouring for two days straight, actually.

But as soon as they'd passed the Wall, the clouds had started to dissipate.

Oscar found that...

Troubling.

To say the least.

Behind him, Saige let out a huff of air and said, "Were you not even looking?"

"Sorry," Oscar said, turning around quickly. "Sorry! I've just... I've never played buzzball!"

---

[88] A game much like basketball, except the ball vibrates in your hands, making it incredibly hard to maneuver.

That was true.

But he'd also never *wanted* to play buzzball, and Saige of course knew that, and gave him a withering look as she pressed the button to fold the hydraulic lift back into the car.

"Come on," she said. "I'll give you the tour."

The inside of the Cleverers' new house was just as impressive as the outside.

For one, everything smelled *new*. There was a pleasant mixture of paint and wood and fresh carpet as Oscar stepped inside. Mr. Cleverer had already retreated somewhere, but Mrs. Cleverer was getting a snack plate together as the baby, Arthur, banged happily on the tray of his highchair.

The downstairs was large and open, with big, airy ceilings and wood paneling on the walls. Saige led Oscar through the kitchen, the living room,[89] the dining room, a bathroom, a sitting room[90] lined with bookcases, and back to the front foyer.

They'd passed one single shut door.

"What's in there?" Oscar asked, struggling to keep his voice casual.

"Oh, that's my dad's office," Saige said, shrugging. Then,

---

[89] Back in the Alley, Saige had owned a small keyboard, but here, in the living room, was a massive grand piano.

[90] With a phone! The average household in the Alley didn't have a phone, although each building did have a shared phone in the lobby that sometimes worked and sometimes didn't. Saige gave Oscar her phone number now and he memorized it: 1024.

lowering her voice, she added, "Definitely am *not* allowed back in there."

"Saige, honey, take this up to your room. I'm sure Oscar's famished," Mrs. Cleverer called from the kitchen.

Oscar *was*, actually, quite hungry, but he didn't like the way Mrs. Cleverer had said that. It made him feel...weird. Why would she assume he was hungry? Why wouldn't she have asked him instead?

Saige returned with the plate of food and handed it to Oscar as she maneuvered Dot onto a platform at the bottom of the wide, sweeping staircase. She shut herself in by closing a sturdy metal bar, then pressed a button, and Oscar watched as the platform moved quickly upstairs.

"Wow," he said. "That's so cool, Saige!" He followed her upstairs, shoving a cracker into his mouth.

The upstairs of the Cleverers' house consisted of Saige's bedroom, Arthur's bedroom, Mr. and Mrs. Cleverer's bedroom, and another big bathroom with a tub in it.

The door to Saige's bedroom was closed, and she made sure Oscar was looking before she pushed it open gently.

Oscar stepped inside and he couldn't help it; he actually gasped.

"I know," Saige said from behind him. "Isn't it so cool?"

To say it was *cool* was the understatement of the year. It was exactly the sort of bedroom Oscar would have dreamed up for Saige. There was a massive drafting table in one corner, art supplies everywhere, two huge windows that took up much of the far wall, a complicated bunk bed with another hydraulic lift built into it, and a closet wide enough for her wheelchair.

The walls of the room were painted the same robin's-egg blue as her bedroom in the Alley—except for one corner, which had been painted to look like an actual forest at night. There were brown trees rising up out of the carpet and dots of yellow fireflies swirling around a midnight-blue sky. There was even an *actual tent* set up there. And two overstuffed beanbags in front of it.

Saige saw Oscar staring and said, "I told them I wanted a fort. I know it's not the same as Fort Cleverbuckle, but it's nice to be able to pretend."

Oscar went and peeked into the tent. It was filled with comic books. He straightened and turned around.

"Saige, this is officially the coolest room I've ever seen."

"I never wanted to leave the Alley, you know?" she said. "But this isn't so bad. Right?"

"Not bad at all," Oscar agreed. He sat down on one of the beanbags and Saige came over to join him. They made quick work of the snack tray, then Saige pointed Oscar over to a bookcase stuffed with different board games. He chose one based on a popular comic and they spent the next hour lost in the game.

Eventually, Mrs. Cleverer stuck her head into the bedroom and suggested they get outside for some fresh air.

"I'm sure Oscar wouldn't mind getting a bit of sunshine while he can," she said, and although her voice was light and airy, it gave Oscar the same weird feeling he'd gotten downstairs.

There was just something in her voice that made him think she felt...

Guilty?

But also, she wasn't wrong.

Oscar *did* want to spend some time outside.

They decided to explore the neighborhood.

Oscar wasn't surprised to find that each house was just as big and impressive as the Cleverers'. The lawns were neatly manicured, the flowers were bright and healthy, the trees were green and full, and—of course—the sky was still blue. There wasn't a hint of rain in the air.

"Saige," Oscar said. "Don't you find it weird that it's . . . Not raining here? But when you came to pick me up, it was—"

"Rouring," Saige finished. "I know. I asked my parents about it. They said it's because of a weird geographical anomaly. Something about the sea level of Roan Piers and the way the harbor is shaped."

"Yeah," Oscar said slowly. "I've heard the same thing before. It's just weird because . . . They're really quite close, you know? The Alley and Roan Piers, I mean. Just a couple of miles."

Saige shrugged. "I don't understand it."

Oscar didn't understand it, either.

And a few weeks ago, he might have accepted the existence of a geographical anomaly without questioning it at all, but now . . .

Now something just felt a little fishy to him.

And although he knew it was wrong, although he knew it was the deepest invasion of privacy he could possibly think of . . .

He knew he had to get into Mr. Cleverer's study.

That was obviously the locked door Eunice had mentioned.

He had a feeling he'd find something interesting in there.

Apologies

THAT NIGHT, AFTER A dinner of lasagna and salad, Saige and
Oscar went up to Saige's bedroom to continue their game.
They had just about finished when Mrs. Cleverer poked her
head into the room and held up two mugs of hot chocolate.

"A little something for the almost-birthday guy?" she said
lightly, but Oscar noted how she never *quite* looked him in the
eyes. Was he imagining that?

But no. He didn't think he was. He thanked her for the
drink and she nodded and placed them both on Saige's nightstand, then slipped out of the room again.

"Is your mom all right?" Oscar asked hesitantly, handing
Saige one of the mugs. They were playing on the floor, using
the beanbags as backrests. Saige took a sip of the hot chocolate
and sighed happily.

"She says she's just adjusting," she replied. "I think she misses the spice store. She doesn't have a job here, you know. Dad says she doesn't need one."

"Do you think she misses the Alley in general?" Oscar asked, because he knew *he* would, if he had to leave it. No matter how nice and big and new and bright Roan Piers and Commerce City were, the Alley was Oscar's home. He couldn't imagine living anywhere but Dove.

"She says she doesn't," Saige replied.

"Do *you*?"

Saige paused at that. She took another sip of hot chocolate. "I miss parts of it," she admitted. "I miss our fort. I miss East Market. I miss Bleak Beach. I miss riding the bus with you, around and around, not even having anywhere to go. I miss our bedroom windows and how we could wave to each other before we left for school. I miss EBA. I miss seeing my dad."

Mr. Cleverer hadn't joined them for dinner. He'd left the house shortly after Oscar had arrived, and as far as Oscar knew, he hadn't yet returned.

"He's working a lot?" Oscar asked.

"A *lot*. And when he isn't *at* work, he's working here, in his study. He shuts himself in. He's always on the phone or the typewriter. Mom leaves food outside the door and tries to keep Arthur as quiet as possible."

"What does a chief engineer do, anyway?"

"I'm not really sure," Saige admitted. "When I do see him, he doesn't like to talk about it. We play buzzball or go explore the neighborhood or something. But he's really quiet. Like he's not paying attention."

"I'm sorry," Oscar said.

Saige just nodded in a vague kind of way and took another sip of her hot chocolate. Then, brightening, she said, "Oh!" and pointed at the elaborate board game set up in front of them. "Duh."

"Duh?"

"Our next move. We can defeat the dragon in three steps. Don't you see it?"

Oscar studied the pieces, laid out in such a complicated manner that it almost looked like they'd just thrown them all on the floor, letting them fall wherever.

"The cleric?" he guessed.

"Yes!" Saige said. She used her turn to move the cleric to the Abandoned Boardwalk. And *then* Oscar saw it.

They defeated the dragon in two more moves.[91]

After a brief celebration, Mrs. Cleverer reappeared in the doorway. "About time to get ready for bed, okay kids?"

"Sure, Mom," Saige replied.

---

[91] The game in question is called Burgeoning Bloomrackers and, as I mentioned, is based on a popular comic book. *Burgeoning* means "something that is growing rapidly" and the Bloomrackers were a fictional group of children who banded together to fight petty crime in their city of Smolder.

They took turns using the bathroom, brushing their teeth and washing their faces. Saige was excited to show Oscar how her bed worked. The hydraulics lifted each bed into the air in a rotating circle, almost like a Ferris wheel, so that Saige could move from Dot to the bottom bunk, then press a button and transform the bottom bunk into the *top* bunk.

"Cool, right?" she said.

"Super cool," Oscar agreed. He got onto what was now the bottom bunk, and Saige pressed another button, then stopped the rotation of the beds when they were on the same level, about two feet apart from each other.

"Hey," Saige said.

Oscar laughed. "Hey."

"Thanks for coming," she said. "To visit. I didn't know if you would."

"Why wouldn't I?"

"Because."

"I'm kind of surprised you invited me at all."

"Why wouldn't I?"

"Because."

A long pause.

"I thought you wouldn't want to be friends with me anymore," Oscar admitted. "Now that you live here."

"Honestly, I thought *you* wouldn't want to be friends with *me* anymore."

"I'm sorry."

"I'm sorry, too."

"I guess things have just gotten a little complicated."

"Yup."

"Do you think we'll be able to do it? Still be friends?"

"I do," Saige said after just a moment's hesitation. "Don't you?"

"Yeah," Oscar said. "I do."

Oscar looked over at her a few minutes later, but she was already asleep, her eyes closed, her breathing even and deep. He turned off the bedside lamp and listened into the silence and darkness of the house. Mrs. Cleverer was still moving around downstairs; he could hear her footsteps on the tile floor of the kitchen, and every now and then he heard a cabinet or a door shut.

About fifteen minutes after they'd turned the lights off, Oscar heard a car pull into the driveway. The front door opened and closed. Oscar heard Mr. and Mrs. Cleverer's muffled voices. After another few minutes, one set of footsteps padded softly upstairs.

Oscar sat up.

He was suddenly wide awake.

He knew he couldn't miss his chance.

He'd wait until Mr. Cleverer went to bed.

And then he'd break into his study.

The Secret Compartment

As it turned out, Mr. Cleverer didn't come upstairs for at *least* another hour. And although Oscar had felt wide awake at the beginning of the wait, by about halfway through, he had to pinch himself to stop from falling asleep. He made a game of lifting one leg off the bed for as long as he could, then the other, then an arm, then the other arm. He thought he might have dozed off once, and he jerked awake at the sound of a door closing nearby.

Mr. and Mrs. Cleverer's bedroom door.

He got out of bed as slowly and quietly as he could, managing to avoid tripping over Saige's wheelchair.

He poked his head into the hallway. All the second-floor lights were off. The house was like a dark abyss. Quiet and pitch-black.

Oscar tiptoed over to the stairs, remembering to avoid the side with the track on it, keeping a good grip on the railing as he made his way down. The Buckles' stairs were creaky and loud and impossible to sneak down, but *these* stairs were new and absolutely soundless as he made his way to the first floor.

All was dark down here, too.

It actually might have been a little creepy, had Oscar's body not currently been a vessel of pure adrenaline. He couldn't feel much of any other emotion; there simply wasn't enough room to contain it. His fingers buzzed with it, his feet hummed with it, his body was practically vibrating as he reached the bottom of the stairs and turned right to enter the living room.

The windows were wide here, and there was enough moonlight to see by, so as not to run into the couch or the armchairs or the coffee table. He crossed the room quickly, pausing at the far end of it just to listen, to make sure everything was still silent.

The study was at the back of the house, and Oscar held his breath as he reached out and gripped the doorknob, saying a silent prayer before he turned it . . .

And found it locked.

Well.

He had expected that.

And he'd come prepared.

He removed his lockpicking pin[92] from his pocket and took a deep breath, steadying himself.

He held the pin up, watching it glint in the moonlight.

There was never this much moonlight in the Alley.

Most nights there were so many clouds, you couldn't see the sky at all.

And that is what Oscar thought about as he gently maneuvered the pin into the lock.

That is what he thought about as he closed his eyes, concentrating all of his senses on the tiny movements his fingers made.

The twist. The catch. The jiggle.

The soft sigh of the lock as it gave way.

Oscar pushed into the room, almost closing the door behind him before he decided to leave it open a crack.

Just a crack.

So he could hear if anybody was coming.

There was a switch on the wall that Oscar assumed controlled the overhead light, but he avoided that, moving instead to the desk and turning on a much smaller lamp. Then he paused and tried to decide where to start.

Aside from the desk, there were wooden filing cabinets on either side of a long bookshelf against the far wall. There

---

[92] This is the same lockpicking pin Oscar used to open the door that led to Dove's roof.

were also boxes lining an adjacent wall, some of them with lids half hanging off, revealing piles and piles of paperwork in each of them.

Oscar sat in the desk chair and decided to start with what was right in front of him: the desk. It stood to reason that the most important papers would be within reaching distance, right?

Wrong.

He went through every single drawer of the desk,[93] finding nothing of any real importance.

Aside from the lamp, there were only four objects on the desk: one fancy-looking typewriter with a fresh sheet of paper set into it, a phone, one framed photo, and one unframed photo. The framed photo showed Saige and Arthur sitting together in their old kitchen in Woodpecker. The unframed photo was propped up against the framed photo, and this showed an expanse of green grass with a small dog sitting in the middle of it. Oscar picked up this photo. The dog must have belonged to Mr. Cleverer when he was a boy, since the photo was old and worn and the Cleverers had never had a dog as long as Oscar had known them.

---

[93] There were six of them. He found, in no particular order: doctor's slips, an X-ray of a broken arm, receipts for most of the new furniture in the house, report cards from Saige's Lowers and Middles, multiple manila folders of artwork and blueprints Saige had completed over the years, anniversary cards from Mrs. Cleverer to her husband, a few paperback romance novels, and lots of new office supplies.

He turned over the photo. On the back was a single word: *Scrappy.*

He set the photo back how it was, just so.

Then he started with the filing cabinets.

Nothing. There was more to do with Brawn Industries here, at least, like umbrella sketches and office memos, but nothing really *important.*

The boxes that lined the wall were daunting, and Oscar figured he'd probably already been in the study for forty-five minutes.

His back was hurting from spending so much time hunched over, rifling through papers. He needed to rest, to regroup. He lay down on the floor and stretched his arms over his head, making his body as long as possible. His bones cracked and popped so loudly that he thought someone might actually hear them. But the gaping, enormous silence of the house stayed silent. The darkness outside of the study door stayed dark.

He was the only one awake in the house.

Of that he was certain.

He didn't think it was physically possible to go through all the boxes in the room. There were dozens, and papers were spilling out of the tops of them. Some of them had unhelpful writing on the side, like *1390 Project—Canceled* or *Canopy Specifications* or *Rib Materials.*

The longer he lay on the floor, the more he thought he ought to just give up entirely. There was no point in wasting any more time.

Plus he was *tired*.

And that was when he realized, with something of a shock, that it was his birthday.

He guessed it was around two or three in the morning. So he'd been twelve for a few hours and hadn't even realized it.

Bilius had once told Oscar that his mother thought it was good luck to start every birthday with a wish.

It should be the first thing that comes out of your lips, Bilius had said. *The first thing you whisper when you wake up in the morning.*

Oscar didn't know what to wish for.

He wanted so many things.

He wanted Saige to move back to the Alley, he wanted Buckle Umbrellas to be as successful as it used to be, he wanted Brawn Industries to go out of business, he wanted to find time to carve the block of monkwood in his room, to carve *anything*. He wanted to carve wood for the rest of his life, to find the hidden lines locked inside it, to run his blade over the grain and reveal the secrets it held within. He wanted Gregory Fairmountain and Tim Klint to fall into a big puddle of slime or boogers or mud. He wanted whoever had painted Saige's bedroom wall such an ugly color to move out of Woodpecker immediately.

But you had to pick *one* thing for your birthday wish.

So Oscar closed his eyes, inhaled slowly, and whispered into the stillness of the room: "I wish I knew what to do."

It might have been a vague wish, as far as wishes go,[94] but it felt right to Oscar. He kept his eyes closed for a few seconds, letting the wish fill his body, imagining it as a ball of light moving underneath his skin.

And then he opened his eyes.

And saw the hidden compartment in the underside of Mr. Cleverer's desk.

It was an exceptionally clever secret compartment, as far as secret compartments went.

You wouldn't have been able to see it unless you knew it was there, as Mr. Cleverer surely did, *or* unless you were lying flat on the floor, which Oscar *was*.

It blended in perfectly with the underside of the desk. He could just make out the almost invisible line that separated the door of the compartment from the rest of the wood of the desk.

And because it was so cleverly hidden, it wasn't even locked. Obviously Mr. Cleverer wasn't worried about anyone ever finding it.

Oscar scrambled to his hands and knees and crawled

---

[94] In previous years, Oscar had wished for a bike, a million skiffs, a sailboat, super-powers, and an unlimited supply of wood for his carvings.

toward it. The door was slanted at a downward angle, so that when he pulled it open, a fat white envelope slid out and smacked him directly in the face.

He sat back, rubbing his nose, scooting a few inches so that the small circle of light from the desk lamp reached him.

There was no writing on the outside of the envelope. It was fastened shut with a piece of string wound around two small metal disks.

Oscar unwound the string carefully, then removed a thick stack of papers from inside it. There were folded blueprints here, along with a few handwritten pages of notes and scribbles and a thick, stapled-together booklet. He laid everything down in three piles.

The first thing he did was unfold the blueprints.

They were quite big, and he had to move a little to find

a spot on the floor where he could lay them out. There were three sheets, stapled together in one corner.

The top sheet seemed to depict some kind of building or structure. It was complicated, with lots of inset diagrams and boxes and smaller drawings within the larger drawing and tiny, neat writing labeling everything with numbers and letters that didn't make any sense to him.

Oscar blinked a few times, then stood up to see it at a bit of a distance.

Whatever it was, it was *big*.

It was taller than it was wide, shaped almost like Mr. Cleverer's desk lamp, actually. There were a bunch of little squiggles around the base of it that Oscar couldn't identify. A piece of the thing was x-rayed, so that you could see inside of it, and the inner workings were so complicated that Oscar felt overwhelmed just looking at them.

It was almost like...Some sort of machine inside some sort of building?

But what kind of building was so tall and skinny?

Oscar rubbed at his eyes. He really *was* tired now. His brain felt mushy and slow.

He looked back at the blueprint, scanning it again, starting at the bottom.

Oh, the squiggles.

Were they . . .

Waves?

And the desk lamp thing—of course! It was a lighthouse!

The only lighthouse Oscar knew of was Gray Lighthouse, which stood on a small island[95] off the coast of Bleak Beach and had been shuttered and dark for years now.

He couldn't be sure these blueprints were for Gray Lighthouse, but it seemed like the most probable answer.

But why would Mr. Cleverer have blueprints of a lighthouse in his desk? As far as Oscar knew, Brawn Industries had nothing at all to do with Gray Lighthouse.

Oscar turned to the second blueprint page.

The outline of the lighthouse was there, but now you could see the inside of it. There was a spiral staircase that wound around the walls, leading up to the top of the building.

And there was the strange machine. It was seamlessly integrated into the interior of the lighthouse, making use of all the available space.

Which made it *huge.*

Oscar had no idea what it did.

There was more writing on this blueprint, but again, it was all in weird shorthand and codes.

---

[95] The island is so small that it doesn't have an official name, but most people refer to it as Gray Island (since it is in the Gray Sea and home to the Gray Lighthouse).

Oscar flipped to the third and last page.

This one was zoomed in on the top of the lighthouse, where the actual light should have been.

It was hard to figure out what he was looking at, but it seemed almost like there were dozens of skinny little cannons poking through holes in the roof of the building. The space around these cannons was filled with hundreds of little dots. They looked a bit like stars in the night sky.

He left the blueprint on the floor and turned back to the other two piles.

First he picked up the typed pages. There were about twenty or thirty stapled together. The cover read, simply: *Project Gray.*

Project Gray.

That sounded a little creepy.

He turned the page.

Then turned that page.

Then quickly fanned through all of the pages.

Well, these weren't going to be helpful at all.

Basically all of the text was blacked out with thick, permanent marker.

He thought there was a word[96] for that.

---

[96] There is, and that word is *redacted*. It's for when things are *really* secret. So secret that the person writing about it can't risk someone else actually *reading* it. Which sort of makes one wonder—why write it down in the first place?

There were only a few words in the entire stack that weren't blacked out:

Gray. Sea. Atmospheric. Conversion. Patterns. Increase.

Oscar laid that stack of paper down and picked up the handwritten notes. There weren't as many of these, only five, and they were written in faint pencil, in a sloppy script that Oscar found almost impossible to read.

He thought he could pick out a few words—something that might have been *heather*? What was heather? A type of plant, maybe.

Another word that might have been *secret* or *sacred*?

Another word he thought was *maintenance* but could also have been *machinery* or *macadamia*.[97]

He was beginning to feel like this whole thing was a big waste of time.

He'd broken into Mr. Cleverer's office, gone through all of his things, and all he had to show for it was some weird blueprints for a lighthouse, a stack of paper that was more black marker than words, and unreadable notes.

He'd *broken into* Mr. Cleverer's office.

What was he thinking?

All because a random Farsouthian had told him some cryptic nonsense about a locked door?

---

[97] The handwriting was really *quite* bad.

Oscar was done with all of this.

He just wanted to go to bed.

And that was when he heard the footsteps upstairs.

He froze.

And then he leapt into motion, hurriedly gathering everything up, refolding the blueprints as the footsteps moved from the upstairs hallway to the stairs.

He slipped everything back into the envelope. And as he did, a page of notes fluttered to the floor. Oscar picked it up and just before he shoved it into the envelope, he paused.

Because he could read one line of the notes.

And it said—*request for ongoing maintenance reports for w.m.*

W.M.?

What did *that* mean?

But there wasn't time to look for even a second longer—the footsteps had reached the first floor. Oscar shoved that single piece of notepaper into his pocket, then crammed all the other paperwork back into the envelope, wrapped the string to close it, and slipped everything back into the secret compartment. He dove for the desk light and turned it off, then listened with horror as the footsteps paused, then picked up speed. He threw himself across the room, slipped out the door, and didn't dare close it as he moved deeper into the house, sticking to the shadows at the edges of the hallway.

His heart was racing as he did the only thing he could think to do—

He ran into the bathroom, turned the light on, and began washing his hands in the sink.

A moment later, Mr. Cleverer popped his head around the open door.

"Oscar? What are you doing down here?"

"Just using the bathroom," Oscar said, trying to keep his voice cheerful and light. "I didn't want to wake anyone by using the one upstairs."

Mr. Cleverer glanced behind him, back in the direction of his study. "There was another light...," he said.

Oscar cleared his throat. "No, I don't think so. Just this one."

"And my study door is open," Mr. Cleverer continued, turning back to Oscar. "I never leave my study door open."

Oscar turned off the water and dried his hands with a towel. He did his best to make himself look sleepy and confused as he turned to Mr. Cleverer and said, "Sorry, sir, but can I get a glass of water?"

Mr. Cleverer looked at Oscar for just a moment too long, then he relaxed and shook his head, softly chuckling to himself. "Of course, of course, Oscar. I'm sorry. I think you just startled me a little. I'm half asleep myself."

"No problem, Mr. Cleverer. Sorry."

Oscar slipped past him and made his way to the kitchen, his heart beating so hard within his chest that he felt like he might collapse or throw up or do both, in either order.

Because while he'd been in the bathroom, trying desperately to look normal in front of Mr. Cleverer, he'd figured it out.

He'd figured out what those blueprints were *for.*

Those dots surrounding the top of the lighthouse—those weren't stars at all.

They were *rain.*

The word *heather* had actually been *weather.*

Secret. Machinery. Conversion.

The note he had shoved into his pocket: *request for ongoing maintenance reports for w.m.*

W.M.

It stood for weather machine.

Brawn Industries had turned Gray Lighthouse into a *weather machine*!

No Friend of Mine

Oscar did not sleep a wink that night, and when Saige finally woke in the morning and rolled over and said, sleepily, "Happy birthday, Oscar," he pretended to be just waking up, stretching and yawning as he thanked her.

"Did you sleep okay?" she asked.

Oscar didn't know how to answer her. What would she have said if he admitted that he *hadn't* slept okay, that he'd actually spent half the night breaking into her father's locked study and the other half of the night feeling weird and guilty about it?

"Um, yeah, I slept okay," he made himself say. "What about you?"

"Great," she said. "It was fun to have someone to share the bunk bed with."

Oscar got off the bed and waited while Saige used the hydraulic lift to lower her bed to the floor. She gripped the handles of her wheelchair and carefully moved into the seat.

"Hungry?" she asked. "Mom said she'd make waffles for breakfast, for your birthday."

"Sounds great," Oscar said.

Mr. and Mrs. Cleverer and Arthur were already downstairs in the kitchen, and although Oscar tried to act normal and sleepy, like he'd just woken up, he was actually suddenly feeling very awake, and extremely self-conscious and fairly uncomfortable and just a bit...

Scared.

But that was ridiculous, right?

He had no reason to be *afraid* of Mr. Cleverer.

Did he?

No. No. He was overreacting.

There was a perfectly reasonable explanation for why Mr. Cleverer had the blueprints for a weather machine in the hollowed-out shell of an abandoned lighthouse.

There must have been.

The waffles were excellent, anyway, and after they'd eaten, Oscar opened up a small pile of gifts, including a few new comic books, new woodworking tools with lovely, smooth handles, and a five hundred–piece puzzle.

He couldn't shake the feeling, through all of it, that

Mr. Cleverer had looked his way too much, kept letting his gaze fall on Oscar just a *bit* too often.

It made Oscar feel unsettled. Exposed.

He was happy when Saige suggested they go to her room and play another game of Burgeoning Bloomrackers before it was time to drive Oscar back to the Alley.

Mrs. Cleverer called upstairs a few hours later and told them it was time to go. Oscar was relieved when he reached the foyer and found that Mr. Cleverer had taken Arthur out for the afternoon. It would just be Mrs. Cleverer and Saige driving him back to the Alley.

Saige was sad to see him go, and he was sad to be leaving her, but it felt like a much deeper sort of sadness, one that extended past just this visit, just this car ride.

Oscar couldn't help but feel like he was leaving her forever. That he would never see her again.

When they got to the Alley, Mrs. Cleverer eased the car into a parking spot.

"I just want to pop over and see my friends at Rainy Season," she said. "Saige, would that be all right with you? I won't be too long."

"Of course, Mom," Saige said. "I'll go with Oscar to Dove. It will be nice to say hi to Bilius."

Oscar grabbed his overnight bag from the car and waited while the car's lift lowered Saige and Dot to the pavement.

They were quiet as Oscar held the door of Dove open for Saige, quiet as they crossed the small lobby to the elevator, and quiet as they saw the sign taped crookedly to its door: OUT OF ORDER.

"Nice to see some things never change," Saige said with a huff.

"Sorry," Oscar mumbled.

"It's not your fault."

"Let me run up and grab my dad. He'll want to come down and say hi to you."

Oscar took a step toward the stairway door, but Saige moved Dot so she was facing him, blocking his way forward.

It was shlinking[98] out. Saige still had her umbrella open, and there were drops of liquid falling off the tips of the ribs.

W.M.

He squeezed his eyes shut.

He wanted to stop thinking about what he had found in Mr. Cleverer's office, but he couldn't.

"You've barely said a word since breakfast," Saige said. "You've barely said a word all day. What's wrong?"

"I'm sorry," he said. "I just, um . . . I don't really like my birthday."

---

[98] This is that gentle and steady rain that's just shy of a spillen.

"Oscar, you *love* your birthday," Saige said. "I've known you since we were babies. I know when something's wrong."

"I'm just tired."

"Are you going to keep trying different lies until you find one I believe?"

"What? No, of course not!" [99]

"I know you were in my father's study last night," she said, and Oscar froze, not even blinking as he stared at her. "I heard you get out of bed. I figured you were just using the bathroom. I thought you took kind of a long time, but I was falling in and out of sleep. But then this morning, I heard my dad whispering to my mom. He said his study door was open. He said he found you downstairs. I wanted to give you a chance to tell me what happened yourself, because we tell each other *everything*, but now you're barely looking at me or talking to me. So before you try and think up another lie, tell me what you were *really* doing last night."

Saige stared at him, unblinking. Oscar *tried* to blink but found himself unable to. He was still frozen.

He didn't want to tell Saige what he'd found. This was her *father*, and the allegations Oscar was about to make were pretty serious.

But he didn't want to lie to Saige.

---

[99] That is actually exactly what he had been planning to do.

Not when she was looking at him so intensely, so fiercely.

But *how* could he say what he wanted to say? He didn't think he'd actually be able to get the words out.

So he didn't.

Instead, he took the piece of paper from his pocket, and he handed it to her.

She looked confused as she glanced over it.

"What is this?"

"I took it from your father's study," Oscar said. "He was right. I *was* in there. I picked the lock."

"Why?"

"When we were supposed to meet at the Night Market, Gregory and Tim showed up instead," Oscar began, taking a deep breath to steady himself. "They chased me through the market, into this weird section called the Others."

"The Others," Saige repeated. "I don't remember that part of the Night Market."

"Right. Nobody does. I even tried to go back and find it and...I don't know...I don't know how to explain it. It was there, and then it wasn't. But Gregory and Tim, that's where they chased me. I ran into this pole and completely knocked myself out. When I woke up, I was in a tiny tent. This Far-southian girl—Eunice—had pulled me inside. Gregory and Tim got taken away by the guards. She totally saved me from getting beaten up. She called herself a Teller. She gave me a

Interception

OVER THE NEXT TWO weeks, Oscar wrote Saige three letters,[100] dropping them into the mailbox before he headed to the shop in the mornings.

He didn't hear back from her.

In the first letter, he apologized and said he'd been wrong about the whole thing.

In the second letter, he insisted he'd been right about everything but apologized again for the way he'd sprung it all on her.

In the third letter, he'd told her he was a bigger jerk than Gregory Fairmountain and Tim Klint combined.

His days fell into a colorless routine.

---

[100] He didn't want to risk calling and have Mr. Cleverer answer the phone.

June faded into July.

He was worried that he would never carve again.

He *tried* to.

Saige had given him those beautiful new tools for his birthday, but when he held them in his hands, he found his fingers frozen and unwilling to cooperate.

He stopped carrying the monkwood around in his pocket. What was the point?

All he had time for was the apprenticeship, eating, and sleeping.

It rained for fourteen days straight, without a reprieve, which even in the Alley was something of an unusual occurrence.

He wrote a fourth letter.

It contained only two lines:

Don't you want to know either way?

and

Sunday. Dawn. Bleak Beach.

He dropped it in the mailbox on Thursday morning. It would be picked up in a few hours and would hopefully reach her by Saturday. Which would give her some time to think about it.

On Saturday evening, he filled a backpack with some things he thought he might need. He went to bed early. "I'll be gone in the morning," he told Bilius before he went upstairs. "Some kids from school are getting together to hang out."

"As long as you're at the shop by noon," Bilius replied, not looking up from his mug of tea.

"Yeah, Dad," Oscar said. "I'll be there."

He rose from his bed at five o'clock the next morning, strangely awake and alert, and he brushed his teeth and grabbed an apple from the fruit bowl before pushing out into the retroclining[101] rain.

The bus didn't run until six, so he walked to Bleak Beach. He was a ball of energy and nerves. He made himself eat the apple, even though he didn't feel the slightest bit hungry, and he paused at the entrance of Piteous Park to hand the apple core to a stray dog that had trotted up to him with hopeful eyes.

"Hey, buddy," Oscar said. The dog's fur was matted and wet and it swallowed the apple core whole. "Wish I had something else for you."

He left the dog and continued onward. The retrocline had slid into a sluice,[102] and Oscar turned up his collar and shoved his hands into his pockets, trying to keep warm.

The beach was empty when he arrived except for one lone car pulled to the side of the road.

Oscar's stomach gave a little flop as he recognized the

---

[101] This type of rain is quite rare and seems to fall upward rather than downward (but that is, of course, impossible...I think).

[102] Which, if you don't remember, is a particularly cold type of rain.

shiny new, jet-black paint job on the big and fancy vehicle that sat with its engine idling before him.

For one second he had the wild thought that Saige had stolen her father's car....

But nope.

Because as Oscar froze just across the way from the sandy start of the beach, the driver's door of the car opened and Mr. Cleverer got out, smoothed his shirt and suit jacket, gave Oscar a little nod, and waited for him to cross the street.

Which Oscar did, despite everything in his entire body telling him to RUN.

Oscar realized, as he crossed the street, a few things in quick succession:

One: How had he expected Saige to get from her house to Bleak Beach on a Saturday morning before any buses were running?

Two: He probably should have put a different return address on the four letters he'd sent to her house, because *clearly* Mr. Cleverer had read them all and Saige probably hadn't even seen a single one.

Three: Mr. Cleverer was smiling, but there was something about his smile that was a little *too* big. A little *too* happy.

It made Oscar's stomach hurt.

But he crossed the street.

He had no other choice.

Even if he took off running...

Well, Mr. Cleverer had a car.

So Oscar wouldn't get far.

He stopped a few feet from Mr. Cleverer and tried his best to sound as casual as possible as he said, "Good morning, sir."

"Good morning, Oscar," Mr. Cleverer said. He was holding an umbrella, and Oscar couldn't help but notice that it was a Brawn model, one of the bigger ones. It sold for four skiffs and this one was already pulling apart at the seams. Oscar tried not to stare at it. He tried not to stare at the ground, either, which was his next choice. He tried to act natural but he felt a rising desire to burst into tears. "I assume you know what brings me to Bleak Beach so early on a Sunday morning?"

Oscar didn't know what to say to that. To say *no* would be lying. To say *yes* would be admitting fault.

He settled for a noncommittal shrug.

Mr. Cleverer nodded. He looked off into the distance, out past Bleak Beach, past the choppy waters. It was too cloudy today—Gray Lighthouse wasn't even visible.

"How were you planning on getting there?" Mr. Cleverer asked.

"The boatyard," Oscar said in a small voice that was almost carried away by the wind. He pointed down the beach a little, and Mr. Cleverer turned to see the small, abandoned cemetery of boats, all fairly small, some with holes in their bottoms, some with oars, some without, others with barnacles and slimy sea mold clinging to their hulls.

"Oscar," Mr. Cleverer said. "I cannot stress to you how dangerous that would have been." He looked serious now, turning back toward Oscar, crouching a little so they were on the same level. "Those boats haven't been used in years. The Gray Sea is unpredictable and fierce. Professional sailors died in these waters all the time, often enough that they closed entire *ports* to spare any more loss of life. And you wanted to bring my daughter on one of *those*? I don't think I need to express to you how even the strongest of swimmers would hardly stand a chance if their boat capsized a hundred feet from shore. What would have happened to you, Oscar? What would have happened to *Saige*?"

Oscar couldn't speak.

A large lump was forming in his throat, a thick blockage that was making it hard to breathe. Mr. Cleverer seemed really scared now, not at all angry, just earnestly, earnestly, scared, and his eyes were wide as he stared at Oscar, waiting for him to respond.

"I would have picked a good boat," Oscar said, and even as he said it he realized how weak of a plan it was, how little he'd thought this through. What did he know about boats, anyway? Absolutely nothing. *Less* than nothing. He'd never even been *on* a boat.

He would have gotten them both killed.

Mr. Cleverer closed his eyes. He rubbed his hands over his face and straightened up. He was back to looking angry. "Oscar, I don't know why you were in my office or what you think you saw there, but I *assure* you, you are completely off base."

"If you don't know what I saw in your office, how do you know I'm off base?" Oscar asked, and he knew it was the wrong thing to say the moment it left his mouth.

Mr. Cleverer leaned in, his face so close to Oscar's that Oscar could smell the coffee he'd had that morning.

"I like you, Oscar," Mr. Cleverer said, his voice soft and low. "I've always liked you. And Saige likes you. And *that's* why I'm going to give you one more chance. Now. I assure you. You are completely off base. Don't you agree?"

Oscar saw no other way out of the situation. He nodded.

"I think you're right, Mr. Cleverer," he said.

Mr. Cleverer straightened up. His mouth melted into an easy smile, his eyes brightening. He looked completely normal again. Completely happy.

"Perfect," he said. "Can I give you a ride back to the Alley, son?"

"No, no," Oscar replied quickly. "That's okay, thanks. I can walk."

"Suit yourself. I never could stand a sluice. Cold as hell."

Mr. Cleverer turned back to his car, then stopped himself and patted the breast pocket of his jacket. He pulled out an envelope and handed it to Oscar. "Almost forgot. Saige wanted me to give this to you. Feel free to send a reply back by post. You'll forgive me if I read it first, though."

Mr. Cleverer winked, slid into the driver's seat of his fancy black car, and pulled away from the curb.

He was gone in another minute, and Oscar shivered, a full-body convulsion that felt like the release of a long, painful breath. The letter was getting wet, so he shoved it in his pocket and started back toward Dove.

A Better Plan

OSCAR COULD BARELY FEEL the ground beneath his feet; he could barely feel the rain against his skin. He was soaking wet by the time he walked into Château Buckle. Bilius was wearing his flannel robe and stoking a fire in the stone fireplace. When he saw Oscar, he tut-tutted loudly.

"An entire world of umbrellas at his fingertips, and the boy is always wet," he muttered. "Are you already done with your friends?"

"We rescheduled," Oscar said, his teeth chattering (although he didn't feel the least bit cold; he didn't feel the least bit *anything*).

"Go upstairs and change, then, you're making me cold," Bilius said, shooing him off.

Oscar kicked off his shoes and went upstairs to the

bathroom. He shed his layers of soaking-wet clothes and hopped into the shower. The warm water gradually brought back feeling to his skin, and he stayed under the spray for a long while.

After the shower, he changed into warm pajamas and went downstairs to sit in front of the fire. Bilius was reading the Sunday newspaper at the kitchen table, nursing a mug of coffee. Oscar had Saige's letter in his hands.

He was scared to read it.

Obviously Mr. Cleverer had read it.

He had made it clear that Saige and Oscar wouldn't be allowed to communicate without his direct supervision.

With slightly shaking fingers, Oscar opened the letter.

This is what it said:

Dearest Oscar,

We were so happy you came to spend your birthday with us. Need to say sorry that it took me so long to respond to your letters! A lot has been happening and I've been so busy. Better late than never, though, right? Plan as I might to sit down and respond sooner, it just didn't happen!

Come back to Roan Piers whenever you want! Next time I'm definitely going to beat you in Burgeoning Bloomrackers. Saturday or Sunday usually work for me. Morning or afternoon, whenever! East of here we can go visit a cool park I like. Mark my words! Ten skiffs says you love it.

Don't be a stranger! Tell you what—next time you write, I promise I'll respond sooner! Anyone else who needs me will just have to wait :)

Yours,
Saige

By the time he finished the letter, Oscar's heart was pounding so hard he thought it might jump out of his chest.

It seemed like a normal letter, right?

Anyone who read it would think it was a perfectly normal letter.

But Oscar knew better.

Because Saige had said *dearest*.

Oscar jumped up from the hearth of the fireplace and ran to the kitchen table, where Bilius kept a pen to do the newspaper's messword[103] puzzle. Oscar snatched it up and ran back to the fire, then he circled the first word of every sentence of the letter.

When Saige and Oscar had first built Fort Cleverbuckle, they'd decided that any good fort needed a foolproof code for sending secret messages back and forth.

"But how will we know when a letter is just a letter and when it's a secret code?" Oscar had asked.

"We'll start any coded letters with the word *dearest*," Saige had responded. "It will be easy to remember, because neither of us ever says *dearest*. So we'll know right away that the letter has a secret message!"

The code itself followed this simple rule: The first word of every sentence of the letter was pulled out to reveal the secret message. Each paragraph made up a complete sentence.

Which meant that Saige's secret message was:

We need a better plan. Come next Saturday morning East mark ten. Don't tell anyone.

East mark ten.

Obviously that was East Market, at 10:00 a.m.

And even though Mr. Cleverer had read this letter, he wouldn't have been able to decipher the secret message.

"Brilliant!" Oscar exclaimed.

---

[103] This is sort of like a mashup between a crossword, a word seek, and Scrabble.

"What now?" Bilius asked, only half paying attention.

"Oh, nothing. Sorry, Dad," Oscar said.

He had to write Saige at once, to let her know he'd gotten her message.

He hopped up again and found a clean piece of paper, then sat back down.

This is what he wrote:

> *Dearest Saige,*
>
> *I got your letter and no worries about the late reply! Will you let me know if the first weekend in September works for a visit? Be ready for me to beat you in Burgeoning Bloomrackers! There is no way you'll win!*
>
> *Yours,*
> *Oscar*[104]

Oscar read the letter over, then nodded to himself and folded it up. He found a blank envelope, addressed it to Saige, put a stamp on it, and headed downstairs to drop it in Dove's mailbox.

Now all he had to do was wait a week.

---

[104] I'll leave you to decipher this one yourself!

Frederika's Collection

IT WAS IMPOSSIBLE FOR Oscar to concentrate on anything while he waited for his secret visit with Saige, which resulted in the following mishaps:

On Monday, he burned dinner so badly they had to throw the entire thing out and go back to East Market for something else to eat.

On Tuesday, he cut a canvas for a Wib umbrella when he was supposed to be cutting a canvas for a Spillen.

On Wednesday, he spilled an entire mug of hot coffee on the kitchen table.

On Thursday, he put his shoes on the wrong feet and didn't notice until halfway through the day.[105]

---

[105] When he had already developed some pretty impressive blisters.

And on Friday, he was so jittery that he kept dropping Bilius's tools, over and over, until finally Bilius dismissed him altogether, and sent him over to the factories to pick up a new roll of canvas.

"You're like a bull in a china shop," Bilius complained loudly after narrowly escaping impalement from a pair of scissors Oscar threw across the room.

"Sorry," Oscar said, and he really *was* sorry, of course, because he hadn't *meant* to launch the scissors at his father.

"It's fine, it's fine. I've been meaning to send you to the factories, anyway. It will be good for you to run an errand and get the lay of the land."[106]

Oscar had ridden past the factories on the bus plenty of times, but he'd never actually gotten off at the stop before. Bilius found a scrap piece of paper and drew Oscar a quick map, outlining the six factories and which one Oscar was meant to visit. He labeled each building with a letter, A through F. Bilius had drawn one of them, C, significantly larger than the others. Oscar stared at it. That must be Brawn Industries. All the other factories were leased and used by multiple companies. Brawn Industries was the only one that owned an entire building, just to themselves.

---

[106] But Oscar didn't really *want* to get the lay of the land when it came to the factories, because they had always creeped him out. Just being near them made his throat itchy (from all the smoke) and his skin sweaty (the air always seemed to be five degrees warmer over there).

"There will be a loading dock here," Bilius said, pointing to building D with the tip of his pencil. Oscar tried hard to pay attention. "You'll ask for Frederika. Introduce yourself and she'll get you what you need. Got it?"

"Got it," Oscar mumbled.

"See you in a couple hours," Bilius said. "And for goodness' sake, Oscar, try not to throw any sharp objects at the bus driver, okay?"

Oscar cracked a smile at that. "I'll try," he said. "No promises."

By good fortune, Oscar arrived at the bus stop just as the bus was pulling up, and he waved a hello to the driver as he took a seat near the middle of the vehicle. He studied Bilius's map, then put it in his pocket. Now that he thought about it, he was actually happy for the distraction this errand provided. As it was, he could hardly sit still—he kept bouncing up and down in the bus seat—but at least he was out in the world and not trapped in the umbrella shop, where time sometimes seemed to slow down so much as to stop entirely. This was much better. There was a little breeze coming through the cracked-open windows and it wasn't even raining that hard.

The bus meandered[107] its way around the Toe, stopping

---

[107] The bus driver never seemed to be in that big of a hurry, driving slowly and sometimes taking quite random wrong turns, doubling back, and eventually continuing on again.

at Bleak Beach, where a few people shuffled off and on, then swinging back around to the west side and heading north to the factories. When they reached the factory stop, Oscar filed off with a half dozen other people.

Within a minute, his throat had become scratchy, and his skin had become clammy and warm. In front of him, the factories spat their foul smoke into the air, darkening the sky above, and all around him, workers hustled and bustled, coming to and from lunch breaks and clocking in and out of shifts. There was so much energy and movement that Oscar felt a little overwhelmed, and once he'd passed buildings A and B, he took a moment to stop and get his bearings.

Building C was right in front of him. The enormous doors were thrown open, and a sign above them confirmed what Oscar had guessed, because there, in massive letters, were the words BRAWN INDUSTRIES. The building was wider and taller than any other factory, and the smoke that gushed from its smokestacks seemed to be even blacker, even thicker, even fouler. Oscar couldn't tear his eyes away from it. How was this sort of rampant pollution even legal?

He started walking again, keeping to the right of building C, just like Bilius had instructed. Beyond building C were buildings D and E and, past those, building F. Oscar made his way around the left side of building D and found the loading dock, which was buzzing with activity. There were a few

trucks being loaded with large, heavy-looking boxes, assembly lines spitting out more boxes from the belly of the building, and people everywhere who moved like bees in a hive, in a perfectly coordinated dance that seemed to make sense to them but just felt a bit like chaos to Oscar.

Eventually, he became aware of a tall, striking white woman in an ankle-length gray skirt, gray button-up linen blouse, and gray linen vest. Her hair was fixed into a severe bun and she held a clipboard as she moved throughout the crowd. She had to be Frederika, so Oscar waited until she was free and hesitantly approached her.

"Yes?" she asked, sensing his presence but not taking her eyes off her clipboard. She was writing so quickly that her fingers were a mere blur of motion.

"Um. Are you Frederika?" Oscar asked.

"Yes. How can I help you?"

She spoke abruptly, quickly, sharply, and she still hadn't looked up at Oscar.

"I'm, um…"

"Spit it out, please. I haven't got all day."

"I'm, um…Bilius's son."

Frederika's eyes snapped up, and she instantly softened, dropping the clipboard to her waist as she looked Oscar up and down.

"My stars," she said kindly. "Why didn't you say so! You're the spitting image. A dear, dear friend of mine, Bilius is. Come right this way. I have what you need."

Frederika turned on her heel and led Oscar through a door to the right of the loading dock. The hallway he found himself in was lit with weak overhead fluorescent lights. One of them flickered in a distracting way. The light they cast made Oscar's skin look yellow.

At the end of the hallway, Frederika turned right, then left, then she removed a large key ring from her pocket and unlocked a door with a plaque on it that read FREDERIKA ROLL-INS, SHIPPING SUPERVISOR. She pushed into the room, flicked on an overhead light, and stepped aside to make room for Oscar.

His eyes widened as he walked into the office. Every inch of wall space was taken up by massive glass aquariums, which held fish of every size, shape, and color. Oscar couldn't help it; he literally gasped. Frederika chuckled.

"That's what most people do when they see it for the first time," she said.

The lights played across the water, sending curvy, squiggly lines of luminescence across the floor and ceiling. It felt like he was underwater.

"I always wanted to be a marine biologist," Frederika said. "Life had other plans. But still, I've managed to assemble this little collection over the years."

Oscar walked over to one tank that was about five feet long and taller than he was. It was absolutely filled with small, brightly colored fish, every color of the rainbow. He thought of Pietra and her Ocspectrascope. She would *love* this.

"Many of these fish came from the Gray Sea," Frederika continued. "Before it became so polluted as to be completely uninhabitable."

"These fish lived in the Gray Sea? But they're so *beautiful*," Oscar said.

"These are some of the last of their kind," Frederika said. "Pollution has wiped out entire species. Look over here."

Oscar walked to the other side of the room, where Frederika was standing in front of a series of smaller tanks. Each one held two fish—one red, one yellow.

"These are called stopentia," she said. "Each pair is a couple. They mate for life, you see, and they don't like to be around any other fish. They get quite feisty. Completely extinct in the wild. I'm hoping they'll have babies. The babies come out a vivid green, then as they mature, they pick a gender and turn red if female, yellow if male."

"Wow," Oscar said. He moved to the next aquarium, which was the biggest in the room and took up the entire back wall.

"I think fish are the most beautiful creatures," Frederika said. "The way they glide through the water, their uncomplicated lives, their simple beauty. My favorite thing in the world used to be walking in the underwater tunnel to Gray Lighthouse, being completely surrounded by marine life outside the glass walls."

Oscar was transfixed by a tiny octopus that had just crawled out from underneath a rock, but he turned now, intrigued by what Frederika had just said.

"Underwater tunnel?"

"It's been closed for years now, unfortunately," Frederika said, nodding. "Not that you would see much anymore. The water is too cloudy. The fish are all gone."

"Sorry, can I just…an *underwater tunnel*," he repeated. "Like…a tunnel. But it's…underwater."

Frederika laughed. "Have you never heard of it? No, I suppose it's before your time. Bilius would have been to it, I'm sure. It led right from Bleak Beach to Gray Lighthouse. Quite the tourist destination, back then."

"And it's still there?"

"Well, it must be, but like I said, it's been closed for years."

"Right, right," Oscar said carefully, keeping his voice light, deciding to lie just a *tiny* bit. "I think I've heard of it, actually. The entrance was near the boatyard, right?"

"No, no, on the other side entirely," Frederika said. "In the basement of the old aquarium, of course."

"Oh, yeah," Oscar said. "That's right. I think my dad has mentioned it."

"And I'm sure he'll be wanting you back soon. I've taken up way too much of your time! I just get so excited when someone is interested in my fish," Frederika said, smiling. "But here you are. One fresh new roll of canvas for your father. Charged to his account, with his usual discount."

Frederika removed a roll of canvas from behind her desk and handed it to Oscar. It was heavy but manageable, and at that particular moment, Oscar could barely feel its weight. Because—

THERE WAS AN UNDERGROUND TUNNEL THAT LED DIRECTLY TO THE LIGHTHOUSE!

He wouldn't have to risk his life navigating a dilapidated[108] rowboat across the Gray Sea!

Just wait until he told Saige!

---

[108] It's not ideal for a boat to fall apart, unless your goal is ending up on the bottom of the seafloor with the fish Frederika loved so much.

Burgeoning Bloomrackers

Oscar could barely sleep that night.

He had wanted to go to Bleak Beach after his day ended at the umbrella shop, but the weather had turned particularly bad, and Bilius had heard rumors that a blanderwheel[109] might be on its way. By the time they got back to Dove, it was tranklumpeting, and after dinner it had picked up to an alfer.[110] Bilius removed the wooden window savers[111] from underneath the couch and fit them over all the windows in the apartment.

---

[109] Oh, do you think this might be THE blanderwheel? The one we've been hearing so much about?

[110] A LOT of rain. Extreme flood danger. The only rain more dangerous than an alfer is a blanderwheel.

[111] It is common for households in the Alley to keep a set of wooden planks cut to fit their windows, to use in the event of a particularly bad storm. They act as an additional barrier to help with flooding, and they also protect the glass from smashing.

"Better safe than sorry," he said. "Statistically, an alfer turns into a blanderwheel sixty-eight percent of the time."

"I might just nip down to the lobby quick," Oscar said. "I want to try giving Saige a call."

"All right," Bilius said. "But be quick. I'll feel better when we're both tucked in safely for the night."

In the lobby, there were just two people in line waiting for the phone, and Oscar shuffled back and forth while they finished up their calls. When it was his turn, he dialed Saige's number, then bounced up and down and *prayed* Mr. Cleverer didn't pick up.

He was lucky; Mrs. Cleverer answered.

"Hi! Mrs. Cleverer, it's me, Oscar!"

"Oscar, dear, how are you?"

"I'm fine. I was wondering, um, could I say hello to Saige?"

"Of course, dear. I'll have her pick up in the living room and I'll just stay on the line here in the kitchen, in case you need anything."

Translation: She was going to listen to the entire conversation. Shoot.

How was Oscar going to manage this? He needed to tell Saige that the weather was bad in the Toe, that she shouldn't come tomorrow, but Mrs. Cleverer didn't *know* she was coming tomorrow and now she was going to stay on the phone while—

"Hi, Oscar!" Saige said brightly.

Oscar took a deep breath. "Hi, Saige."

"What's up?"

"Oh, I just..."

Think, Oscar!

How could he talk about their plans for tomorrow without Mrs. Cleverer understanding him?

On the other end of the line, Mrs. Cleverer cleared her throat impatiently.

Oscar was frozen. He couldn't speak or think.

"I was just playing a solo game of Burgeoning Bloomrackers," Saige said. "I love that game so much. Of all my games, I think it's the dearest to my heart."

Dearest!

Saige had said the code word!

But the code was a *written* thing. How would they work it into a conversation?

"Anyway," Saige continued, "I don't think our connection is that good, but I assume that's why you're calling. You had a question about the rules, right? Didn't you just get a copy of the game?"

"Yeah," Oscar said, playing along. "Yeah, I did. That's why I'm calling."

"Right. Well, I think it gets tricky in the later part of the game, when the main characters are trying to decide whether to go to their secret meeting."

"Exactly!" Oscar said. "I don't think they should go."

"I thought you might say that. But they *have* to go— otherwise, they can't advance to the next level."

"But in the game, you know how you roll that one die[112] and it tells you what the weather will be? I rolled it and it said the weather will be really bad when they meet. It just feels too dangerous."

"Sometimes you know that's how a thing is worth it. Because it feels a little dangerous," Saige said seriously. "It will be fine, Oscar. You have to take some risks in Burgeoning Bloomrackers or else you'll never get to the final level and rescue the entire city from the evil empire."

There was a long silence.

And finally, Mrs. Cleverer spoke. "Was that your only question, Oscar, dear?"

"Yeah," he said. "Yeah, it was. Thanks, Saige."

"Of course, Oscar! Let me know how the game goes!"

"I will."

Oscar hung up the phone, and only then did he realize just how much his hands were shaking. He didn't move for a few seconds, and then someone behind him gently cleared their throat.

---

[112] *Die* is the singular of *dice*. But it *is* just a bit unfortunate that it's spelled and pronounced exactly like *die*, as in "I really hope Oscar doesn't die in the upcoming blanderwheel!"

"Are you done with the phone, son?"

It was Mrs. Carmichael from the fourth floor. She had her pet parrot on her shoulder, as usual.

"Yes, sorry, Mrs. Carmichael," Oscar said.

"I just need to call over to Finch and make sure my sister remembered to put her window savers up.[113] Supposed to blanderwheel tonight! I haven't seen a blanderwheel in a few years now. Oh, I don't love all the noise."

"You know where to find us, if you need anything," Oscar said.

"Sweet boy," Mrs. Carmichael said. "Tell your father I said hello."

Oscar ran up all seven floors to Château Buckle. He burst into his living room, out of breath and red-faced, and Bilius, who was making a pile of towels in the center of the living room,[114] paused, studying his son.

"Everything all right?"

And because Oscar did not know how to answer that question, because he had *no idea* how to possibly convey to his father all the levels on which everything was *very much not all right*, he simply forced a tight smile, nodded, and went upstairs to his bedroom.

---

[113] Mrs. Carmichael, whose name is Lucille, talks to her twin sister, Arden, every evening at the same exact time, which is how Lucille knows that Arden will be waiting by Finch's lobby phone for her call.

[114] In case of leaks.

Blanderwheel
(Part 4)

AND THAT IS WHEN the blanderwheel hit!

Just kidding.

But we're really, really, really almost there now.

Promise.

Weathering the Storm

THE ALFER CONTINUED THROUGH the night, and there were times when the storm came close to tipping into blander-wheel territory, but it kept pulling back, as if dipping a toe into a body of water and deciding it was much too cold to jump in.

But still, an alfer was no walk in the park, and Oscar and Bilius took turns wiping leaks from the windows and making sure the window savers were still sturdy and in place. They filled jugs with water in case the pipes shut off, and sure enough they did, around midnight.

"Go on up to sleep," Bilius said then. "There's no need for both of us to suffer."

"Are you sure?"

"I'll wake you if I need you."

But Oscar couldn't sleep, and for the longest time he lay awake in bed, staring up at the ceiling, listening to the screaming rain outside.

He was scared.

He didn't know how Saige was going to make it to East Market tomorrow.

He didn't know how *he* was going to make it to East Market tomorrow.

Alfers were known to bring flash floods, turning the streets of the Alley into a literal lake.

He'd rolled the die, and it clearly said the weather was too dangerous.

But Saige had insisted....

And the weather north of the Wall was so much different from the weather in the Toe, anyway.

Maybe she'd make it just fine?

Oscar tried to close his eyes, to relax, to fall asleep, but he was just feeling too anxious....

So he got off his bed and looked underneath it, where he stored his wood-carving supplies.

It had been so long since he'd had any energy to work on his carvings, but it was pretty clear that he wouldn't be able to sleep tonight.

He picked up the block of monkwood. Its warm, comforting weight felt good in his hands.

But he put it back under his bed for now. He still didn't know what to make with it, and he knew it had to be *perfect* when he finally started carving.

He picked up an interestingly shaped piece of driftwood instead.

It was long and skinny, with a bit of a bulb on one end.

He turned it over in his hand, studying the grain of the wood, letting it speak to him. . . .

And then, suddenly, he could see the animal hidden in the wood.

It was a walrus!

Oscar grabbed the new wood-carving tools Saige had given him for his birthday and jumped back on his bed.

The anxiety and fear left his body as he concentrated on the carving, releasing the walrus from the wood, watching the animal take form.

He carved for hours, then he took a small square of sandpaper and smoothed the walrus's skin, going over every inch of the animal until it was perfect.

His bed was covered in wood shavings by the time he was done.

But he was happy with how it had turned out.

He set the walrus down on his nightstand, next to Wib, and fell asleep almost instantly.

A Treacherous Journey

OSCAR WOKE EARLY THE next morning, and the first thing he did was detach the savers from his bedroom window to check the state of things.

The rain was still crashing down, but Oscar was relieved to find it wasn't a blanderwheel.[115] He wasn't even convinced it was still an alfer; it might have downgraded to a heller,[116] but it was hard to tell those two apart. He'd really have to be outside, to feel the rain, to decide what it was. Sometimes rain was just like that. It insisted that you touch it, smell it, taste it. There was a rain called silk, which felt exactly like silk. There was a rain called grit, which was dirty and coarse between

---

[115] Yet.

[116] The main difference between a heller and an alfer is that a heller is accompanied by *slightly* less rain and the rain itself is *slightly* thinner and *slightly* warmer, which lends itself to a quicker evaporation rate.

your fingertips. There was a rain called lemon, which tasted and smelled exactly like lemons. There was even a rain that somehow fell quite hard but didn't carry any moisture, so nothing actually got wet.[117]

You could live an entire lifetime in Roan and still not know all there was to know about rain.

But Oscar had a feeling he knew more than most people.

He found Bilius soundly asleep on the couch downstairs, and because he didn't know how long his father would *stay* asleep, he decided that it was now or never. He needed to leave.

He dressed quickly, in long pants and a long-sleeved shirt and a waterproof utility jacket and thigh-high rubber rain boots that were pristine and basically brand new.[118] Then he grabbed a few things he thought might come in handy— including a heavy, waterproof flashlight and a roll of water-proof duct tape—and quietly left the apartment. He was immediately glad he had worn the boots, because when he stepped out of the stairway and into the lobby of Dove, he found it flooded with three or four inches of dirty water.

But that was nothing new.

The lobby had certainly flooded before, and if you looked carefully at the walls, you could see the stained lines that marked the height of each previous deluge. Someone had

---

[117] This is probably the rarest rain of all, and it is called sike.
[118] Because, of course, he usually refused to wear them.

even helpfully dated them. It was Dove's own little museum of rain. All the buildings of the Alley were made to withstand rain and flooding and wind, and a little bit of water on the floors was hardly something to be alarmed about, so Oscar took a deep breath and splashed his way across the lobby, then pushed out into the heller.

He knew it was a heller as soon as he felt the first drops on his face.

That was a good sign.

Still, the streets were gushing with shin-high water.

Which was a bad sign.

He doubted the bus to Bleak Beach would be running in this. A few inches of water on the ground and sure, they'd keep the service going, but this was about six inches or so, and Oscar wasn't so confident.

But still.

At least he could make it to East Market on foot.

He started in that direction now and passed just a few people on his way. Some people grunted greetings as they went or waved their hands without looking at him, but one young father with a toddler on his shoulders paused and smiled widely.

"What a morning, huh?" he said. "I have to admit—I love a good flooding. Always have!"

Oscar actually smiled at that. "Yeah," he said. "Honestly, me too."

And he *did*.

It was fun to splash through the streets of the Alley, pretending he was a giant navigating a great, roaring river, but he realized after a few minutes of this that Saige wouldn't have nearly as easy a time as he was having. Although her wheelchair was of course designed to withstand a tremendous amount of water, he wasn't sure it would move easily in this at all.

And it seemed like the water was only getting higher.

By the time he reached East Market, it was almost up to his knees, and it was *slightly* less fun to trudge through it.

Most of the stalls at the market were shuttered and empty, but he did find one open. Mr. Glizzard, an impossibly old white man who Oscar suspected might actually *live* in his market stall, was there, bright-eyed and selling his customary hot coffee and sticky buns.

"Oy! You there!" Mr. Glizzard called when he saw Oscar.

"It's Oscar, sir," Oscar said politely. "Oscar Buckle."

"Ah, Bilius's kid. Knew you looked familiar. What are you doing out on a day like this?"

"What are *you* doing out on a day like this?" Oscar countered.

Mr. Glizzard laughed uproariously. "Touché, son," he

said. "Come here and let me warm you up with a mug of something hot."

Mr. Glizzard poured Oscar a cup of coffee and handed over two enormous sticky buns. He waved away Oscar's money when he tried to pay.

"Thank you," Oscar said.

"We have to stick together," Mr. Glizzard said with a wink. "We who weather the storm, you know."

Oscar smiled and thanked him again, and then went to wait in Neko's empty booth for Saige, because of course she would come there, if she was able to.

The coffee was piping hot and the sticky buns were warm and gooey and soft, and Oscar inhaled everything in about three minutes flat.

Then he waited.

And waited.

He didn't actually know what time it was, and it was impossible to guess, because, of course, he couldn't see the sun. The sky was like an artist's palette of only grays, every shade of gray imaginable, from washed stone to smoke to steel to pewter to ash. There were probably as many names for all the shades of gray as there were for rain. They went hand in hand, Oscar thought. At least in Roan.

He waited some more.

He got up and paced around, then sat again, then stretched,

then sat, then attempted a series of jumping jacks, which ended with him becoming considerably wetter than he'd been a few moments previous.

He sat again.

He waited again.

And then he heard an interesting splashing noise that seemed to be getting closer and closer. Finally he saw Saige turn a corner and paddle her way toward him.

Paddle her way toward him . . .

Oscar wasn't sure exactly what he was seeing.

Saige was sitting in Dot, but the wheelchair was . . . floating on the water?

Oscar leapt to his feet and met her halfway down the aisle.

"Wow!" he exclaimed. "This is *genius*!"

Covering each wheel of the chair were flotation devices, which caused the entire thing to glide easily across the surface of the water. There were weights and counterweights hanging from the front and back of the chair to keep Saige balanced, and she held a short paddle in her hand that she used to push through the water. Her Spillen umbrella was, as usual, open and attached to Dot, keeping everything nice and dry.

"Thanks!" she said, beaming. "I made it!"

"You *made* this?"

"Yup! I drew up the plans last week. They were actually kind of easy to make." She fell quiet, biting her lip before continuing.

"Look, Oscar... When you told me what you found... About the weather machine. I didn't even listen to you."

"Saige, I totally get it. He's your dad. I should have found a better way to tell you, or gotten more proof first, or—"

"I know he's my dad," she said. "And I didn't want to hear anything you were saying. But the truth is...sometimes I feel like I don't even know who he is. He's always worked so much, you know? And when he's home, even before we moved, he's always busy and distracted and...it feels like he likes being at work more than he likes being with *us*."

"Saige—"

"But I should have listened to you. Even though he's my dad, and I do love him, of course I do, I had this feeling…" She looked up at him then, and her eyes were red and shining. "I had this feeling like…I knew you were telling the truth. It's been really hard for me to accept that. And I'm sorry. I wasn't ready to hear any of it."

"You don't have to apologize," Oscar said firmly. "Not for anything. *I'm* the one who should be apologizing."

"It seems like we're both doing a lot of apologizing lately, huh?"

"A lot's been happening."

"Yeah," Saige agreed. "And that's why I broke into my father's study myself, when both of my parents were out at the market. I found the secret drawer you told me about. And I think you're right. I think there's a weather machine in Gray Lighthouse. And I think we need to go there and figure out how to dismantle it, and then we need to tell everybody the truth about Brawn Industries."

"Even though your father works for them?"

"*Especially* because my father works for them," Saige said. "I know it's a long shot but…Maybe there's a chance he doesn't even know? Or he doesn't think it's real? Or he doesn't know the whole truth? I don't know, Oscar. I don't know *what* to think. But I *do* know we have to get to that lighthouse. Here—I brought some supplies…" She gestured to a very stuffed backpack that was hanging from the back of her wheelchair. "I thought we could check out that abandoned boatyard. Maybe I can fix up one of the boats enough so that we can take it out there."

"Actually," Oscar said, "I have a better idea."

And he told her all about his visit to the factories, his conversation with Frederika, and, most importantly, the existence of an underwater tunnel that led right to the lighthouse.

When he was done talking, he realized that Saige had gone quite pale.

"What?" he said.

"I don't *super* love the idea of an underwater tunnel," she admitted.

"Do you super love the idea of capsizing in the middle of the Gray Sea?" Oscar asked. Saige laughed. "Nope. Tunnel it is!"

"Should we go now?"

"No time like the present!"

"I doubt the bus is running."

"Me too. That's why I added this to my design."

Saige turned Dot to the side, revealing a little platform at the back that looked like it was meant for someone to stand on. She adjusted some of the weights, moving more to the front of the wheelchair, and gestured for Oscar to hop on.

"Are you sure you can paddle both of us?" Oscar asked.

"Oh, definitely not," Saige said.

Then she pulled a small prop motor from under her rain jacket.

"Are you *kidding me*!" Oscar squeaked, totally impressed. "Did you make this, too?!"

"Yeah," Saige said, blushing a little. "I've had a lot of time on my hands lately. Just attach it to that hook right underneath the platform, then press that red button. And hold on. It won't go fast, so I can steer up front with the paddle."

Oscar hopped on the platform and waited as Saige adjusted the weights again to make sure everything was perfectly balanced. Then he attached the prop to the hook, pressed the red button, straightened up, and held on.

Dot took off at a respectable pace, and Saige stuck the oar in the water in front of her, using it as a makeshift rudder.[119]

It took her a minute to get the hang of steering, and they bumped into quite a few things as they made their way out of the market, but then it was pretty smooth sailing. The wheelchair boat probably only went about four or five miles an hour, but riding it was *so much fun*.

"Usually rudders go in the back of the boat," Saige called over her shoulder. "But this isn't really a boat, anyway, and since we're going so slow, I thought it would work. And it does!"

---

[119] Which is something that is usually used to steer a boat, not a floating wheelchair.

"How did you make it to the Toe, anyway? Did you take this all the way from Roan Piers?"

"Nope," Saige replied. "I didn't have to. There aren't any floods north of the Wall."

"Right," Oscar said bitterly. "Of course not."

"I took the bus to Central Market. They have these massive storm drains just south of the Wall. All the water goes pouring into them. I'd never really noticed them before; they must be able to cover and uncover them when they need to. Basically, I was able to pass the Wall and then inflate my wheel wraps."

"Saige, I think you might be the smartest person I've ever met," Oscar said.

She flashed Oscar a bright smile.

It took the better portion of an hour to reach Bleak Beach, and their progress slowed considerably the closer they got to the shore. And the water *deepened* considerably the closer they got to the shore. And the rain *increased* considerably the closer they got to the shore. By the time Bleak Beach came into view, it was alfering again and the water was at least two feet deep.

Then, the prop motor gave a sick kind of cough, sputtered, and died completely.

"Out of gas. That actually lasted about fifteen minutes longer than my calculations suggested," Saige said. "But no worries. I can paddle the rest of the way."

Oscar hopped down from the wheelchair's platform and gasped at the sudden chill of the water. It came up to just under his waist, and it poured into his rain boots, rendering them completely useless (and very heavy). Luckily he'd worn his sneakers underneath, so he wasn't completely barefoot when he slid off the boots and abandoned them on a park bench.

"Where's the tunnel entrance?" Saige asked, shouting now to be heard over the roar of the storm.

"This way!" Oscar said.

They figured out that the fastest way to forge onward was for Oscar to hold Dot's handles and push as hard as he could while Saige manned the oar, rowing as hard as *she* could. Still, it was hard and tiresome work, and they were both out of breath and exhausted by the time they reached the old, boarded-up entrance to the old, boarded-up aquarium.

"In *here*?" Saige asked incredulously.

"Yup," Oscar said.

"Creepy."

"Yup."

"Hand me my backpack, please."

Oscar removed the backpack from the handles of the wheelchair.

"Geez, what's in this thing?" he asked as he handed it over.

Then he burst out laughing when Saige pulled out...

A crowbar.[120]

"I came prepared," she said.

"Clearly."

Saige fit the crowbar behind one of the many planks of wood that covered the front door. It took a few good wrenches, but she managed to detach one side of a plank, then the other. She did two more boards, then handed the crowbar to Oscar.

"Can you get those taller ones?" she asked.

Oscar removed a few more planks, and after several minutes they'd managed to uncover a section big enough to squeeze through. The door had once been glass but was now mostly shattered, and they made sure to be careful not to cut themselves on any of its jagged edges.

And then they were inside.

The space was big and open, and there was a fair amount of light filtering in through high windows all around them, in places where wooden planks had become unstuck over the years.

In fact there was *just* enough light to see the massive shark that was swimming through the air, on its way to eat them both!

---

[120] In our world, a crowbar is mostly used to pry things apart or open—like a wooden crate, or two boards that have been nailed together. In Oscar's world, the average citizen of Roan owns a crowbar to assist in weather-related tasks, such as pulling a window saver off if a storm was expected to be so bad that you decided to nail it in place.

Downward

"Oscar, you need to stop screaming," Saige said calmly.

Oscar opened his eyes.

The shark was still in midair, still aimed directly at them, but it... wasn't moving.

Oh.

That was because it wasn't real.

It was a *model* of a shark.

"Shark," Oscar said weakly.

"Actually, that's an orca," Saige said. "A killer whale. It's not a shark. It's not even a whale. It's a dolphin."

"It has as many teeth as a shark."

"Actually, the average great white shark has about two hundred and fifty more teeth than an orca. But I see your point. And at any rate, it isn't real."

"Yes, I can see that now," Oscar mumbled.

"And sharks don't fly through the air," she added.

"Okay, I get it!"

"So where is the tunnel entrance?"

"In the basement, Frederika said." Oscar's heart was still beating *very* fast. He felt a little foolish that he'd thought the giant creature suspended from the ceiling was *real*, but to be fair, he was pretty on edge to begin with.

"Over there," Saige said, pointing. "It looks like a directory."

There was considerably less water in the aquarium than there was outside—only about a foot on this floor.

That probably had something to do with an enormous staircase in the center of the space, which led downward to a lower floor of the building. All the water that made it into the aquarium was rushing wildly down those stairs, transforming them into a literal waterfall. Oscar found himself wishing for an elevator, even though that seemed extraordinarily unlikely.

The directory was in pretty good shape, though, so that was lucky. The entrance to the tunnel was down one flight of stairs, then all the way in the back corner of the building.

"I don't suppose you brought a chairlift," Oscar said weakly, in such a sad and small voice that he and Saige looked at each other before dissolving into a fit of wild, high-pitched laughter.

Then Saige pretended to dig around in her backpack for a chairlift, and that made them laugh even more, and when they stopped, Oscar felt better, like he'd laughed out most of the fear and anxiety from his body. The mood felt lighter as they stood as close to the stairs as they could without fear of being swept away.

"This isn't ideal," Saige said.

"Right."

"But it isn't a total roadblock, either."

She withdrew a coil of sturdy rope from her backpack and held it up for Oscar.

"I don't know about that," he said nervously.

"I have my wheel wraps," she reasoned. "They'll help me glide down the stairs. We can attach one end of the rope to the top of the staircase, and I can lower myself down slowly. We can wrap the rope around my handles and use them as a sort of pulley.[121] Actually, you can come with me, on the platform. The extra weight will make us sturdier, and it will probably be safer for both of us."

---

[121] A pulley changes the direction in which something, like a rope, is pulled, which does in fact decrease the amount of exertion needed to lift the object being pulled (in this case, Saige, Oscar, and Dot). You can use multiple pulleys to further decrease the weight of a load. Physics!

"Saige..."

"Didn't you *just* say I was the smartest person in the world? You should trust me."

Oscar smiled. "I said you were the smartest person I'd ever *met*."

"Close enough. Let's do this."

They set it up like this:

Oscar got close enough to the top of the staircase to tie a knot[122] on the banister. He then tied the same knot to Dot's bottommost horizontal bar, just underneath the standing platform (they took off the prop motor and left it aside). He made sure to thread the rope around both sides of the wheelchair, to keep the weight distribution as even as possible. Next, Saige adjusted her hanging weights to be half on her left and half on her right.

"I have approximately fourteen thousand doubts about this," Oscar said as he carefully stepped onto Dot's platform.

"That's about twelve less than I do," Saige said with a chuckle, but before Oscar could question her, she let out a few feet of the rope, and they went barreling toward the top of the staircase.

---

[122] The knot he uses is called a double figure eight fisherman's knot. Neko had taught him how to tie it once. It is sturdy and, when properly tied, won't come undone.

They were teetering[123] right on the edge now, the wheelchair tilted at a stomach-churning angle.

"You have fourteen thousand and twelve doubts?" Oscar shouted over the crashing of the water.

"Yup!" Saige yelled back.

And then she let go of the rope.

Once again, Oscar screamed.

Once again, Saige asked him politely to please stop screaming.

They'd plunged downward about three or four feet, but Dot was miraculously still upright.

"CAN YOU PLEASE GO A LITTLE SLOWER?" Oscar shouted.

"I'M TRYING!" Saige shouted back. "THIS ISN'T EXACTLY EASY. AND LOOK, IT'S WORKING."

"YES, YES, FINE. GOOD JOB, BUT BE CAREFUL!"

Saige let out a little more of the rope, and they glided somewhat more gracefully down another foot. Then another. Then another.

They were about halfway down the staircase when they heard a tremendous *rip*.

Saige froze.

---

[123] Imagine yourself on a seesaw, the exact weight of the companion across from you. If both of you lifted your feet, you would hang somewhere in the middle, gently bouncing up and down. That's basically what it was like for Oscar and Saige now, right at the edge of the stairs.

Oscar twisted his head around to look up at the top of the staircase, and his stomach sunk when he saw what had made the noise.

Part of the banister had lifted up from the floor—

And as Oscar watched, a second part lifted, and the rope slipped—

And the wheelchair plummeted[124] downward.

---

[124] As a general rule, one doesn't want to *plummet* down a waterfall. This meant that they fell. Quickly. One would do much better *gliding* down a waterfall. Or *floating* down a waterfall. But it seems too late for that now.

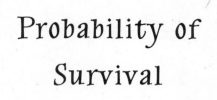

Probability of
Survival

THIS TIME, THEY *BOTH* screamed.

The rope caught about five feet later, and the wheelchair came to a jerking stop. Oscar slipped off the platform and grabbed wildly for something to hold on to, managing to wrap his hand around Dot's right wheel.

"Oscar!" Saige yelled.

"Hurry!" Oscar shouted back. "You have to hurry; let out more rope!"

Oscar's mouth and nose and ears were filling up with water as he struggled to keep his head elevated. He looked downward, but they were still too far from the end of the staircase; if he let go now, he'd be seriously hurt. He tightened his grip on Dot and prayed that Saige could unravel the rope fast enough.

Twenty seconds later, there was another tremendous ripping noise and a third section of the banister pulled up; the rope slid forward and the wheelchair slid with it and they both screamed again, although Oscar's scream was underwater and just came out as a cascade of bubbles.

Oscar inhaled involuntarily and swallowed a mouthful of dirty, freezing-cold water, and then he felt a hand grab his collar. Saige yanked his head up.

"OSCAR!" she screamed.

"FASTER!" he screamed back—or, he *tried* to scream, but it mostly came out as a barking, water-logged cough.

They made it the next few feet in fits and starts, the wheelchair swinging wildly and crashing against the side of the stairway and bouncing up and down. Oscar managed to hold on for most of the way, but finally his fingers slipped and he sank into the rushing, cold water, swept downward even as the banister gave way completely, folding in on itself and finally pulling up completely from the floor. Oscar fell the last ten or so feet down the rest of the staircase and slammed into the water below, only just managing to swim out of the way before Dot crashed directly where his head had just been.

Yes—*swim.*

Because the water down here was much, much deeper. If Oscar had been able to stand, it would have been up to his neck, but he *couldn't* stand, because the water rushing down the stairs created a whirlpool effect, and the churning water sent him spinning around and around, and then Saige's wheelchair was spinning around and around, but *where was Saige?!*

Oscar looked around him frantically even as Dot righted itself and floated calmly away on its inflatable wheel wraps, the backpack still attached to it, the weights all firmly in place.

"SAIGE!" he shouted just as a swirl of water pulled him downward. He came up spitting and gasping for air, and then he saw her, hanging on for dear life, her arms wrapped around the banister at the bottom of the stairs. She was having a hard time keeping her head above water—that was right where the flood was at its most wild, its most dangerous.

Oscar would have to swim through the worst of it to reach her.

He didn't think twice.

He threw his body forward, trying to remember everything Bilius had taught him about swimming.[125]

And it actually worked!

He swam forward a few feet, full of momentum and thrust—

But the churning waters at the bottom of the staircase were

---

[125] Since the Gray Sea had become so polluted, the people of the Alley didn't get many chances to practice their breaststroke. Oscar couldn't remember the last time he had actually been in water like this, and his arms already ached with the effort of staying afloat. He remembered vaguely that his legs should be doing something, too, so he began to kick them in as steady a rhythm as he could manage.

too much for him, and he went under again, tossed about like a broken sailboat on treacherous seas. He heard Mr. Cleverer's voice ringing in his ears:

I don't think I need to express to you how even the strongest of swimmers would hardly stand a chance if their boat capsized a hundred feet from shore. What would have happened to you, Oscar? What would have happened to Saige*?*

What would happen to them?

Oscar knew exactly what would happen to them.

They would both drown here in the basement of the boarded-up aquarium, and nobody would ever find their bodies, because nobody would know where to look.

Oscar was out of time, out of strength, out of chances. The water was too strong for him. He was no match for the churning, swirling flood.

And then he heard another voice.

Saige's voice.

It will be fine, Oscar. You have to take some risks in Burgeoning Bloomrackers or else you'll never get to the final level and rescue the entire city from the evil empire.

The evil empire.

Brawn Industries.

Keeping an entire city perpetually wet and beaten down and storm-ridden just to... what?

Sell more umbrellas?

Make more money?

Was that all the world was about?

Making more money so the rich got richer while everybody else struggled for each skiff they made? Forcing people to buy rain supplies *also* owned by Brawn Industries—rain boots and rain jackets and plastic hats and window savers and flouses, all protection from storms that were *manufactured*???

Not today.

Not if Oscar could help it.

Using a last reserve of strength he wasn't sure he even had, Oscar pushed himself forward. He swam like his life depended on it.[126] He windmilled his arms. He kicked his legs. He took deep breaths and held the air in his lungs, making himself as buoyant as possible.

When he reached Saige, he grabbed her arms and helped hold her afloat. Her eyes were wide and scared.

"How did you *do* that?" she asked, her voice shaky.

"We have to defeat the evil empire," he said.

She nodded. Her lips were a pale shade of blue. Oscar could see Dot, floating in calmer waters just fifteen or twenty feet away from them.

"We're going to swim," he said. "Okay?"

"I don't think I can."

---

[126] And it did.

"I don't think you can, either," Oscar said. "I *know* you can."

Saige nodded again. It was a hesitant nod, like she was trying to convince herself but wasn't quite managing it.

"Here," Oscar continued. "We'll do it side by side. You'll grab on to my neck, and I'll put my arm around your waist. We'll make a human raft."

"Have you rolled for probability of survival?"[127] Saige asked, cracking a thin smile.

"Yeah," Oscar said. "We got a thirty-two."

"But that's the highest roll you can get."

"Exactly."

Saige nodded for a third time, and this nod was more confident.

"Okay," she said. "Let's do this."

Oscar took a deep breath, gathering up every bit of strength he could find in his body. He wrapped his arm around Saige's waist and she put her arm around his neck.

"Use your free arm to paddle and keep us even," Oscar instructed. "I'll kick my legs. Got it?"

"Got it."

Before either of them could change their minds, they let go of the railing.

---

[127] She is referencing Burgeoning Bloomrackers here, in which you often have to roll a die or two to determine the probability of different outcomes.

It was tough going.

There were moments Oscar didn't think it would be possible.

But he refused to give up.

He kicked his legs as hard as he could. He felt Saige tighten her grip around his neck. Inch by inch they crawled forward, skirting the worst of the tumultuous water, keeping close to the hallway walls.

When Oscar finally felt his fingers close around one of the bars of the wheelchair, his heart leapt in his chest. He twisted Dot so the seat was facing them. The water here, away from the bottom of the staircase, was much calmer, and only up to his chest. The problem was that the wheelchair was floating on top of the water, so it would be nearly impossible for Saige to climb into the seat, even if Oscar tried to balance everything and give her a boost.

"Over there," she said, pointing, and Oscar turned to see what he could only describe as a mountain of *stuff* sticking out of the water. It was comprised of old plaques, diagrams, broken models of sea creatures like the orca that had scared him half to death, benches, tables, and a variety of other things that had obviously once been used throughout the aquarium but had now followed the path of the flood and ended up here. "I can crawl up that, if you hold Dot steady," Saige continued.

"Are you sure?"

"I think it's our best option."

Oscar and Saige maneuvered Dot over to the pile of junk and Oscar did his best to hold the wheelchair at a good angle while Saige pulled herself up, putting her knee on the back of a sea turtle as she paused to take a break.

"I did not properly prepare for where this day would take me," she observed.

Oscar snorted. "I don't think I did, either."

With some difficulty and a small avalanche of aquarium garbage later, Saige managed to hop into Dot's seat. She leaned over and hugged one side of it.

"I love you very much, Dot," she said.

"I love you, too," Oscar said, making his voice high and squeaky.

"Is that what you think Dot sounds like?" Saige asked, laughing.

"It felt right."

"Yeah. It does, doesn't it?"

"All right, so, I think the entrance for the tunnel is down this way," Oscar said, pointing down the wide hallway. "Luckily the water is calmer over here."

"But *unluckily*, we've lost the paddle."

"Oh, crap."

"Yeah." Saige leaned forward and started sorting through

the top of the junk pile. She removed a long, flat, skinny fish. "Was this alive once?"

"I have no idea," Oscar said.

"Well. It will work in a pinch. Hop on!"

Oscar took his place on the platform and held on as Saige began paddling down the hallway.

The water rushing down the stairs created a gentle current that helped them along, and in no time at all they reached the end of the hallway. Saige turned right and continued down a second hallway, and at the end of *that* hallway they found the entrance to the tunnel.

There wasn't as much water here, just a foot or so. The tunnel itself had a wide, open entranceway with just three stairs leading down to the start of it. After the staircase they'd just navigated, Oscar felt no anxiety at all about these small steps, and Saige hardly paused before she pushed them over the edge. A gentle *whoosh* later and they were at the beginning of the tunnel.

"Kinda dark down here," Saige said uncertainly.

Oscar removed the flashlight from the inside pocket of his jacket, clicked it on, and pointed it ahead of them.

They both gasped quietly.

The tunnel was about ten feet high by ten feet wide, and it stretched onward in front of them in a seemingly endless expanse. The flashlight's beam ended abruptly after fifteen or so feet, and beyond it, there was only darkness. An abrupt line of darkness.

Just like Frederika had said, the entire tunnel was made of glass. Not that you could see much *beyond* the glass, of course, but when the flashlight's beam fell across it, they could just make out the murky greenish-black water of the Gray Sea.

"Wow," Saige whispered.

"Yeah."

"Creepy."

"Yeah."

"Do you think it's...safe?"

"I mean, it's been here a long time," Oscar said.

"Right. The glass is probably really thick."

"It has to be."

"And what are the chances it would pick *this moment* to crack," she said, struggling to keep her voice light.

"Want me to roll for probability?"

"I think we better just go for it."

And so they went for it.

A Necessary Distraction

IT WAS NOTICEABLY CHILLIER in the tunnel.

There were only a few inches of water on the ground now. Oscar got off the wheelchair's platform and walked beside Saige instead. Each step he took echoed strangely around them. He tried not to look anywhere but straight ahead, because the glass around him was spooky and weird. And he tried not to think about the fact that they were *literally underneath the sea* because, when he did, his heart started to race and his palms grew sweaty.

"That Farsouthian girl," Saige said suddenly, when they'd been in the tunnel for a minute or two. "Eunice. What did she call herself?"

"A Teller," Oscar replied.

"She said she knew about me. How did she know about

me? How did she know you'd find something in my father's study?"

"I have no idea. She said she couldn't really control her visions. And it wasn't like she was out looking for me; she just dragged me into her tent after Gregory and Tim chased me into that weird part of the Night Market."

"And you weren't even going to *go* to the Night Market. But that Farsouthian came into the umbrella shop and spent all that money...Which meant you *could* go..."

"That's right..."

"So some Farsouthian just happens to walk into Buckle Umbrellas and buy all these umbrellas so you could go to the Night Market and then another Farsouthian just *happens* to rescue you from Gregory and Tim, who just *happened* to chase you into this part of the Night Market that nobody has ever heard of before?"

"Well, when you put it like that it sounds kind of weird."

"Oscar, it's *super* weird," Saige exclaimed.

"So what are you suggesting...?"

"I'm suggesting that the Farsouthian who came into your shop was *probably* Eunice!"

"Not tall enough," Oscar said thoughtfully, but then he remembered Eunice's brother, Garner. Hadn't Oscar thought there was something familiar about him? "Her brother. It was her brother!"

"Which meant this was all completely orchestrated—"

"And she knew before she even met me that there was a weather machine—"

"And she must have known enough about you to know that you'd go—"

"But she said she has to have some kind of connection to the person she's trying to do a reading on—"

"And you had never met her before, obviously—"

"But everything she told me was about *you*—"

"And I've never met her before, either! At least I don't think I have," Saige said. She paused. It was impossible to tell how far they had gone. The tunnel disappeared into darkness in front of them and behind them. Oscar tried to keep his breathing calm and even.

"I'm starting to feel a little nervous," he said.

"Me too," Saige admitted. "That's why I started talking about all of this. For a distraction. But then it sort of occurred to me that everything that's happened...Doesn't it just feel a *little* too coincidental?"

"Yeah. It does."

They were quiet.

And then Oscar's flashlight flickered off.

And they found themselves in complete darkness.

Bioluminescence

Oscar DID NOT SCREAM this time.

He found that he was quite screamed out.

He did, however, silently reach over and take Saige's hand.

"Well," Saige said. "This is perfect."

"I just changed the batteries the other week," Oscar said, and hit the flashlight against his thigh a few times. It spluttered back to life for just a second or two, then shut off again and didn't come back on. "Great."

"It's okay," Saige said, and Oscar noted the slight tremor in her voice. "It's fine. It's just straight ahead. We can make it."

"I'll get behind you and push," Oscar said. "Hold the fish out in front of us so we know if we're about to run into a wall or something."

"Okay," Saige said. "Good idea."

Oscar moved behind Dot, gripped its handles, and started to push.

It was incredibly eerie.

Oscar's echoing, splashing footsteps were the only noise. He took steady, deliberate steps and tried to ignore his rising panic. Eventually he closed his eyes, because it didn't make much of a difference to have them open, anyway, and it was easier to keep calm with them closed.

When he heard Saige gasp, he assumed the worst.

He assumed the tunnel had collapsed in on itself.[128]

He braced himself for the water to hit.

But when Saige said, "Oscar, *look*," it did not sound like she was scared of impending water death doom.

It sounded like she was...

Oscar opened his eyes and found himself in the center of Virginia.[129]

The tunnel was alight with sparkling, luminous blue-green orbs that floated and twinkled all around them.

Oscar didn't have words for it.

He couldn't explain it.

"They're alive," Saige said.

---

[128] It didn't occur to him that he might have *heard* something if the tunnel had collapsed in on itself. But sometimes when we are in a state of deep stress, logic takes a back seat.

[129] If you don't remember, Virginia is the name of the solar system Oscar lives in, and of course they weren't *actually* floating out in space—it just looked like that.

Oscar's eyes struggled to make sense of what he was seeing, but gradually the tunnel came back into focus, and it became clear that the glowing pinpricks of light were *outside* the glass, in the Gray Sea itself.

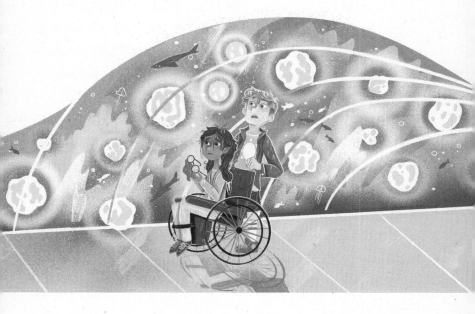

"What do you mean they're *alive*?" Oscar asked.

"It's bioluminescence," she explained. "They're living organisms that produce light to communicate with each other."

"I don't understand."

"Like a firefly," Saige said. "Except these live in the sea."

"Frederika said the Gray Sea was too polluted to sustain life."

"I guess she was wrong. Maybe these guys never come to

the surface. All the way down here, it's possible that people just don't know about them."

"They're . . . *glowing*."

Saige laughed. "Yeah. That's kind of what they do."

For a long time, Saige and Oscar didn't move. They stood as still as statues at the bottom of the sea, in a tunnel that weaved its way across the seafloor, surrounded by tiny creatures that glowed like stars and danced around them like, well, fireflies in the night sky.

Finally, without a word, they continued down the tunnel. The rest of their journey was lit by the soft glow of impossible marine creatures, and when they reached the far side of the tunnel, they were both relieved to find an accessible ramp waiting for them.

"Well *this* would have been nice back in the aquarium," Saige said as she let the air out of her tire wraps, pulled them off, and folded them up. There was no water at all on the ramp, and Saige and Oscar went up side by side.

"Kind of don't want to leave them," Oscar said, glancing back at the tunnel.

"We'll see them on the way back," Saige said.

At the top of the ramp, there were double doors with an old and rusted chain wrapped around the handles. Oscar lifted up the chain weakly, then let it drop.

"Great," he said.

No, there was no way around it—

Making a split-second decision, Oscar turned around and dashed toward the fallen backpack. He grabbed it and pivoted back toward the lighthouse in one movement.

And *that*, my friends, is when the blanderwheel started.[130]

---

[130] Finally!!!

Blanderwheel (Part 5)

O<small>SCAR</small> B<small>UCKLE</small> <small>RAN LIKE</small> his life depended on it.

Because his life *did* depend on it.

Because everybody knew—

You didn't go outside in a blanderwheel.

So Oscar ran.

And ran.

Never mind that he couldn't see more than a foot in front of him.

Never mind that he had no idea where the lighthouse was or where Saige was or where *he* was or where even the *ground* was.

He ran as the skies darkened.

He ran as great bolts of lightning shot across the sky.

He ran as the clouds split open and dumped buckets of rain down over the earth.

He ran as the ground beneath him began to shake and tremble with violent quakes and jolts!!!

The lighthouse must be close now, and he knew he had to reach it or else he'd be swept into the Gray Sea, carried away by the rising waves that were crashing viciously across the small island. Could an entire island flood? Would the lighthouse and Oscar and this tiny outcrop of land end up at the bottom of the sea?

As he continued to run, he thought he heard a voice screaming on the wind...

But then he realized it was *him.*

It was *his* voice.

He was screaming.

And even as he realized that, a wild wail of wind stole his voice away.

Suddenly he could hear nothing except the white noise of the storm.

And then everything went black....

His ears roared with sound.

Was he dead?

No.

You probably couldn't hear things if you were dead.

And he could *feel* things, too.

His cheek and chest and hips were pressed against something hard.

The ground! He had fallen to the ground.

Ouch.

The wind was violent, whipping his hair around his face.

He struggled to open his eyes, to push himself up. He needed to find Saige. He needed to keep going. If he stayed out here in the storm for much longer...

Well. Then he really *might* die.

He managed to get to his hands and knees, but the wind was too strong for him to stand up. It pressed down on him like a physical thing, like a hundred strong hands were pushing against his back.

The closest thing to a blanderwheel in our world is a monsoon.

The last blanderwheel to hit Roan had been three years ago.

The storm had lasted for twenty-three terrifying minutes.

Oscar had been *inside*, of course.

Dove had lost power.

He and Bilius had lit candles and put up their window savers and sat together on the floor of the living room, listening to the roar of the storm outside.

Dove had swayed in the violent winds.[131]

Oscar's heart had beat so fast he could feel it pulsing in his fingertips.

---

[131] Which had been scary, but buildings in Roan were *designed* to sway in heavy winds. Otherwise they might just snap in half.

And still, the next day, after Bilius replaced one of Mrs. Carmichael's shattered windows,[132] he'd said, "That wasn't the worst blanderwheel I've seen."

What would Bilius say about *this* blanderwheel, Oscar wondered as he struggled and failed to pull himself to his feet.

Was *this* the worst blanderwheel Bilius had ever seen?

And where was Bilius now? Was he safe?

What if he had noticed Oscar was gone?

What if he had gone to look for him?

Had Oscar put Bilius in danger?

Oscar could feel himself starting to panic. His strength had been depleted. He collapsed, pressing his cheek into the ground, breathing hard into the dirt.

The backpack had fallen somewhere next to him; he couldn't see it in the darkness.

Why had he gone back for it?

Why hadn't he changed the batteries in the flashlight?

Why hadn't he told Bilius or Neko or Pietra or *anybody* else about the weather machine?

Why did he think he and Saige would be able to stop the biggest company in the entire city?

Oscar thought he might have been crying. But there was so much rain on his face, he couldn't be sure.

---

[132] Despite her window saver!

He lay on the ground for a long time as the rain continued to beat down, turning the dirt to mud and flooding the small island, first by an inch, then two, then three...

The blanderwheel was showing no signs of slowing down.

He hoped Saige had made it to the lighthouse okay.

If she hadn't...

He would never forgive himself.

This was all his fault. Why had he listened to a random Farsouthian in a random part of the Night Market that didn't even *exist*?

Maybe he'd hit his head so hard he'd imagined the whole thing? Maybe Eunice was a figment of his brain-rattled imagination?

Oscar squeezed his eyes shut.

He couldn't keep lying here and spiraling and feeling bad for himself forever. He had to move or he would never be able to. He'd be stuck there in the mud and dirty rainwater forever.

He didn't know where he found the strength.

But he did.

Little by little, inch by inch, he made it onto his hands and knees again.

He had to find that backpack.

Crawling, Oscar made a series of circles, larger and larger, hoping he was covering enough ground. He felt with his hands in the darkness.

And then a *huge* bolt of lightning shot across the sky. And he saw it—

The backpack!

He lunged for it, his fingers closing around one of the straps.

He slipped it onto his back.

He had to get up. *Now.*

Still on his knees, he straightened his torso.

He got one foot on the ground.

Then the other.

Then he straightened his legs, bit by bit, until he had somehow managed to stand.

The storm was all around him.

It consumed everything. It *was* everything. It filled his ears and his eyes and it pressed against every inch of his skin.

The wind was incredible. Oscar had felt a *lot* of wind in his lifetime, and this was unlike anything he'd ever experienced. It smashed against him from every angle, first crashing into his right side, then pummeling his left side, then knocking into his stomach so hard it took his breath away, then pounding his back so strongly he almost folded over.

He forced himself to take a step.

Water sloshed around his ankles, and with each next step he took, he swore he could feel it rising.

Gray Island was flooding.

He wanted to run.

He *tried* to run.

But the wind was just too strong.

Every few seconds, the earth was rattled by a tremendous *boom* of thunder.

The lightning split the sky apart, making everything suddenly so bright that it was hard to focus on anything, hard to get his bearings.

But then—there it was!

The lightning flashed low across the sky to his left, and the dark outline of the lighthouse popped into view.

Oscar corrected course and trudged onward, step by brutal step.

He developed a sort of mantra[133] as he went.

He forced himself to keep his eyes open, to wait for every flash of lightning, to make sure he was still headed in the right direction.

It was nothing short of a miracle when, several grueling minutes later, completely soaked to the bone and shivering uncontrollably, Oscar crashed into something hard and chair-shaped.

It took him a moment to realize what it was.

And then—

---

[133] This meant he repeated, with every single step, "I have to find Saige, I have to find Saige, I have to find Saige."

Dot!

"SAIGE!" he screamed.

"OSCAR!" she screamed back.

"I THOUGHT YOU WERE DEAD!"

"I THOUGHT I WAS DEAD, TOO!"

"ARE WE CLOSE?"

"THIS WAY! IT'S RIGHT HERE!"

Oscar felt Dot move, and he followed as closely as he could, knocking his shins against the wheelchair, squeezing Saige's hand so hard he might have ripped it off.

And then he saw the door.

Right in front of them.

Not even boarded up, just *there*. Saige reached out a hand and pushed it open, and in another moment they were inside a small vestibule, and Oscar had shut the door behind them, and they were ALIVE—somehow they were ALIVE!!!

Oscar dropped to his knees.

His whole body was shaking and he couldn't seem to catch his breath.

It was pitch-black. Outside, the wind howled and the rain fell and the thunder boomed and the walls of the lighthouse shook around them.

"How sturdy do you think this thing is?" Saige asked. Her voice was small and quivering.

Oscar couldn't answer her. He couldn't *breathe*.

"I didn't think I was going to make it," he said finally, once he'd found his voice again.

"I know," she said.

"I just kept thinking that it would have been my fault if anything happened to you. And then I started thinking about my *dad*. What if he went looking for me? And your parents. What if *they* went looking for *you*? What if somebody got hurt? All of this is just a mess, and it's all my fault...."

"Oscar, I found the same stuff in my dad's study that you did. It was *my* decision to come here. And we're okay. We're going to be okay. No matter what we find here, we can wait out the storm. We're safe now."

But the lighthouse groaned around them and the floor vibrated and Oscar couldn't help but feel like they *weren't* safe. Not at all.

"Why didn't I bring a *flashlight*," Saige mumbled. "That's the one thing I forgot."

And then Oscar thought of something!

He searched the pockets of his jacket frantically, just now remembering that the last time he'd worn it, he'd been inside Château Buckle. They'd lost heat for a night and Bilius had lit a fire. Afterward, he'd handed Oscar a book of waterproof[134] matches, telling him to keep them safe and on hand.

---

[134] Obviously any matches produced in Roan were of the waterproof variety.

And *here they were!* Oscar's fingers closed around the small book and he withdrew it from his pocket, ripped off a match, and dragged it against the striker.

The space was tiny, so the small flame lit it well.

"Hi," Oscar said to Saige when her wet, scared face came into view.

"Hi," Saige said. "That's better."

"They only burn for a minute or so," Oscar said. Then, "I think I'm starting to feel a little better."

"You were right behind me, and then you were gone...."

"Your backpack. It fell off the wheelchair. I thought we might need it."

"My backpack," Saige repeated, noticing Oscar wearing it for the first time. "You know, I slept through the last blanderwheel."

"How did you sleep through a blanderwheel?"

"My dad asked me the same thing."

At the mention of her dad, they both fell silent.

The match burned out in Oscar's fingers.

He lit another one.

Then—

"Wait, what is *that*?"

He pointed behind Saige, to the wall opposite the front door. There was nothing on the wall, not a door or a blemish or a sign. Nothing except just one small black box. A keypad.

Oscar moved closer to Saige, throwing more light on it. It

was a standard numerical keypad, and underneath each number were three to four letters, just like on a telephone.

"Um," Oscar said. "You wouldn't happen to know the code...would you?"

"No," Saige replied.

Oscar's heart sunk.

They had made it *so far*. It had never occurred to him that there might be a *code* to get into the lighthouse. There was nothing they could do now. They didn't know how long the code was, so there were, quite literally, an infinite number of possibilities. They would never be able to guess it.

"Let's think," Saige said. "If my dad is the chief engineer, and he's the one with the blueprints in his office, then he must be in charge of all this now. Of the whole weather machine and stuff."

"Maybe."

"Then *he* probably chose the code."

"Maybe."

"So it could be something, like...his birthday!"

Saige entered her father's birthday into the keypad. A small red light flashed once.

"Nope," she said, disappointed.

"Your birthday?" Oscar suggested, just as the match's flame snuffed out.

He lit a new match.

Saige tried, in this order: her birthday, Arthur's birthday, her mother's birthday, and her parents' anniversary.

"Although, I guess it doesn't have to be numerical," she said after each code had prompted flashes of red light. "There are letters, too."

"Try your names," Oscar said.

So Saige tried her name, Arthur's name, her mother's name, and her father's name.

Red. Red. Red. Red.

The third match burned out. Oscar lit a fourth.

"How many of those do you have?" Saige asked nervously.

"A few more. Do you have any other ideas?"

"No. You know how private my dad is."

Oscar thought of Mr. Cleverer's office. How *bare* it had been. Nothing on the walls, very few personal touches. Granted, they hadn't lived in that house all that long, and maybe he had plans to spruce it up later, but...

It was just empty.

The only things in the entire room had been the picture of Saige and Arthur and the picture of the dog.

The dog.

The dog!

The fourth match's flame burned down so low that it singed Oscar's fingers; he yelped and dropped it on the floor, where it extinguished.

"That's it!" he said into the darkness as he fumbled for a fifth match.

"What's it?"

"Scrappy!" Oscar exclaimed.

"What's scrappy?"

"*Who's* Scrappy! Your father's childhood dog!"

"The dog from the picture? On his desk? How do you know its name?"

"It was written on the back!"

"You're a better snoop than I am," Saige said.

Oscar managed to get the match lit with shaking fingers. He punched the following numbers into the keypad: 7272779.

The light flashed green.

And before either of them could say a word, a section of the wall next to the keypad sunk backward, then glided smoothly to the side.

"Ohmygoshwhatishappening," Saige said.

"I believe that is a secret doorway," Oscar replied.

And they stepped into Gray Lighthouse.

Gray Lighthouse

As SMOOTHLY AND SOUNDLESSLY as it had opened, the door slid shut behind them, and at the same time, the lighthouse lit up in a warm, buttery golden-yellow light that spread from the bottom upward in a motion as gentle and seamless as the door.

"Wow," Oscar and Saige whispered.

The space was an odd mix of old and new. There was a spiral staircase that hugged the outermost wall, crawling upward, around and around, until it reached the top. This was made of old, worn-smooth wood and it had a rickety banister and Oscar just knew every stair would hold its own specific *creak*. This was clearly original to the lighthouse, as old as the building itself. What *wasn't* old was the machinery that took up most of the middle of the space. It was shiny and spotless and its base was a perfect circle, leaving about six feet of free space around it. It stretched upward just as high as the staircase, ending at the top. Even now, the machine was alive, in motion. Pistons fired; gears turned; small levers tilted up, then down. The space had a metallic smell to it. The air was charged. Electric.

Everything was quiet.

Saige said, "Have you noticed you can't hear—"

"The storm?" Oscar interrupted. "Yeah. It's creepy."

"The outside walls are original," Saige said thought-fully, taking a step into the space. "And the inside walls, too, that brick...But you see there, on the far wall, that slightly disturbed area? My guess is that someone disassembled the entire interior, insulated it, then carefully built it up again."

Saige, of course, had always wanted to be an architect, so of course she would notice a detail like that. And she *also* noticed—

"That square, there, of wood. With the ropes attached. That's for hauling heavy equipment up to the top floor. That's how I can get up there."

"Wait...did I just hear you right?" Oscar asked. "You want to get onto a tiny, four-by-four square of wood and have me...*pull you through the air*?"

"Yup. It's perfect. Obviously I would have preferred an elevator, but this is the next best thing."

"The *next best thing*? Saige, suppose for a minute that I was even *strong enough* to lift you—"

"Pulleys," she said calmly.

"What?"

"There are pulleys. Actual ones this time. You see how the ropes crisscross their way up the length of the space? That platform is designed so one person can lift really heavy things by themselves. You'll be fine."

"And if I *drop you*?"

"Oh gosh, please don't," she said seriously. "I'd definitely die."

"Saige, this is a terrible idea," Oscar said.

"If you give me a minute, I'm sure I can recount all the terrible ideas each of us has had in the past few weeks," Saige deadpanned.

"Right."

"Climb those stairs. I'll get myself on."

"We should secure Dot, at least. Do you have any more rope in here?"

Oscar was still holding Saige's backpack, and he lifted it higher now. Saige actually snorted. "Do I have any more rope," she repeated, chuckling to herself as she pulled more rope out of the backpack.

"Right," Oscar said. "Should have known."

He zipped up the backpack and hung it on the back of

the wheelchair, then followed Saige as she went over to the wooden platform and got herself situated in the middle of it. The platform had four metal hooks, one at each corner, clearly designed for securing cargo. Oscar used these to tie Dot down, looping the rope around and through the hooks and finally tying everything up with another double figure eight fisherman's knot.

"Are you absolutely, positively, super incredibly sure about this?" he said when he was done.

Saige looked him dead in the eyes. Her mouth was set in a thin, straight line. "Yes," she said.

Oscar knew better than to argue with her.

He nodded, double-checked his knot, then walked over to the bottom of the spiral staircase and began climbing up.

Truth be told, the spiral staircase made him a little dizzy.

Gray Lighthouse was, Oscar knew from school, three hundred and twelve feet high. It had been designed and built eighty-three years ago by an architect named Florence Perchance.

Oscar had always liked that name.

Florence Perchance.

The lighthouse contained three hundred and forty-eight steps, and by step thirtysomething, Oscar was out of breath.

"This is not as easy as it looks!" he shouted down to Saige, who was waiting for him with a rather bored expression on her face.

"Totally," she called back. "Probably easier than agreeing to be hauled into the air on a wooden platform not designed for human use, though."

Oscar grumbled to himself.

He kept climbing.

Around the one hundredth stair,[135] Oscar had to stop and massage a stitch in his side.

At stair two hundred and something, he let himself sit down for thirty seconds. He put his head between his knees and took deep, filling breaths.

At stair three hundred–ish, he made the terrible mistake of looking over the railing at the floor beneath him.

The floor *so very, very far* beneath him.

"Are you almost there?" Saige shouted. She was blocked by the machinery and Oscar couldn't currently see her.

"Almost," he called back weakly.

He looked up.

There weren't that many stairs left now, but still, Oscar struggled to get his legs to cooperate. They simply didn't want to do what he had told them to do. They seemed to have other ideas entirely, and their ideas mostly sounded like *Stop moving forever.*

Still, he won in the end, and he began his slow crawl up the remainder of the stairs.

---

[135] This was a complete guess; he had given up counting at sixty-three.

Oscar had never considered himself to be wary of heights, but at the top of the staircase, he found that he didn't love looking down. The floor was so far beneath him and the platform he stood on was so insubstantial in comparison. There was a door to his right that he assumed led to the rest of the lighthouse, the tippy-top, where the actual light would have been.[136] In front of him was a square-shaped hole that allowed the wooden platform to be raised flush with the rest of the floor. The end of the rope was tied off on a metal hook in front of him.

"Oy!" Saige called up. "Are you ready?"

Aside from being a little dizzy and a little out of breath and a little skeptical of this entire plan, Oscar was completely exhausted. He wasn't sure he was physically able to lift anything much heavier than a pencil.

But he had to try.

He had made it this far.

Carefully, he unwound the rope from its hook. He gave a gentle tug—

And was surprised to find it was *much* lighter than he expected.

He chanced a look over the low railing. Saige was giggling.

"That took me by surprise!" she shouted.

---

[136] Before it was replaced by a weather machine, that is.

"Are you okay?"

"Totally fine! Keep going!"

Just like Saige had said, the pulleys made the load *very* light. Oscar was able to slowly and surely raise Saige and Dot through the air. His arms started to ache when they were about halfway up, but it wasn't anything he couldn't handle.

Every few pulls, he paused to carefully wrap the rope around its hook. This was for two reasons: One, it kept the rope neat and out of the way, and two, if something happened and

Oscar were to *drop* the rope, the hook would catch it and Saige would be fine.

He gave the rope a few more pulls, paused to wind the excess, then peeked over the balcony again. Saige was pretty close now.

"You okay?" he asked again.

"Fine," she said. "It's a great view from up here."

Saige and her love of heights.

Oscar smiled to himself and gave the rope another pull.

The closer Saige got to the platform, the heavier the load felt. Oscar wasn't sure if it was because he was tired or if it was because of physics,[137] but he took no chances, wrapping the rope around the hook after every pull now.

"Almost there!" Saige sang. She was just six or seven feet away from the platform now, and Oscar heaved with all his strength. Three more pulls and she slid easily through the hole in the floor.

Oscar tied the rope off, smiled widely, and said, "Wow. I can't believe that actually worked."

"Easy-peasy!" Saige said.

"Well, not *super* easy," Oscar said, showing her his hands, which were quite red and blistery from the rope.

"Sorry," Saige said, wincing. "But on the bright side, you didn't kill me!"

---

[137] It was both!

"That was a big goal of mine," he said, still smiling as he knelt down and began to untie the ropes that secured Dot to the platform.

"I had a long time to think when I was floating through the air," Saige said thoughtfully, rolling up the rope as Oscar untied it. "And I realized that we've never actually talked about what we're *doing* here."

"Oh," Oscar said. "I guess you're right."

"I mean, I just assumed we'll be sabotaging the weather machine?"

"Yeah," Oscar said. "I think we kind of have to."

"Right, right. And we should find some kind of proof, too. Something that we can show everybody in the Alley. Something that will prove Brawn Industries has been controlling the weather. For *years*."

Oscar finished untying the rope and Saige wound the remaining length into a neat oval and slipped it into her backpack. Oscar stood up and the two friends looked at each other. Now that the scary bit was done with and Saige was safely on the platform with him, Oscar felt cautiously optimistic.

"This is actually going to work," he said.

"Yeah," Saige said, smiling. "It is."

And that is when they heard someone clear their throat.

They looked over the balcony to see...

Mr. Cleverer.

Even from this height, they could see that his face was red and he looked very, very angry.

"Now you two just stay right there," he said. His voice was calm and quiet and even but somehow managed to crawl up the entire height of the lighthouse, as clear as if he was standing right next to them. "I'd like to come up and have a conversation with you."

"Saige," Oscar said as Mr. Cleverer strode to the bottom of the staircase. "Um. I think we need to—"

"Go!" Saige interrupted.

So they went.

The Weather Machine

THE ONLY PLACE TO go was through the door right next to them, so Oscar threw it open and he and Saige bolted through and closed it behind them. Lights clicked on to illuminate the space as Oscar scrambled for something to block the door.

"Here!" Saige said, handing him the crowbar. Oscar took it and fit it through the door's handle. Mr. Cleverer wouldn't be able to open it from the outside now, unless...

"Do you think he'll break the whole thing down?" Oscar asked.

"Yeah," Saige said without hesitating. "I do. So we need to hurry."

They turned around at the same time, facing the space in front of them.

"Holy smokes," Oscar said.

There was a short ramp here that spiraled gently upward to the top of the lighthouse. Oscar could tell where the enormous light had once been, but the space had been gutted and replaced with, as he had seen on the blueprints, a series of cannon-like objects that were all connected to a central mechanism. These cannons extended outward through perfectly sized holes in the walls of the lighthouse.

"Something in here must produce whatever they use to control the weather," Saige said, rushing up the ramp. "Then the cannons shoot the mixture into the atmosphere."

"What could do something like that?" Oscar asked, following Saige. "What could change the weather?"

"Historically, this entire area has tended toward the wet side, anyway," Saige said, speaking quickly, maneuvering around the small space to examine the central machine. "Before the rain got *really* bad, it was still rainy, like, sixty percent of the time. So it probably wouldn't be that hard to increase that number. You're already starting from a place of rain. It would be another thing entirely to make, say, a *desert* rainy. They could be using any number of things here. Potassium chloride, magnesium, sodium chloride. Maybe they're supercharging the clouds themselves, adding more moisture directly into them. I'm not sure, but whatever it is, it's clearly working."

"You really *are* the smartest person in the world."

Saige smirked. "I thought you said I was the smartest person you've ever *met*."

"You've just been upgraded."

"That works for me. Aha!"

Oscar jogged over to her, to see what she'd found.

There was a little metal door in the machinery. Saige removed it now, revealing a complicated-looking control panel with—

"A kill switch!" Saige exclaimed.

"What's a kill switch?"

"It will turn off the machine!"

"Do it!" Oscar exclaimed. "Qui—"

The word he had been trying to say was *quick*, but he didn't get to finish, because at that exact moment, there was a tremendous *BOOM* as the door to the room exploded inward. Oscar was knocked backward off his feet, and Dot was rocked sideways, crashing into the wall of the lighthouse.

Plaster and dust and dirt rained down from the ceiling. Oscar's ears were ringing. Had Mr. Cleverer just SET OFF A BOMB?

"Saige?" Oscar said, his voice weak and raspy. In the haze of the space, he reached out for her wheelchair, struggling to find her.

"I'm all right," she said, her own voice thin and scared.

"Did your dad just try to kill us?" Oscar said as his hand finally landed on Dot. He pulled himself over to Saige, sitting up so he was looking into her dust-streaked face.

"I did *not* try to kill you," Mr. Cleverer's voice rang out. "The idea is quite preposterous."

"You just *blew us up*," Saige squeaked.

"I blew up the *door*. I just want to talk with you."

"If you wanted to talk to us you might have KNOCKED!" Saige screamed.

"An excellent point," Oscar piped up.

"Instead you just skipped right to BLOWING UP THE DOOR," Saige continued. "Which, you know, basically translates into you TRYING TO KILL US."

"I have already explained that I did not try to kill you," Mr. Cleverer said. His voice was strained now, like he was trying to keep his temper.

"Sorry, but I'm *super* not into trusting the word of someone who's just tried BLOWING HIS DAUGHTER UP!"

"Saige, this has gotten completely out of hand. I'm sorry for blowing up the door. At the time, I felt it necessary—"

"Just like you felt it necessary to keep the people of Roan under constant *rain* for the past ten years?!"

"I've only been working for Brawn Industries for the past few weeks; *please*, Saige, let's talk about this reasonably."

"Officially," Saige said.

"What?" Oscar asked.

Mr. Cleverer went quiet.

"He's only *officially* been working for Brawn Industries for a few weeks," Saige explained. "In reality, he's been doing contract work for them for *years*. How did they put it? On a trial basis? You'd be brought on full-time once they knew you could be trusted?"

Mr. Cleverer cleared his throat. "How did you…"

"Oscar found the secret drawer in your desk, but what he *didn't* find was the loose floorboard in the back corner of the room. You've been helping maintain this machine for a long time now, haven't you, Dad?"

"Saige, I can explain…"

"It makes sense, though. Brawn Industries would never pull a nobody out of the Alley and give them a mansion in Roan Piers after a couple of interviews."

"Why didn't you tell me this before now?" Oscar whispered.

"Because I was *embarrassed*," Saige said, and when she looked over at Oscar, she had tears in her eyes. "He's been working for the enemy for years. And he's my *dad* and I *love* him and I thought there was a chance this was all a big mis-understanding, but clearly it's *not*!"

Saige burst into tears. All the anger seemed to drain from her body, leaving only a deep sadness behind.

The air was clearing in the small room, and Mr. Cleverer was slowly coming into focus. As Oscar watched, he took a step toward them.

"Don't move," Oscar exclaimed. "Don't move, or we'll hit the kill switch!"

Mr. Cleverer froze.

"Let's all relax and talk about this calmly," he said.

"How could you do this?" Saige said. "You're my *dad*." She was crying harder now, fat tears falling fast down her cheeks.

"Saige...," Mr. Cleverer said. "Sweetheart...I can explain everything. I promise. Please...Please just come with me to the elevator, we'll get inside, we'll go home, and we'll talk about everything."

"Wait," Oscar said. "There's an *elevator*?"

"Of course there's an elevator." Mr. Cleverer sighed, sounding a bit like he was losing his patience. "You think we renovated an entire eighty-year-old lighthouse and didn't put an elevator in?"

"That's it!" Saige said.

"But you took the stairs," Oscar mumbled. Then, to Saige, he asked, "Wait, what do you mean *that's it*? What's it?"

"The dimensions don't add up," Saige said, sniffing loudly, pulling herself together. "The ramp over there is wider than the space over here, which would mean the lighthouse is lopsided, but it *isn't*, it's perfectly symmetrical, because Florence Perchance would never have built an asymmetrical lighthouse. Which means—there's a hidden room! Quick, Oscar, the kill switch! Hit it!"

Oscar didn't hesitate.

He leapt toward the kill switch and pounded his palm against it.

There was a terrible noise.

The room was filled with it—gears grinding to a halt, metal on metal, a shrieking, angry, crunching sound. Oscar covered his ears with his hands even as Saige grabbed his arm and pushed him forward, through a small door that, like the main entrance, had blended seamlessly into the wall around it. Saige came in after him and the door shut automatically behind her. Without missing a beat, she picked up a desk lamp and smashed it into a control panel next to the door. The control panel sparked and whined, then finally went dark.

"He won't be able to get in this way," Saige said. "Come on, we need to hurry."

"I think I need just one quick second to stop my heart from exploding," Oscar said. He took a deep breath, then looked around the small room they were in. It was skinny and long, and the outside wall fit the curvature of the lighthouse. There was a desk, a now-broken desk lamp, a tall filing cabinet, a blackboard filled with complicated equations and unreadable chicken scratch, and, at one of the skinny ends of the room, the entrance to a small elevator.

"Of course," Saige said. "An office. Look—we need proof, Oscar. We can't leave here without solid, irrefutable[138] proof. I'll take the desk."

Suddenly the door shook—Mr. Cleverer must have thrown his entire weight against it. Oscar and Saige looked at each other for half a second and then leapt into action.

Oscar searched the filing cabinet as Saige took the desk.

He found a lot of things that would have been convincing but not, as Saige had specified, irrefutable.

There were receipts for different pieces of equipment, lumber, and supplies. There were invoices to dozens of different contractors. There were fifteen separate receipts for screws *alone*.

"I don't understand," Oscar said, holding up a stack of these receipts. "Why would they order the same exact screws from so many different people? There's like, fifty from this person, twenty from this person..."

"An abundance of caution," Saige said. "So nobody in Roan could have figured out what they were doing. This is virtually untraceable. And *completely* useless to us. Keep looking!"

---

[138] This meant proof so good that *nobody* would be able to argue with it, like a piece of paper that said, "I'm Mr. Cleverer and I'm guilty!"

Mr. Cleverer kept pounding on the door and then—abruptly—stopped.

Oscar and Saige froze.

"He could be setting up another bomb," Saige said.

"In this small space? That would kill us!" Oscar exclaimed.

"I know."

"Do you really think—"

"I don't *know*," Saige said, her voice tight and scared. "I don't think I know him at all."

And that is when they became aware of a beeping sound on the other side of the door.

A beeping that sounded suspiciously like...

A countdown.

"Oscar!" Saige shouted. "Abort mission! We have to go!"

But at that exact second, Oscar's hand closed around a piece of paper. Not pausing to double-check what he had just read, he shoved it into his pocket, dove across the room, and hit the button for the elevator.

It took an eternity[139] for the doors to open.

The whole time they had to listen to the beeping sound outside the door. When the elevator doors slid open, they scrambled inside. The doors shut behind them and the

---

[139] About three seconds.

elevator began its descent and for a few seconds everything was quiet and peaceful—

Then they heard a tremendous *BOOM* from above them. The elevator shuddered violently, stopped moving, went completely dark, then plunged downward.

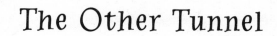

The Other Tunnel

It was a strange feeling, Oscar noted.

Dying.

It was a strange feeling indeed.

It was sudden, and quiet, and pitch-black, and heavy, and ears-ringing, and throat-thick, and soft-orange light, and sharp-pain-in-side, and eyes-bleary, and face-hurting, and arm-maybe-broken—

"Oscar, *answer me!*"

It was nice, at least, Oscar thought, to have Saige with him in the world of the dead. It was lucky they had patched things up between them. It would have been horrible to be alone.

"Oscar, ANSWER ME!"

"Oh, actually, please don't yell at me," Oscar moaned. "I'm just going to need a minute to get used to being dead."

"Right, that's the thing, though—we're NOT dead," Saige insisted. "We only dropped five or ten feet or something before the emergency brakes kicked on."

"Wait...are you sure?"

"I'm sure," Saige said. "You were knocked to the ground but Dot is heavier; she didn't move that much at all. I think you...Oscar, I think you broke your arm."

Oscar attempted to move his left arm and was met with a stomach-churning jolt of pain.

You probably didn't feel pain if you were dead, he thought.

"Ouch."

"Can you stand?"

"I think my arm is broken."

"Yeah, I noticed. Oscar, I think you need to try and stand up. We have to get out of here before my dad catches up to us."

Oscar nodded, and his head instantly swam with bright lights and sparks of pain. He gritted his teeth and shakily pulled himself up to a sitting position.

"That looks really bad," Saige said, eyeing his arm.

"It *feels* really bad," he replied through gritted teeth.

"Here—"

Saige reached into her backpack, fumbled around inside it, and pulled out a big, square silk scarf. She folded it into a triangle and tied it around Oscar's neck, and then, moving carefully, they guided Oscar's broken arm into it. It was the perfect makeshift sling.

"I understand the crowbar and the bolt cutters," Oscar said, forcing a smile, "but a silk scarf?"

"I sort of panicked at the end of my packing and just threw a bunch of stuff in here. But it came in handy!"

Something in the elevator made a sick, groaning sound. Oscar looked around him warily. "Do you think we're stuck?"

"I do. But *hopefully* we're close enough to the ground that we can jump. Ugh—if only we still had my crowbar."

"It's okay," Oscar said. "We can do it together. My right arm and both of yours."

"Are you sure you can?"

"It doesn't matter if I *can*. I *have* to."

He used Dot to pull himself to his feet. The world tilted dangerously on its side and he fell backward into the wall.

"Oscar!"

"I'm fine. I'm fine. Come on."

Oscar crammed the fingers of his right hand into the crack between the elevator doors. The skin on his fingers burned as he scraped it, but he managed to make the slightest crack, enough for Saige to fit both of her hands in, too. Gritting his teeth, Oscar pulled as hard as he could while Saige tugged in the opposite direction.

And little by little, they opened the doors wide enough

that Oscar could stand between them, using his legs to push them open the rest of the way.

They were only about two feet from the ground, on the opposite side of the floor from the main entrance. Oscar jumped down nimbly, just as Mr. Cleverer appeared at the top of the staircase.

"Are you *kidding* me?" Oscar shrieked as he looked around for something to fashion into a ramp for Saige's wheelchair.

He needn't have worried, though, because she crashed down next to him a second later.

"Saige!"

"Ouch," she said. "I'm okay! Dot's okay! Let's go!"

They started to make their way toward the main door, back to the vestibule with the keypad, back outside across the small island, back to the aquarium tunnel—but then Oscar spotted *another* door.

It was slightly ajar. He pushed it open and found a ramp that led downward to a second tunnel. This one was clean and dry and lit by rows of orderly yellow lights.

"Saige, look—this must be how your dad got to the lighthouse!" Oscar exclaimed.

There was even a flamingo cart[140] in the tunnel. Oscar ran down the ramp and started searching it for keys.

---

[140] In our world, a flamingo is, of course, a bright pink bird. In Oscar's world, flamingo is a game that is fairly similar to our golf. Much like golf, flamingo is played over long distances, hence the need for a cart!

"Oscar, quick!" Saige shouted, coming down the ramp and situating herself in the middle of the tunnel. "Get on Dot's platform!"

"Get on the platform? Saige, we need to *move*! Can you hot-wire[141] this thing?"

"This seems to be a really good time to tell you that in addition to making a prop engine for Dot, I *also* made a jetpack."

"You made a—I'M SORRY, WHAT?"

"Look—I told you—I've had a lot of time on my hands, okay?! I don't have any friends in Roan Piers yet and school won't start for weeks and I can only play with Arthur so much! Now GET ON!"

It did not make sense how the backpack held the contraption that Saige pulled out of it now. It was a small, complicated-looking motor, smaller than the prop engine, with a harness on it that she quickly fixed over Oscar's shoulders. He winced terribly when it accidently hit his left arm.

"Sorry, sorry, sorry," she said, pulling the straps tighter.

"Is this safe?"

"My father keeps setting off bombs," she hissed.

"Right. Point taken. Let's go!"

---

[141] If anyone could start a vehicle without having the vehicle's keys, it was Saige.

Oscar hopped onto the platform, Saige turned around and pressed a button on the side of the jetpack, and—

They were off.

I mean, they were *really, really* off.

Dot and Oscar and Saige shot down the tunnel like a bullet.

Aside from a bit of warmth on his back, the jetpack was really quite comfortable.

Once Oscar got used to the sensation, it was even... enjoyable.

And it honestly helped take his mind off the terrible throbbing ache of his broken arm.

They must have been going twenty-five or thirty miles per

hour, a steady pace that wouldn't have worked had the tunnel been anything but completely straight. Saige couldn't really steer the wheelchair at all. If she had tried to grab the hand-rims, she would have burned the skin off her palms.

"Where do you think this lets out?" Oscar shouted over the wind.

"Judging by the trajectory of this tunnel in comparison to the other tunnel . . . I don't think it lets out anywhere good."

"What do you mean?"

"I think we're headed toward the Brawn Industries factory. They must have built this tunnel for easy access to the lighthouse."

Oh.

Yeah.

That made sense.

And Saige was right.

It wasn't anywhere good at all.

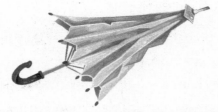

Brawn Industries

"THE GOOD THING," SAIGE said as they continued down the tunnel, "is that it's a Saturday. Hopefully the factory will be mostly empty."

"You mean hopefully we won't arrive to an army of Brawn guards waiting to haul us off to an underground prison in the middle of the Distant Ocean[142] with no hope of escape or parole?"

"Yes, Oscar," Saige said. "That's exactly what I'm hoping for."

Oscar could practically feel Saige roll her eyes at him, and that made him smile, but his smile quickly turned into a wince, because his arm hurt *a lot*.

---

[142] The proper name for the Distant Ocean is actually the Dennimeyer Ocean, but those in Roan call it the more poetic Distant Ocean because it is, to be fair, pretty far away.

If he took a moment to pull back from himself, to see himself and Saige and Dot from an aerial view, he saw two frightened kids riding a modified jetpack wheelchair through a futuristic underground tunnel that would lead them directly into the arms of an enemy that had been controlling the weather in their city for years and years and years.

Oscar's heart skipped a beat, and he leaned closer to Saige and shouted into her ear, "I think I might be having a bit of a panic attack."

"This is not the best place to have one of those," Saige shouted back.

And Oscar knew that, but somehow it did nothing to help.

After a few more minutes of traveling down the tunnel, Oscar became aware of a light at the end of it.[143]

"Do you see that?" he asked Saige.

"It's the end," Saige said. "Get ready to press that button when I tell you to, okay?"

Oscar found the button with his right hand and rested his finger on it until Saige shouted—"NOW!"—then he pressed it, turning off the jetpack. Dot's speed decreased gradually, until finally they were going slowly enough that Saige was

---

[143] The irony of seeing a literal "light at the end of the tunnel" did not escape him, and he probably would have laughed under different circumstances.

able to grab the handrims and bring the wheelchair to a safe, gentle stop in front of a large door at the end of the tunnel.

"I really wasn't convinced we were going to survive that," Oscar admitted as he hopped down from the platform.

"Me neither!" Saige said brightly. "It's a nice surprise, though."

Oscar laughed, because, yes, surviving *was* a nice surprise.

What *wasn't* a nice surprise was the tunnel door opening suddenly and no less than ten people in smart suits and sensible shoes filing out of it, surrounding Oscar and Saige and offering them absolutely no hope of escaping.

"If you try anything funny, we will be forced to use force," a tall man with a handlebar mustache said.

"You'll be forced to use force?" Saige repeated. "Well, we'd hate to force you into feeling forced to use force."

"Saige, it is perhaps *not* the right time to be antagonistic,"[144] Oscar hissed.

"You are both very funny children, I'm sure," said a woman with a tall beehive-like hairdo. "Now, are you going to come quietly, or are we going to have to try something different?" She pulled two syringes out of her suit jacket and held them up to the light. They were filled with a red liquid that

---

[144] This meant that Saige was being hostile and rude to these people (even though, to be fair, they deserved it).

seemed to swirl and shimmer. Both Saige and Oscar pressed their lips together.

Mustache placed himself behind Dot, taking control of the wheelchair, as Beehive put her hand on Oscar's right shoulder and guided him through the doors. There were four people leading the way, then Saige and Oscar and Mustache and Beehive, then four people bringing up the rear.

The group walked through the inner labyrinth of the Brawn Industries factory, passing many closed doors and winding corridors. Every so often Oscar caught a glimpse of something through a window or an open door—a series of cages, a row of Erlenmeyer flasks filled with neon-green liquid, a bookcase crammed with five-foot-tall books, a large vat of something noxious and bubbling.[145]

Oscar's stomach was in absolute knots, his arm was pounding in the sling, and he was finding it difficult to breathe.

Eventually the group reached an elevator. Oscar saw that they were on basement level four, and that made him feel claustrophobic and heavy. When the elevator doors slid shut and trapped them all inside, he found that he couldn't hold his weight anymore. He sunk down to his knees. Beehive squeezed his shoulder harder and said, "Get up."

---

[145] Almost definitely poisonous.

"Leave him alone," Saige spat. "He's having a panic attack."

Oscar didn't think he was having a panic attack; it was more likely that he was having a total system failure. His palms were sweaty and his breathing was even more labored now and his heart was slamming against his rib cage painfully. His left arm hurt so much he had the irrational thought that he should just rip it off his body completely.

Then there were hands under both of his armpits and he thought someone actually *was* ripping his arm off his body, that was how intense the pain was, and he was hauled to his feet and half led, half dragged out of the elevator and down another hallway. Saige was screaming from somewhere behind him and he was dipping in and out of consciousness, aware of nothing except pain and pain and pain forever, and then there was a booming, impossibly loud voice he recognized but couldn't place except it made him feel safe and at ease and although he tried to open his eyes, he found he couldn't, and aside from that, he felt blackness creeping in from every angle, a warm, comforting, velvet-soft blackness that finally reached his heart and, with a firm, gentle caress, pulled him into its embrace.

The Sun

THE FIRST THING OSCAR became aware of was something warm and soft on his face. It was a feeling he didn't find familiar at all, and he would have described it almost like water pooling softly over his skin, except he didn't feel particularly wet. He tried to move his hand, to touch his face, but he was met with a sharp pain. Oh. Right. His broken arm. So he tried to move his other hand and he found that someone was holding it in place. Oh. Right. They were being held captive.

Neither of those things explained, though, how warm and comfortable[146] and *nice* he felt.

---

[146] Aside from the broken arm.

"Are you awake?" Saige asked, her voice quiet but close to him.

"No," he mumbled.

Saige laughed at that, and Oscar had to admit, he found it a little strange that she was laughing, given their current circumstances.

"Can you open your eyes?" she asked.

"No," he repeated.

"Come on, Oscar," she said. "Try."

So he did try, and with some difficulty he managed to open both his eyes to small slits. He was instantly accosted by a bright, burning light.

"Ow," he said. "Can you turn off that lamp?"

"It's not a lamp," Saige said, and her voice was almost... giddy? "Oscar, open your eyes. It's the sun!"

The Sun the Sun the Sun

It took Oscar's eyes some time to adjust to the brightness around him, but when they finally did, he forgot about the pain in his arm, the panic in his chest, the terror of the past few hours. He sat up slowly. Someone kept their hand on his back, gently supporting him. He looked up.

Up at the blue skies.

Up at the puffy white clouds.

Up at the bright, yellow, burning sun.

The sun.

The sun.

The *sun*.

Irrefutable Proof

"IT'S A BEAUTIFUL THING, isn't it?" said a new voice. Not Saige. The hand on Oscar's back patted him tenderly and Oscar turned his head to the side and felt his mouth drop open when he saw—

"Neko!"

"Whoa, whoa, calm down there, small friend," Neko said, because Oscar had tried to throw his arms around Neko's neck, forgetting once again about his broken appendage. He looked down at it now and found that it was still tucked safely and securely into the sling.

"I broke my arm," Oscar said.

"Yes," Neko said. "You did. But we'll take you to the doctor soon, and you'll be right as rain in no time."

"Rain," Oscar repeated. "It's *not raining,* Neko!"

"I think he hit his head," Saige explained. "He fell over in the elevator."

"And those people dragged me out…those people… NEKO, BRAWN INDUSTRIES IS EVIL AND THEY'VE BEEN CONTROLLING THE WEATHER! WE HAVE TO STOP THEM!"

Oscar launched himself sideways off what ended up being the bed of Neko's truck, and upon crashing to the ground,[147] he became aware of a few things all at once.

One: He and Saige were no longer being held captive.

Two: Bilius was just a dozen or so feet away, talking to a number of functionaries of the Roan Assistance Bureau.[148]

Three: The ten people in suits, including Mustache and Beehive, were nowhere in sight.

Four: Saige's wheelchair was damaged, with one wheel tilted inward at an angle that made Oscar's stomach hurt.

"Dot…," he said.

"She's been through a lot," Saige said, but then she smiled. "Don't worry. Nothing I can't fix."

Oscar let Neko help him to his feet.

His head was slowly un-fogging.

His heart was slowly un-freaking-out.

---

[147] Thankfully on his right side.

[148] The closest comparison to the Roan Assistance Bureau (RAB for short) in our world would be police officers, although the RAB do not carry weapons. Individuals of the RAB are elected by public vote and are called functionaries.

He looked upward again.

"We stopped the machine," he said.

"As soon as the blanderwheel ended, your father called me and we set out in my truck to find you. Bilius was worried sick," Neko said. "We drove all around the Toe and were just about to head north, past the Wall, when we noticed something strange...a number of identical black, fancy-looking cars all making a beeline for the factories. Something told me to follow them. So we did. And we waited here, out of sight, while they went into Brawn Industries. And just a few minutes later...you came out."

"You passed out," Saige explained helpfully. "I think it was the combination of extreme pain, exhaustion, and your panic attack. It would have been a lot for anyone to handle. When the suits saw Neko and Pietra and your dad—"

"Pietra's here?" Oscar interrupted.

"She's around the back with some more RAB."

"And where are all the Brawn employees? Were they arrested?"

"They booked it," Saige said. "Just dropped us and ran back into the building."

"Someone needs to go get them!"

"There's not a single trace of them," Neko said gravely, shaking his head. "The RAB said it's like they all vanished."

"They must have more tunnels...," Oscar said. "They

could lead *anywhere*. Neko, the RAB need to search the building!"

"They're taking care of it, Oscar," Neko promised.

At that moment, Bilius noticed that Oscar was awake. He hurried over to his son and, as gently as he could, embraced Oscar, kissing the side of his face.

"My boy," he said. "I was so scared when I woke up and you weren't there."

"I'm sorry, Dad," Oscar said. "But we had to find the weather machine! Mr. Cleverer, he and Brawn Industries—"

"Saige told us everything," Bilius said, putting a hand on Oscar's chest to calm him down. "We believe you. And I'm sure the assistance bureau will find irrefutable proof that—"

"Irrefutable proof!" Oscar shouted.

"Sorry?"

"His head," Saige said apologetically, but Oscar shushed her, then shoved his hand into his pocket.

"I totally forgot!" he said. "You know, probably because Saige's dad almost blew us up and then our elevator plummeted to the ground and I broke my arm and then we attached a jetpack to Saige's wheelchair and then we were captured by ten people in suits and—"

"Oscar, move it along," Saige said.

Oscar pulled a piece of badly crumpled paper out of his pocket.

He unfolded it.

He smoothed it out against his leg.

And then he read it aloud.

This is what it said:

Angus,

Your point is well taken. Believe me, I haven't gleaned any joy in prolonging the process of your official appointment, but you must understand how sensitive these things can be.

I did, however, mean what I said. Your point is well taken.

We will begin preparations for your promotion immediately.

Your family will, of course, be moved to Roan Piers. I am sure the accommodations will be to your liking.

Please await further details of your security briefing, but it will include taking full control over Project Gray and, yes, that includes the *lighthouse itself. Your work over the past six years has been exemplary. Rainfall has increased twenty-eight percent in the past three years alone. I know you will continue to do good work, and with the additional security clearance, it should be less of a headache for you.*

As to your query regarding scheduling the upcoming blanderwheel—you're quite right. It has been a while since the last one, and I think we are well deserved for another. Just let me know the date you choose so I can make sure to stay out of the Toe that day!!

I don't need to tell you to destroy this letter in the usual manner.

> *With regards,*
> *Dominious Brawn*

Angus was, of course, Mr. Cleverer's first name.

And Dominious Brawn, as you might have guessed, was the head of Brawn Industries.

Oscar lowered the letter.

"I would say that's irrefutable," Saige said. "And they

should search my house as well. My father's study. They'll find a lot of interesting things in there."

Bilius took the letter from Oscar. "This stationery...it's official Brawn Industries letterhead. It would be near impossible to fake. Why would Angus have kept this?"

"Pride," Saige retorted immediately. "He finally got what he wanted. Promoted to an official position. He would have wanted to save that forever."

Bilius nodded, then said, "There have been whispers about Brawn Industries for years, of course, rumors and tall tales, but...I never imagined I would actually be holding proof of their involvement in all of this."

"Ten years..." Neko said. "I just can't wrap my head around it."

"It will take some time, I imagine," Bilius said. Then, still holding the letter, he walked back to the RAB.

"He scheduled the blanderwheel," Saige said softly. Neko pretended to be busy with something around the front of his truck, in order to give her and Oscar privacy. "Which means he could turn it on and off whenever he wanted, which means he turned it on because he knew we'd be trying to reach the lighthouse. He must have been able to turn it on from the factory. He was trying to stop us. He could have killed us. He almost did."

Oscar reached over and took Saige's hand. "I'm sorry," he said.

She brushed away a tear from each cheek, then sniffed loudly and said, "I miss Woodpecker. I miss my old bedroom. I miss our windows. I miss the Alley."

"Maybe you can come back now," Oscar said.

"I don't think we can ever come back," she replied sadly.

And there was nothing he could think of to say to that.

So he just kept holding her hand.

Sunset

ONCE THE FUNCTIONARIES OF the Roan Assistance Bureau
had asked all their questions and taken all their notes, everyone got into Neko's truck and they drove to the hospital in
Commerce City, where a nice doctor named Melody put
Oscar's arm into a stiff cast. Afterward he sat in the waiting
room with Saige and Pietra while Bilius and Neko went off
to find sandwiches. It was around seven o'clock in the evening and Oscar couldn't decide what he felt *more*: hungry
or tired.

Saige had called her mom from a payphone and when
Mrs. Cleverer arrived, her eyes were red and wet. She wordlessly handed Arthur to Pietra and fell to her knees in front of
her daughter, laying her head in Saige's lap and hugging her
around her waist.

Pietra stood up and motioned for Oscar to follow her outside.

The sky was clear and blue and the sun was low in front of them, setting over Roan Piers.

Oscar reached up and squeezed Arthur's hand. The baby laughed sweetly, burbling a stream of nonsensical words.[149]

"You okay, Os?" Pietra asked, shifting Arthur to her other hip.

"Sort of," Oscar said. "It's all just..."

"A lot?"

"A lot, yeah."

"You want to see something cool?"

Oscar nodded, and Pietra reached into the pocket of her jacket and removed her Ocspectrascope. She held it out to Oscar.

"Look at the sunset," she said.

Oscar fit the Ocspectrascope over his head, adjusted it until it felt comfortable, and then looked up.

He actually gasped.

Next to him, Pietra chuckled softly.

"I know," she said.

It was unlike anything Oscar had ever seen.

---

[149] Which loosely translates to "Usually I have my bath around this time, but this seems like a fun and unusual adventure!"

Without the Ocspectrascope, the sunset had been truly beautiful, with shades of pink and red and orange and gold.

With the Ocspectrascope, it was . . . hard to process, at first.

All of those shades were there, of course, but there were *more* shades, colors Oscar didn't have words for—warm tones that seemed to shimmer and shift as he looked at them and cooler tones that hugged the horizon and metallic tones that haloed out from the low, glowing sun like so many layers of icing.

"The coolest thing about the Ocspectrascope is that it begins to train your eye," Pietra said. "Take it off; you'll see what I mean."

Oscar reluctantly took the Ocspectrascope off his head and for a beautiful, lingering moment all the colors he saw remained. As he watched, they faded a little, losing a bit of brightness. But they were still there, now that he knew where to look.

"Someday I want everyone in Roan to have one," Pietra said. "Just like a fridge or an oven. I think art and color and beauty are just as important as eating."

Oscar handed Pietra the Ocspectrascope and nodded. "I think you're right."

"You gave everyone this sunset, Os," Pietra said. "Not just the people in Commerce City and Roan Piers. But *everyone*. The Alley, the Toe. You gave this to them. You and Saige."

Oscar felt his cheeks start to burn with embarrassment. "Mostly Saige," he mumbled.

Pietra shifted the baby again and put her free arm around Oscar, squeezing him quickly.

"I think you're very cool," she said. "I can't wait to see what you do next."

She smiled, then turned and walked back into the hospital with Arthur.

Oscar continued to look at the sunset—

Until he became aware of a figure standing across the street, half-hidden in the shadows.

They wore a cloak with a heavy hood pulled over their face.

Just like a . . .

Farsouthian.

Oscar dashed across the street and the figure stepped further back into the shadows, darting down a small, skinny alleyway.

"Wait!" Oscar said, struggling to keep up.

The alley hit a dead end.

The hooded figure turned around and bowed their head dramatically—

And then pulled their hood down and burst into laughter.

"Eunice!"

"You should have seen the look on your face!"

"What are you doing here?"

"I had to come congratulate you. You did it! Not like I ever had any doubts, of course. Well . . . Maybe, like, the *smallest* doubt."

"I have about a thousand questions for you."

"Like what?"

"Was it Garner who came into the store and bought all those umbrellas so we could go to the Night Market?"

Eunice grinned. "Yup. I mean—Buckle umbrellas make the best Yuletide[150] presents. So it really killed two birds with one torchball."

"And the Others? How come nobody else had heard of it? How come I couldn't find it again?"

"Well, obviously all the Farsouthians know about the Others,"[151] Eunice said. "But as for *non*-Farsouthians...you just need to be invited in."

"You invited me in...."

"Yup. And those two bullies, which was unfortunate," Eunice added. "But they wouldn't have remembered much about it, once they were gone. *You*, on the other hand—I let you remember everything."

"And why me, exactly? If your readings have to do with energy, but you'd never met me before..."

"We're connected," Eunice said. "All of us. Have you ever paid attention to your friend's left ear?"

"What do you..."

Oscar trailed off.

---

[150] A holiday much like our Christmas (it also happens to be Saige's birthday!).

[151] Aha! Oscar *knew* Innis had been lying!

Saige's left ear was slightly pointed. She had slammed it in a door.

Eunice wiggled her own pointed Farsouthian ears now.

"Oh my sun," Oscar whispered. "Are you saying that Saige is—"

"I'm saying we're all connected," Eunice said. "I can't help what my visions reveal to me. I just know they revealed *you*. You and Saige." She smiled. "And I was right. You did it. And I can't wait to see what you do next."

I can't wait to see what you do next.

Pietra had said that, too.

But Oscar couldn't help but wonder—after Eunice had hugged him goodbye and left him alone in the alley and promised him they'd see each other again one day[152]—what *would* he do next?

The only thing that sounded nice to him was a long bath and a nap that lasted about nine days. And after that...he guessed he would go back to being an umbrella maker's apprentice.

In a city where it mostly rained but didn't *always* rain.

Sometimes there was sun.

---

[152] "Trust me," she'd whispered into his ear. "I can sense these things."

A Very Silly, Noble Thing

WHEN OSCAR GOT BACK to Château Buckle that night, he took a long bath, his cast wrapped in plastic and awkwardly sticking out of the water to keep it as dry as possible. When the water turned cold, he got out of the tub and slipped into clean pajamas and crawled into his bed.

Then he took Wib from the nightstand and held the dog in his hand.

"Hi," Oscar whispered into its small wooden ears. "It's been a really, really hard day."

A light knock at the door announced Bilius's presence.

"Come in," Oscar said.

Bilius came into the room and sat on the edge of Oscar's bed.

"All clean?" he asked.

Oscar nodded.

"Comfy?"

Oscar nodded.

"Okay?"

Oscar burst into tears.

Bilius gently took Wib from Oscar's hand, set the dog back on the nightstand, and hugged his son.

"You did a very silly, reckless, dangerous thing today," Bilius said. "But you also did a brave, selfless, noble thing today."

"Are you mad at me?"

"Not at all. I wish you had told me what you'd found in Angus's study. I wish you had let me help you. But I understand why you didn't. I am so grateful that you are safe. And unharmed." Bilius pulled away and gently tapped Oscar's cast. "Relatively," he added.

"What if they never find any of the people who worked at Brawn Industries? What if they never find Mr. Cleverer? What if nobody ever has to answer for what they did and the bad people just get away and nothing ever *changes*?"

"Oscar, the truth will win out in the end. I have no doubt of it."

"But what if it *doesn't*?" Oscar said. He was still crying, and now he had started to hiccup, too. "What—*hic*—if— *hic*—they all—*hic*—get away—*hic*—with it?"

"They *won't*," Bilius said firmly. "I won't let them. Neko won't let them. And I know you won't let them, either."

Oscar took a deep breath, trying to calm himself down. Finally, he whispered, "I just can't believe Mr. Cleverer would do any of this."

"I know," Bilius said. "But sometimes people...lose their way. He just lost his way."

"Understatement of the year," Oscar said, and Bilius chuckled sadly.

"Get some sleep now, all right, Oscar? You need your rest. It's been a long, difficult day."

But Oscar didn't go to sleep.

He found that as soon as he was alone, as soon as Bilius had left his bedroom, he was wide awake.

He couldn't seem to get Pietra and Eunice's words out of his head.

I can't wait to see what you do next.

And what *would* he do next?

He wouldn't let Brawn Industries get away with this.

He would make sure each and every person responsible was caught and punished.

He would never stop looking for them.

Oscar opened his curtains and let the silver moonlight fall across his bed.

He held Wib again.

And then he did what he loved more than anything in the world.

He got a block of wood, and he made a carving.

It wasn't the easiest thing in the world, to carve mostly one-handed, but Oscar managed. He held the wood in his left hand and used his right hand to whittle.

He didn't really know what it was at first.

Sometimes it was like that. He would let his whittling knife move with the slightest pressure from his hand. It was like the knife itself had a mind of its own, a heart of its own, a soul of its own. He watched long, thin shavings of fragrant wood fall onto the bed around him. He saw a body start to form—plump and round and long. He saw a fin and eyes and the smooth slice of a gill.

When it was done, it was a fish.

Oscar hadn't carved a fish; rather, the fish had unearthed itself from the wood, springing to life, shedding its outer layers to reveal its true form.

It was a long and sturdy carving, about eight inches in total length, and the fish's tail was curved as if in mid-stroke, giving it the shape of a hook or a—

Or a...

And then, sitting on his bed with a broken arm and shower-wet hair and tired eyes, Oscar Buckle had the best idea in the history of all the ideas that had ever been had on the entire planet of Erde.[153]

In one fluid motion, he jumped out of his bed and ran to find Bilius.

He was still holding the fish.

---

[153] In his opinion (and in my opinion, too).

The Handle

THE NEXT MORNING, VERY bright and very early, Oscar and Bilius set off for the Buckle Umbrellas shop.

The sun was out, but Bilius still carried an umbrella at his side.

Out of habit, maybe.

Or maybe because even before the weather machine, things in Roan *did* tend toward the rainy side. And you never knew what a sunny morning might turn into.

Oscar had the fish carving in his right pocket, and he kept patting it with his hand to make sure it was safe.

When they reached the storefront, Oscar got to work immediately.

Bilius was quiet, watchful, amused.

He helped Oscar when Oscar needed help[154] and he stepped back when Oscar said he could do something on his own.

Luckily, there were a few almost-completed umbrellas for Oscar to work with.

He chose a Spillen, which was the umbrella Saige carried.

It took him about forty-five minutes, and when he was done, he handed the umbrella to Bilius.

Bilius took it reverently, opening the umbrella's canopy,[155] holding it in his hand, closing it up again.

---

[154] The cast kept getting in the way of things.
[155] In Roan, there are no silly superstitions about opening an umbrella indoors.

And then he looked up at Oscar and said, "This is perfect."

And Oscar could tell from the expression on Bilius's face that his father was telling the truth.

Oscar took the Spillen back from Bilius and stroked the soft wooden handle, which was, of course, the fish that Oscar had carved the night before. It was the perfect shape, the perfect weight, and the perfect whimsical addition to the Spillen's length and size.

He hadn't known at first what he was carving, and then he'd thought he was carving a simple fish, and then he'd realized what it had *really* been.

The handle of an umbrella.

Curious Things

THAT AFTERNOON OSCAR WALKED to East Market for lunch. The day had stayed fair and warm but there was a certain smell to the air. It would wib[156] later, Oscar knew. But it would be a welcome wib. Nobody in the Alley ever really minded a wib.

Oscar was just passing Crow when the front door of the apartment building opened up and Gregory Fairmountain and Tim Klint came striding outside.

The three boys saw each other at the same time, and they all froze.

Oscar tensed to run.

But then something curious happened.

---

[156] This is, of course, Oscar's favorite rain of all—a gentle, welcome sprinkle.

Gregory stepped forward and gently scuffed the ground with the toe of his shoe, not quite looking at Oscar when he spoke.

"I heard my mom talking to Saige's mom," he said. "I heard what you did. That was really, really cool."

"Thanks," Oscar said. His mouth was dry and he still felt like running away, but he made himself hold his ground.

"I still think you're a dweeb," Tim said, but he was smiling.

When Oscar reached East Market, he felt light and happy.

And then another curious thing happened.

It seemed that everyone he passed in the market[157] either reached out to touch his good arm, or else smiled at him, or else nodded their head as he passed, or else pressed their palms together and bowed their head at him in quiet respect.

By the time he reached Neko's booth, he was feeling overwhelmed, and he was happy to find that Neko was there.

"My small friend," Neko said warmly. "How are you feeling today?"

"Everybody is looking at me," Oscar said quickly. "It's like...I think they all *know*."

Neko laughed his signature deep, booming laugh.

"Oscar," he said. "This is the Toe. News travels fast here.

---

[157] And, being Sunday, it was quite busy.

Of *course* they all know. Now, come here. I have a little something for you."

Oscar stepped into Neko's stall and sat on a wooden stool while Neko rummaged around in a crate.

When Neko turned around, he was holding not one, not two, but *three* stonefruits.

Oscar's mouth dropped open.

"Neko! Are those all for *me*?! I can't take those!"

"Oscar, you brought back the sun," Neko said. "And *that* is worth all the stonefruit I can get my hands on."

A Surprise Visitor

THAT NIGHT, AROUND DINNERTIME, there was a knock on Château Buckle's door.

Oscar answered it, and he gave a happy squeal of surprise to see Saige and Dot.[158] Behind Saige stood Mrs. Cleverer, holding Arthur.

"The elevator was working," Saige said with a grin. "Can you believe it?"

"Hello, Oscar," Mrs. Cleverer said, stepping forward. "Hello, Bilius. I hope you'll pardon the intrusion. Bilius, I thought we might go for a bit of a walk? It's wibbing outside now, but it's a nice night."

She gave Bilius a look that clearly meant—*let's give them a few minutes alone.*

---

[158] Repaired!

"Sure thing," Bilius said, slipping into his shoes.

Saige came into the living room and Oscar closed the door behind her. It had only been twenty-four hours since he'd seen her, but it had felt like an eternity, and it was so nice to be with her now. He sat down on the couch, and she faced him, her hands folded on her lap.

"Hi," she said.

"Hi," Oscar said.

He wanted to show her the umbrella he'd made and he wanted to tell her about his encounter with Gregory and Tim and he wanted to tell her about everyone in the Toe touching him or thanking him or smiling at him, and maybe most importantly, he wanted to tell her about seeing Eunice again, but he didn't say anything. Because he knew, just by looking at her, that she had big news to share.

"We're moving," she said finally.

"Great!" Oscar said. "Back to the Alley?"

But Saige smiled sadly and shook her head.

"Commerce City?"

She shook her head again.

"Well... where?"

"We're moving to Baudelaire,"[159] she said quietly.

---

[159] Baudelaire is the closest city to Roan and the largest city in Terra. It is about a half day's car ride to the southeast. Between the two cities there isn't much of anything other than farmland and the occasional small farm town.

"Baudelaire," Oscar replied, not sure he'd heard her correctly.

"My mother thinks, after everything that's happened, that it would be best to have a fresh start. And she has family there, too," Saige explained. "Her mom, her sisters. I've never met them. She's from Baudelaire, originally. Did you know that?"

"No," Oscar said.

"I've never actually been," Saige continued. "I've always wanted to go. Did you know they have an entire school just for architecture?"

Oscar smiled. "Saige, that sounds amazing."

"It won't be so bad, being that far away," Saige said, and Oscar couldn't help noticing how her lower lip had started to quiver. "Look, I brought you something."

She twisted around and reached into her backpack. Oscar half expected her to pull out a crowbar, but instead she removed . . . a telephone.

"It's from the house in Roan Piers. I took it. When I get to Baudelaire, I'll send a letter with my number. This way we can keep in touch. We can still send letters and stuff, but this is nice to have too, right?"

Oscar took the telephone. It was a soft butter yellow and he wanted to hug it to his chest.

"This is perfect," he said.

"They haven't found him," she continued, her voice

quieter now. "The RAB have been keeping us posted. But it turns out, the house in Roan Piers is in my mom's name, anyway. Almost like my dad wanted to . . . protect us. If something like this happened. But we don't want it, obviously. So we thought . . . we thought you and Bilius could have it instead."

"You want to give us your *home*?" Oscar squeaked.

"It might have been our house for a moment," Saige corrected him quietly. "But it was never our home."

Oscar and Bilius, living in Roan Piers? In a big, fancy mansion with a buzzball hoop and a lawn?

Wasn't that supposed to be the dream?

Wasn't Roan Piers supposed to be the end goal?

And Oscar swore he opened his mouth to say *yes*, but he was surprised to find himself saying *no* instead.

"No, I don't think we want to move," he said.

Saige smiled. "I had a feeling you'd say that." She bit her bottom lip, and it destroyed Oscar to see how sad she was, how broken. "I asked my mom how much she knew. About what my dad was doing, about what Brawn Industries was doing, about everything."

"And?"

"She said she didn't know anything. She thought he was working on factory updates, engineering a new assembly line. That sort of thing."

"Do you believe her?"

"I do," Saige said. "She seems just as sad as I am."

"I'm so sorry, Saige."

She shrugged, not quite meeting his eyes. "It's a lot," she said. "It's a lot to try and process. And there's more, too...."

Oscar didn't know how there could possibly be *more*, but he waited patiently as Saige shifted, gathering her thoughts.

"We were talking about family. I'm kind of nervous to meet my grandmother for the first time, my aunts. I have some cousins, too. And we were talking about my father and what he did and then she showed me this photo. Of *her* father."

Saige reached into the pocket of her jacket and pulled out a black-and-white photo. She handed it to Oscar. It showed a tall, skinny man standing in front of the clocktower at the Night Market. He wore robes and sturdy boots and he had...

"This is a Farsouthian," Oscar said, noting the man's slender, pointed ears.

"Right," Saige said, tucking her thick, curly hair behind her left ear. The slightly pointed ear.

"So Eunice was right. You *are* part Farsouthian!"

Oscar told Saige all about his encounter with Eunice outside the hospital. Saige didn't seem that surprised.

Saige took the picture back and looked at the Farsouthian man. Her grandfather. "I guess he abandoned the family when my mom was young, and she always found it too painful to talk about. So she just made up this story about shutting my ear in a door and decided never to tell me the truth. Until now."

"Eunice said we were all connected...Do you think she could be..."

"A cousin, maybe. Who knows."

"Wow."

Saige laughed. "*Wow* is the exact right word for it." She smiled, but then her smile faded and she just looked sad again. "My mom...She said he's not a terrible man, you know? My dad. But that over the years, he just became obsessed with money and status and power, and he loved me, he loved all of us, but he loved all that stuff just a little bit more."

Oscar reached over and took Saige's hand. He didn't know what to say, so he didn't say anything, and they just sat in silence for a few moments.

"I should probably go," Saige said. "We're leaving early in the morning."

"I'm going to miss you," Oscar said. It felt like the most useless, obvious thing in the entire world, but he thought it was important he say it.

"I'm going to miss you, too," Saige said. "But we're going to talk every day. Okay?"

"Deal," Oscar said. He leaned forward and they hugged each other, and when they pulled away, Oscar's eyes were red and Saige's eyes were wet.

"Going to leave now," she said. "Before I start crying."

A few minutes after Saige had left, Bilius came back. He seemed a little flustered and out of sorts, and before he could say a word, Oscar said, "Don't worry, Dad. I said we didn't want it."

Bilius froze. "You did?"

"Yeah. I did."

"Me too," Bilius said. "I said we didn't want it, too."

"Leave Château Buckle? No, thank you."

Bilius nodded. "I feel the same exact way."

Monkwood

AFTER DINNER AND A game of flock, Oscar took a long bath and then went into his room.

His bed was covered with sawdust and wood shavings from the night before, and he smiled to himself as he cleaned it up, sweeping everything into a small wastebasket. He wasn't feeling super tired yet, and he thought he might try carving another handle—a bird with a wing curved to fit perfectly in one's hand, or a long, curled up cat.

And then he remembered the block of monkwood.

He fished it out from under his bed and held it in his hands.

He had forgotten how almost-black the wood was, how smooth the grain was. Like a block of butter or ice, but slightly warm to the touch.

He sat on his bed and held it, wondering what it wanted to be, what secret shape was hidden inside it.

I'd love to know what you find in that wood, the owner of the monkwood shop had said.

The Night Market felt like a hundred years ago. Oscar wondered when the next one would be. Would he be able to go? Would Saige come back for it?

Saige.

He missed her already.

He'd taken a couple of her drawings from Fort Cleverbuckle[160] and hung them on his bedroom wall. Fireworks.

The block of monkwood hummed in his hands.

He started carving.

The wood was unlike anything he'd ever worked with before.

It was soft but strong, giving but firm, and almost entirely free of grain or knots.

His carving started to take shape, and even though there was still work to be done and sandpaper would be needed to smooth the skin of the animal, the magic of the monkwood was already apparent. The beast's chest rose and fell with its deep, powerful breathing. Every few minutes, if you listened carefully, you could hear the crash of waves on a distant shore.

---

[160] He'd been pleasantly surprised to find that the fort had survived the blanderwheel.

It was an orca. A killer whale.

Oscar smiled, remembering their journey through the abandoned aquarium, the way the life-size orca had almost given him a heart attack.

Not Saige, though.

She hadn't been rattled at all.

She would love this.

He'd mail it to her new home in Baudelaire.

Oscar put the carving aside and snuggled under his covers.

The wib had stopped, and the night was quiet and peaceful.

It was strange, learning how to fall asleep without the sound of rain outside his window.

But for the second night in a row, Oscar managed to do just that.

Partners

OVER THE NEXT FEW weeks, Oscar carved a dozen more handles for his father's umbrellas. All manner of beautiful and intricate wooden pieces that perfectly complemented Bilius's work.

The RAB stopped by Château Buckle often. They had found multiple tunnels in Brawn Industries, just like Oscar had predicted. Some of these were miles and miles long, leading straight out of Roan and into the country beyond it.

"But we're not giving up," the RAB promised. "We'll find them."[161]

One morning when Oscar and Bilius arrived at the shop,

---

[161] Oscar wasn't giving up, either. He had taken to visiting the Alley's library whenever he had a free hour, researching the history of Brawn Industries. He was sure he'd find *something* that would give them a clue as to where everybody had gone...

they found a small line of people waiting outside for them to open.

The next day, a woman brought her dog into the shop and asked if Oscar could carve a handle in the pup's likeness.

Oscar did, and the woman paid handsomely for it.

People came from all over.

From the Alley, from Commerce City, from Roan Piers.

Business boomed.

Oscar was happy. Really happy. He was doing what he loved more than anything else in the world. He was carving.

Then one day, Bilius sent Oscar to the shop ahead of him.

"I have an errand to run," Bilius said.

Oscar didn't think much of it. He went to the shop and opened it, turning on the lights and flipping over the CLOSED sign to read OPEN. He sat down at the workbench and took up a carving he had started the day before. It was a giraffe. The long, slender neck would make the perfect curved handle for a lighter umbrella, like a Gennal or a Mist.

He quickly lost himself in the art of carving, and he was hardly aware when the bell above the door tinkled and Bilius finally arrived, holding two cups of hot chocolate and a pastry for each of them.

"Put that down, will you?" Bilius asked. "I'd like to talk to you about something."

Oscar set the giraffe aside. He took his hot chocolate and waited for Bilius to speak.

"I've just come from a meeting with Principal Gundersen," Bilius said.

"Oh," Oscar said, taking a bite of the pastry. "How's he?"

"He's fine, just fine," Bilius said. He seemed a little flustered, and he kept pacing around the front of the workbench. "He says he's excited to see you back in two weeks. For your Uppers."

Oscar dropped the pastry onto the workbench.

"Sorry?" he said, convinced he'd heard his father wrong.

"I never wanted to pull you out of school, Oscar. I hope you know that. I did what I thought I had to do to survive. But things have changed now. Business is good—really good." Bilius paused. He cleared his throat, and Oscar thought his father might have been trying not to cry. "Your mother would have wanted you to finish school. It's what I want for you, too. And I think it's what you want."

"It is," Oscar said.

Bilius lifted an Enmeral umbrella off the workbench. Yesterday, Oscar had attached the handle: a bear, stretched tall on its hind legs. "These handles, Oscar...They are a stroke of genius. I'm so proud of you. You've been carving for your entire life, working on your craft since you were old enough to safely hold a knife. I hope you'll still carve handles for my umbrellas. But I *also* hope you'll carve whatever you want to, whenever the inspiration hits."

"Of course I'll carve more handles, Dad," Oscar said. "But...I don't think I can go back to school. The shop has been so busy lately. You need someone to help you!"

"Yes, the shop has been busy," Bilius agreed. "That's why I am interviewing people today. For an apprentice position."

"But...*I'm* your apprentice."

"No," Bilius said gently. "You're not my apprentice anymore. You're my partner."

And, as if on cue, the door pushed open, the bell tinkled again, and a young woman danced into the shop. She was smiling and rosy-cheeked as she said, "I'm here for my interview! Oh, I'm Sally. I should have started with that. Are you Bilius? It's so nice to meet you. Wow, it smells so nice in here! Okay, I'll just be quiet until you're ready. Oh, hello, are you Oscar? I'm such a big fan of your carvings! Oh, wait, am I interrupting you? I think I'm interrupting you. Okay, I'll really be quiet now. Don't mind me; you won't even know I'm here."

Sally turned around and busied herself with a barrel of Tranklumpets, examining one under the pretense of giving Oscar and Bilius time to finish their conversation.

I like her, Bilius mouthed to Oscar.

Me too, Oscar mouthed back. Then he said, in a quiet voice, "Are you sure?"

"Positive," Bilius said. "Now get back to work, please. I want that giraffe finished by noon. Sally? Let's take a walk around the block, shall we? It's such a lovely day."

And it *was* a lovely day.

Oscar stood in the open door of the shop, watching Bilius and Sally as they walked south through the Alley. Around them, people bustled in and out of Finch and Cardinal. Some of them had beach bags, heading to the shore to catch a few rays of a newly liberated sun. From Bleak Beach, they'd be able to see Gray Lighthouse, clear as day now that there weren't any clouds.

Maybe Oscar would head to the beach when he was done at the shop. He could wade into the water, calmer now without so many storms. Maybe—if he waded out far enough, and was still enough, and patient enough—he could catch a glimpse of the bioluminescent fish.

Oscar closed his eyes.

There was a soft, warm breeze in Roan today.

The sun fell on his face, warming his skin.

The sun.

The sun.[162]

---

[162] The *sun*.

GLOSSARY

Rain

There are forty-seven different types of rain in Roan. Here are a few of my favorites:

ALFER—A LOT of rain. Extreme flood danger. The only rain more dangerous than an alfer is a blanderwheel.

BLANDERWHEEL—A rain of epic, monsoon-like proportions. Dangerous. Avoid at all costs.

BLIGGOT—Quite a lot of rain, and particularly unexpected.

CATERWHAIL—A summer thunderstorm.

ENMERAL—A summer shower that begins and ends with a brilliant double rainbow.

FLINNER—A rain that doesn't appear to really want to fall at all; sort of hesitant, reluctant, a mediocre drizzle.

GENNAL—A warm rain that occurs on a bright-blue day with not a cloud in the sky from which it might have fallen.

GRIT—A rain that feels dirty and coarse between your fingertips.

HELLER—Similar to an alfer, the main difference between them is that a heller is accompanied by *slightly* less rain and the rain itself is *slightly* thinner and *slightly* warmer, which lends itself to a quicker evaporation rate.

LEMON—A rain that tastes and smells exactly like lemons.

MIST—A mist in Oscar's world is the same as a mist in our world. Barely raining at all.

PLINKER—A very ticklish kind of rain that slithers down the back of your collar and crawls into the cuffs of your socks.

RETROCLINE—This type of rain is quite rare and seems to

fall upward rather than downward (but that is, of course, impossible... I think).

ROUR—This is pronounced like *roar* and it's basically a combination of raining and pouring. It's raining, it's pouring! You get the idea.

SHLINK—Just shy of a spillen. A modest but persistent rain.

SIKE—Probably the rarest rain of all, which somehow falls quite hard but doesn't carry any moisture, so it doesn't get anything wet.

SILK—A rain that feels exactly like silk.

SLUICE—A very cold, almost freezing rain.

SPILLEN—A steady shower.

TRANKLUMPET—A rain characterized by its sudden bursts of downpour lasting a few seconds at a time, creating a distinctive pulsating effect.

WIB—A gentle sprinkle. The nicest kind of rain. Warm and welcome.

Food

What I wouldn't give for a good stonefruit right about now....

BUTTER LEMON—Much like a regular lemon, although less tart; more of a smooth, buttery flavor.

DEVIL'S APPLE—A small, baseball-size fruit with vicious-looking spikes growing from its red-black skin. A single poke from one of the spikes will send a grown man to sleep for a full day. A devil to eat, they are, which is probably how they got their name.

FLACK—A flack is a type of nut known for its creamy, buttery flavor. It is often used to make nut butter.

FLOATING APPLE—A totally normal apple with a tiny hovering enchantment that doesn't affect the taste at all.

GLAMP—A root vegetable similar to a potato.

LAVENDER BANANA—These taste exactly like regular yellow bananas, except they look a lot cooler.

Midnight Orange—These taste like a cross between an orange and a blueberry and are the color of the sky at—you guessed it—midnight.

Ollin—A root vegetable similar to an onion.

Quickbread—It is what it sounds like: quick bread.

Shooting Star Fruit—A wonderfully rare, sweet fruit that is a bit like a lemon mixed with a mango.

Stonefruit—A very rare fruit that, true to its name, looks and feels exactly like a stone. Chocolatey and sweet with just the perfect amount of tartness.

Svin—A root vegetable similar to honestly nothing we have in our world. I can only say that it is Oscar and Bilius's favorite food in the whole wide world, as it is versatile and yummy, and a little bit goes a long way.

Games and Sports

Flock is by far the most popular household game in Roan, and I'm not too proud to admit that I'm absolutely terrible at it.

Burgeoning Bloomrackers—A popular roleplaying board game based on one of Saige's favorite comic books.

Buzzball—A game much like basketball, except the ball vibrates in your hands, making it incredibly hard to maneuver.

Flamingo—A game that is fairly similar to our golf. Much like golf, flamingo is played over long distances, hence the need for a cart!

Flock—A two-player strategy game, not unlike chess, where each player receives ten pieces, each with their own complicated move requirements. First to make it to the other side of the board wins.

Messword—This is sort of like a mashup between a crossword, a word seek, and Scrabble.

Spanner—The name of one of the pieces in flock.

Torchball—A lot like our soccer, except the ball is on fire and most of a player's time is spent running away from it, so as not to get burned.

Geography

We've only seen a tiny, rainy corner of Erde. There's so much more to explore!

THE ALLEY—An apartment complex located south of the Wall, in Roan. This is where Oscar and his father live.

THE ANKLE—This is what people from the Toe sometimes call Roan Piers and Commerce City, although most people from Roan Piers and Commerce City would never refer to it as such.

BAUDELAIRE—The closest city to Roan and the largest city in Terra.

BLEAK BEACH—Located at the southern tip of Roan.

CENTRAL MARKET—A large farmer's market north of the Wall.

COMMERCE CITY—A bustling city located in Roan, north of the Wall.

DENNIMEYER OCEAN—An ocean on the opposite side of the world. The people of Roan refer to it as the more poetic Distant Ocean because it is, to be fair, pretty far away.

Dorn—A city in the Far South. The umbrellas that come from Dorn are short, thick, and square.

East Market—Oscar's neighborhood farmer's market.

Erde—The name of the planet where all of this is happening.

Far South—Where the Farsouthians are from.

Galla—A country north of Terra that makes long, skinny, delicate umbrellas.

The Goms Apartments—Another set of apartment buildings south of the Wall, near the factories.

Gray Island—The small island that is home to Gray Lighthouse. (The island is so small that it doesn't actually have an official name, but this is what most people called it.)

Gray Sea—This dark and stormy body of water surrounds Roan on three sides.

High North—A place on Terra where many wild creatures still roam, including woolly mammoths!

Monkland—A swampy country in the Far South; the only place in the world where monkwood trees grow.

Northern Wastelands—A great stretch of land to the North of Roan.

Piteous Park—A small, rather depressing park just north of Bleak Beach.

Roan—The city where Oscar Buckle lives.

Roan Piers—A fancy neighborhood north of the Wall.

Sun Island—An island that is as sunny as Roan is rainy. It's known for its light, protective, and colorful *sunbrellas*.

Terra—The country where Roan is.

The Toe—In Roan, everything south of the Wall is referred to as "the Toe," because it looks like the toe of a stocking.

Virginia—This solar system contains twelve planets, including Erde.

The Wall—The city of Roan is shaped a little bit like a stocking, and this stocking is divided into two parts by the Wall, which is twenty feet high and slices the city in half from east to west, just underneath the heel. There are three doors in the Wall: East, Central, and West.

Miscellaneous

Can you imagine how cool it would be to look at a rainbow through an Ocspectrascope??

Alder—A tree that, in Oscar's world, has certain healing properties.

Flouse—A thin rubber scarf worn around the head to keep one's hair dry.

Monkwood—This special tree grows in the swamps of Monkland and becomes infused with the magic of the water there. A carving made from monkwood will take on certain characteristics of its likeness.

Ocspectrascope—A cross between eyeglasses and a monocle that allows you to see more colors than is possible with the naked eye. Farsouthian-made.

ROAN ASSISTANCE BUREAU—The closest comparison to the Roan Assistance Bureau (RAB for short) in our world would be police officers, although the RAB do not carry weapons. Individuals of the RAB are elected by public vote and are called functionaries.

SKIFF—The exchange rate of one skiff to one dollar is confusing and varies greatly depending on what you're trying to buy. But for our purposes, let's say it's more or less one-to-one.

STOPENTIA—These fish used to be found in the Gray Sea, before it became too polluted to sustain much life. The fish mate for life, in pairs, and are now completely extinct in the wild. Stopentia babies are born a vivid green, then as they mature, they pick a gender and turn red if female, yellow if male.

WINDOW SAVERS—It is common for households in the Alley to keep a set of wooden planks cut to fit their windows, to use in the event of a particularly bad storm. They act as an additional barrier to help with flooding, and they also protect the glass from smashing.

YULETIDE—A holiday much like our Christmas (it also happens to be Saige's birthday!).

ACKNOWLEDGMENTS

This story has been in my head for such a long time, taking different forms, evolving and changing and coming into its final shape just like one of Oscar's carvings. I am so grateful to those folks who helped me find the animal inside the wood.

I would like to thank Wendy Schmalz, my agent, for guiding me through my first middle-grade book and falling in love with Oscar and the Alley. You are always my biggest supporter, and I'm so happy to continue our literary journey together.

To Samantha Gentry, my editor, for making this book so much stronger and seeing the details—both big and small—that I didn't.

My team at Little, Brown Books for Young Readers continues to be supportive, communicative, and all-around lovely.

Thank you to Nicole Wayland, Kerry Johnson, Esther Reisberg, Alvina Ling, and Virginia Lawther for your close attention to detail. The marketing and publicity team at LBYR is unparalleled: Thank you to Cassie Malmo, Stefanie Hoffman, Savannah Kennelly, and Christie Michel for your constant championing.

The art of *The Umbrella Maker's Son* is everything I could have dreamed up in my own head. Davide Ortu, I am eternally grateful for your beautiful illustrations! And thank you to Gabrielle Chang for an absolutely perfect cover design and to Karina Granda for your art direction.

Thank you to S for helping me navigate the last few months of writing and editing this book. They were the hardest months, and you were my lighthouse (but not the converted, weather-machine lighthouse—the lighthouse that Florence Perchance intended: steady, beautiful, strong, and with a light so bright it guides you home).

This book is for Alma and Harper, my nieces, who have each asked me over one hundred times in the past year, "When does your book for kids come out?" I am so excited for you to read this, just as I am so excited to watch you both grow up and defeat the evil empire.

And to the rest of my family and friends—thank you for being there for me during those aforementioned hardest months. Oof.

Lastly, it might be strange to thank a cat, but thank you to my cat, Milo. You were the best cat, and this book will always feel special to me because it will be the last book I wrote with you on my lap. I hope it is rainy where you are, but you are safe inside, looking out a window, and waiting for me.